"Just Kiss Me, That's All I Ask,"

Travis whispered. "A single kiss. Just one. You know you can trust me. Say you trust me, sweet Cat, show that you trust me. A kiss. Just one kiss for the well-behaved pirate who wanted to steal you and sail over the edge of the world but brought you back to your own room instead."

Cat felt herself succumb to the gentle power of his words, pulled like a bright leaf into the whirlpool of desire. No man had ever wanted her like this. His need was as irresistible as dawn. Slowly she bent her head until her lips touched his.

Dear Reader:

Silhouette has always tried to give you exactly what you want. When you asked for increased realism, deeper characterization and greater length, we brought you Silhouette Special Editions. When you asked for increased sensuality, we brought you Silhouette Desire. Now you ask for books with the length and depth of Special Editions, the sensuality of Desire, but with something else besides, something that no one else offers. Now we bring you SILHOUETTE INTIMATE MOMENTS, true romance novels, longer than the usual, with all the depth that length requires. More sensuous than the usual, with characters whose maturity matches that sensuality. Books with the ingredient no one else has tapped: excitement.

There is an electricity between two people in love that makes everything they do magic, larger than life—and this is what we bring you in SILHOUETTE INTIMATE MOMENTS. Look for them wherever you buy books.

These books are for the woman who wants more than she has ever had before. These books are for you. As always, we look forward to your comments and suggestions. You can write to me at the address below:

Karen Solem
Editor-in-Chief
Silhouette Books
P.O. Box 769
New York, N.Y. 10019

The Danvers Touch

Elizabeth Lowell

Silhouette Intimate Moments
Published by Silhouette Books New York
America's Publisher of Contemporary Romance

Other Silhouette Books by Elizabeth Lowell

Summer Thunder

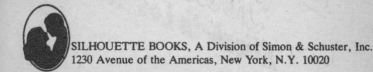

SILHOUETTE BOOKS, A Division of Simon & Schuster, Inc.
1230 Avenue of the Americas, New York, N.Y. 10020

ISBN: 0-671-47537-1

First Silhouette Books printing September, 1983

10 9 8 7 6 5 4 3 2 1

America's Publisher of Contemporary Romance

Printed in the U.S.A.

for Evan

man to my woman

The Danvers Touch

Chapter 1

CAT COCHRAN WAS TOO CAUGHT UP IN THE SENSUAL
beauty of ocean and sunset to realize that the tide
was sliding higher with each blue-green wave. She
had picked her way out on the rocky point in the late
afternoon, set up her camera and waited for the
moment when the sun would set fire to the smooth
face of the sea. Behind her, ragged lines of rock
thrust out of the water, gathering height and power
until they finally became a headland braced against
the seductive rush of waves. In front of her the point
dissolved into random low formations of black rock
that wore thick beards of mussels and slick green
water plants.

The textures of shells and seaweed, waves and
slanting light were what had lured Cat out beyond
the tidepools and slippery intertidal rocks to this
spot midway between land and sea. The top of the
rock she crouched on was dry, deceptively safe,

9

beyond the reach of all but the biggest waves. The rocks behind and in front of her, however, were below water most of the time. Their rough, powerful faces only emerged during an unusually low tide. As soon as the balance of sea and moon shifted, the rugged rocks would again sink into the ocean's liquid embrace.

As the evening sea swept toward the outer rocks, Cat, who had been counting the intervals between waves, braced herself more securely and let out her breath. At the exact instant the fluid curve of water met the rocks, she triggered the camera. Through the lens she saw the wave pour over rock, water exploding into creamy cataracts. Fountains of iridescent bubbles licked over black stone.

That was the moment she wanted to capture: the fragile caress of foam and the rock that had broken a billion waves . . . the rock that was itself being melted by rainbow bubbles until it was one with the sea it had so long withstood. Not defeat, but equality, for wave and rock defined each other. Without the wave, the rock would never know the power of surrender. Without the rock, the wave would spend itself quietly on the shore, never finding the catalyst that would transform its smooth perfection into a fierce explosion of beauty.

Cat lost count of the waves, of the times she had triggered the motor drive on the camera, the rolls of film she had threaded into the Nikon's compact body. Her legs cramped, protesting their unnatural position. She didn't notice. Until the light was gone, she wouldn't notice anything except the changing images coming through the lens.

Water leaped up over the rock, stinging her legs with a cold diamond spray. She looked up and finally realized that she had stayed too long. Behind her, the path to the shore was an impossible gauntlet of churned waves and slick black rocks. It was less than thirty feet to the beach. It might as well have been thirty miles. She would have to cling to the rocks with teeth and nails to keep from being swept off her feet by the powerful waves; but she needed her hands to hold her camera gear up out of the water.

Water foamed up toward her, then hissed down the hard rock. The wet stone looked almost gold as it reflected the setting sun. For once Cat was not enjoying the rich light. She looked at the water with clear gray eyes.

"Damn!"

Even if her hands were free, she would be lucky to keep her feet underneath her. But her hands weren't free. She had thousands of dollars of equipment to carry, equipment she needed to earn her living, equipment she could not afford to replace.

She wasted no more time on curses or regrets. She measured the height of the water against the rocks. Even in the trough between waves, the water was well above her knees. Add more than three feet of wave onto that, and she was in trouble. But she had no choice. All she could do was hold her equipment above her head, abandon the treacherous rocks entirely and wade a diagonal course to the sandy beach that curved back from the headland.

And pray very hard she wasn't knocked off her feet by the deceptively frothy waves.

Cat didn't look around for help. She had been on her own so long that the thought of someone else helping never even occurred to her. She checked the fastenings on her carrying case to be sure that nothing would come unstuck, spilling her cameras into the waves. The most valuable lens—a Novaflex as long as her arm and mounted on a stock that fit against her shoulder—was too big for her camera case. Reluctantly, she decided she would have to make two trips. She set down the case that held cameras and smaller lenses. Holding the Novaflex above her head, she began to climb down the rock.

The first wave wasn't bad. She was still clinging to the rock, so the water reached only to her waist. The wave was cold, though, and powerful. The cut-off jeans and cotton halter top she was wearing offered little protection from the sharp edges of rock, barnacles and mussels.

Watching the sea rather than the shore, alert for the occasional larger wave, Cat eased all the way down the rough shoulder of the rock. She had to cross a narrow sandy trench, then a smaller ridge of rocks before she reached the sandy shelf leading to the beach. The waves were coming so quickly she would be able to take no more than two steps in the lull between breakers.

The next wave slammed her back against the big rock. She scrambled desperately for balance on the slippery, uneven surface. One of her canvas deck shoes was wrenched off. She felt a searing pain along the side of her right foot as unprotected flesh scraped over sharp barnacles. Her arms waved erratically, trying to balance her straining body. It was impossible. She felt herself falling and cried out at what would be the certain destruction of her lens.

Just when she would have gone into the wave, she was yanked upright. At the same instant the Nova-flex was taken from her hand. Reflexively, she fought losing her grip on the precious lens.

"Hold still, wildcat. I'm not going to steal anything."

The deep drawl startled her, but not as much as the lazy amusement reflected in the man's sea-colored eyes as he turned her in his arms. He was standing easily in the powerful surge of surf, his lips curving in a smile that was as seductive to her senses as sunlight tangled in a breaking wave.

"Well, you have some sense, at least," he said as she stopped struggling. "Turn around."

"What?"

With an impatient sound, the man spun her around so that she faced the rock. "Up."

Cat felt his hand on her bottom. She fairly flew out of the water as he gave her a hard boost.

"Hand me the case," he said.

Cat stared at the man who was holding her Novaflex. She saw a stranger rising out of the foam wearing cut-off jeans and a blue-green rugby shirt that matched his eyes. He was wet to his shoulders. The shirt molded to his body, outlining the strength that had so casually lifted her beyond the reach of the waves. His tawny hair was well cut, thick and sun-streaked. His short beard and moustache were clipped to conform to the male planes of his face, but subtly uncivilized despite the grooming. He wasn't conventionally handsome; his face was too hard, too individual for easy labels. If he hadn't been smiling up at her, she might have been afraid.

It was the beard that decided her. She had an irrational weakness for the way it transformed sunlight into open curves of gold.

"That's my life you're carrying," she said in a calm voice, handing down the camera case.

He looked at her for a moment in startled reassessment before he nodded his understanding. "Stay put until I get back," he said, turning toward the shore. "The waves are stronger than they look."

"So am I," she said dryly.

If he heard, he didn't say anything.

Cat watched him wade toward shore, carrying her equipment above his head. His balance was extraordinary, a combination of strength and animal grace that made her hands itch to hold a camera again. In his own way, the stranger was as powerful and compelling as waves sweeping over rocks.

Then she realized that she was waiting like a docile child for him to return and pluck her off the rock. The idea both annoyed and amused her. It didn't amuse her enough to make her wait, though. It had been seven years since a man had told her to do anything. She hadn't obeyed then, either. But her ex-husband's demand had been degrading, while the stranger's request was merely reasonable.

Impatiently, Cat pushed away the unwelcome memories and began easing down the slippery rock. A wave rushed up, tugging at her with blue-green power, tumbling around her until she felt like a leaf being torn from its branch by a storm. The stranger had been right; the water was much rougher than it looked. Cautiously, she lowered herself further. When she was free of the rock she still moved by inches, never really lifting her feet, always keeping her side turned toward the incoming waves so that the water had less of her to push against.

Once she was beyond the point where breakers could slam her onto rocks, she relaxed. The surf still could tumble her around a bit, but the thought of a dunking didn't particularly dismay her. Keeping an eye on the waves, she edged toward the small sandy beach. Her right foot burned and ached with each step.

"You really don't have the sense that God gave a goose."

The voice came from behind her, startling her

again, but not as much as the arms that lifted her off her feet and held her above the reach of waves. Cat stiffened, suddenly aware of the man's warmth, the feel of his skin against her bare legs, the hard length of his arm supporting her back. She had never sensed a man in such an elemental way. She was not sure she liked the feeling. Yet the photographer in her couldn't help but notice the play of light over his cheekbones, the contrasting textures of curling beard and sculpted lips, the depth and changing color of his eyes. . . .

She had the uncanny feeling that she knew him. At the same time she was certain that she had never met him before. He was not the kind of man a woman would forget. Yet she trusted him. The same instinct that had prompted her to hand over her cameras to him made her relax and accept being helped by the hard-looking man who was simultaneously familiar and a stranger.

"I'm a good swimmer," she said, not an objection to being carried by him, simply the truth.

Unbidden, memories surfaced. A two-mile swim through a midnight ocean, her only beacon a glittering yacht, her only strength the rage that had goaded her into diving over the railing of her husband's boat wearing nothing but moonlight.

Yes, she was a very good swimmer.

She realized that the man was watching her, his eyes intelligent, speculative. "I'll bet you've got a temper to match your hair," he drawled.

Cat smiled slightly. Her rich auburn hair was as close as she came to beauty. The rest of herself she dismissed as average. She had the normal number of fingers, toes and everything else in between, and it was all in working order. Well, almost all.

And that was another thing she would not think about.

"Don't you have any happy thoughts?" he asked softly.

The question went through her like a shock wave. Her eyes widened, revealing the shadows in their gray depths. Then her dark lashes came down, shutting him out. He was far too perceptive for her comfort.

"I have thoughts that aren't unhappy," she said in a clipped voice.

"Not quite the same, is it?"

"Close enough."

Cat tried to keep the bitterness out of her voice, and almost succeeded. With a feeling of relief she saw that the beach was only a few feet away. Soon she would be out of reach of the unnerving man whom she had just met and felt like she had known forever.

"Do you always settle for second best?" he asked.

"It's called growing up."

"It's called giving up."

Anger raced through her. With an unexpected, supple twist of her body she slipped free of his arms. She landed on her feet and splashed out of the water to retrieve the camera equipment that he had left well above the high-tide mark. With every step, her right foot felt as though she were walking on bees. Sand mixed with blood stuck to her foot, scrubbing against the raw flesh. She slung the camera bag over her shoulder, settled the Novaflex sling over her arm and turned around to head for her house.

"You've had a lot of practice landing on your feet, haven't you, little cat?" he asked, standing calmly in front of her, cutting off her retreat.

She stared up at him, startled again. How could he have known her name? Then she realized that he was referring to the way she had landed on her feet. She smiled in wry acknowledgment. "Thanks for keeping my cameras dry."

"My name is Travis." He stood close to her, ignoring her attempts to evade him.

"Thanks for keeping my cameras dry, Travis," she said, trying to walk around him. She winced as her cut foot landed on a shell.

He moved again, putting himself across her path. "Don't you at least owe me a name?"

"Several," she agreed coolly, "but my mother taught me not to swear."

Travis smiled. "The cat has claws. Not even a purr for me? Such gratitude."

"On the contrary," she said, stepping around him. "I'm so grateful I'm not even going to tell you to go to hell."

His laughter was as unexpected as the strength that swept her up off the sand again.

"Put me down," said Cat, her voice cold.

"Your foot is bleeding." He looked down at her face, lingering over her wide gray eyes and the generous curve of her lower lip. "Buy a postcard next time. It's safer."

"Postcards lack staying power."

He stared at her as though seeing her for the first time. "I'm beginning to believe you aren't just another pretty face."

"And I'm beginning to wonder how you keep your feet out of your mouth long enough to brush your teeth."

"Come and watch me some time," he offered. "I'll even let you squeeze the toothpaste."

His slow smile was a parody of a sexy leer, and he knew it. It was his way of inviting her to share a joke that was on him.

"You're impossible," she said, laughing despite her irritation.

"Actually, I'm very easy."

Cat groaned at the ancient double entendre. Any other man she would have warned off with a single cold glance, but Travis was too outrageous to take seriously. He clearly did not expect anything from her but a shared moment of mutual amusement. She gave him that, succumbing easily to the lure of laughter, realizing as she did that it had been too long since she had really laughed.

His expression changed as he saw the lines of her face softened by laughter. Her gray eyes were luminous, as warm in their own way as her hair with its hidden fire.

"Tell me your name," he said softly.

The sudden huskiness of his voice was like a caress. Cat's eyes widened. She saw the male intensity of his look and wondered how she had made the mistake of taking him lightly. She blamed the shiver that coursed through her on her wet clothes.

"Cat," she said. Then, quickly, "Catherine."

"Do your friends call you Catherine?"

"No."

"Cathy?"

"Yes."

"And your men," he said smoothly, "do they call you Cat?"

There was no mistaking the cynical calculation in his sea-colored eyes.

Cat was surprised at the regret she felt. The corner of her mouth turned in a sad smile. "Joke's over, Travis. Put me down."

"What do your men call you . . . *Cat.*"

She lifted a dark brow and watched him with unblinking eyes, waiting to be released. After a long moment he loosened his grip on her legs, letting go of her in such a way that she slid intimately over the length of his body before her feet touched the ground. Even when she was standing, his arm stayed around her back, holding her against his body. To struggle against him would not only be futile, it would increase her awareness of his disturbing male strength. She waited with a coolness she did not feel, for her skin was burning with the tactile memory of his body rubbing over hers.

Finally, slowly, Travis removed his arm. She unconsciously readjusted the weight of the camera bag, shifted the Novaflex sling to a more comfortable angle, and studied Travis as though he were an interesting rock formation she wanted to photograph.

The sunset light transformed his hair and beard into fine, radiant wires. His eyes had changed color again, green tourmaline now, so deep that they were like a sea without a shore. His wet clothes clung to every line of tendon and sinew, curved over muscular shoulders and thighs. She realized that he was much taller than he seemed; like a perfectly proportioned tree, she had to stand close to him to appreciate his size. He was too hard, too obviously self-sufficient to be called good-looking. Yet she knew that she could look at him for a long, long time and still find new aspects of him to appeal to her. He was a man . . . and she was accustomed to boys.

"I'm the only one who calls me Cat. I don't have any 'men.' And," coolly, "I'm not looking for any." She turned away. "But thanks twice, Travis."

"Twice?" he said quickly, surprise in his voice.

Surprise and something else. He was not a man who took easily to being wrong in his estimates.

She looked back over her shoulder, caught by the odd inflection in his voice, as though he were echoing her own regret. "Once for the cameras, once for the laugh."

"I was right, wasn't I? You don't have many happy thoughts."

She pretended she hadn't heard.

Forcing herself not to limp, she crossed the narrow sand beach that divided the cliff from the water. Houses spilled down the rugged face, trailing stairways like tentacles down to the beach. The bluff was so heavily eroded that ravines separated homes whose outer walls were no more than twenty feet apart. To visit neighbors she either had to climb up to street level and cross over or climb down to the beach and take a different stairway up. The arrangement was not unusual in Southern California cities like Laguna Beach, where waterfront land was so valuable it was sometimes sold by the inch.

A rock concealed beneath the sand made a mockery of her attempts not to limp. She bit her lip against the pain.

"Cat."

She froze. She had not heard him come up behind her, yet he was so close she could feel his warmth radiating against the bare skin of her back.

"Will you let me help you?"

The words were soft, spoken against the braided mass of her hair, his breath as caressing as sunlight on naked skin. When she didn't answer he slowly picked her up again, giving her every opportunity to object.

She could have told herself that it was all right not

to protest, that her foot hurt too much to walk
on . . . but she didn't. She had given up that kind of
comfortable self-delusion when she dove into a
midnight sea seven years ago. She was letting Travis
carry her because it felt right, as though he were an
old friend come to help her out of a temporary
difficulty.

"Thank you, Cat," he said softly.

She shook her head in a gesture of disbelief. "I'm
the one who should be saying thanks."

"Maybe. But I don't think you let many people
help you." He measured the surprise that flickered
over her face.

"How did you know?" she asked.

"I watched you on the rock. The rest of the world
just didn't exist for you. When that wave sprayed
your legs, you knew you were in trouble, but you
didn't look around for help. You didn't even hear me
when I yelled. It took you about three seconds to get
to the bottom line. No whining, no hand-wringing.
You saw your best chance and you took it. That kind
of independence is unusual for a man, much less a
woman. It comes from living alone."

"Like you?" she asked, her eyes watching him
with a feline lack of self-consciousness.

He smiled. "Like me."

"Well, don't cut your feet," she said wryly.
"You're too big for me to carry."

His arms tightened in what could have been a hug.
"Kitten, I—" He stopped abruptly, aware of the
sudden stiffness of her body. "Don't like being
called Kitten?"

"Right the first time, Travie-boy."

Travis laughed aloud. "What happened to the last
man who called you Kitten?"

"The last *boy* who called me Kitten decided it was a case of mistaken identity." She smiled, but her eyes were narrowed against the flood of memories. Billy had called her Kitten. Billy, the pretty, petulant, too-rich boy she had married before she was old enough to know better.

"Another unhappy thought," said Travis.

"You seem to have the touch," she acknowledged.

He winced. "Sorry."

"Why? You can hardly be blamed for my memories."

"You made them, and you'll live with them," said Travis, a statement and not a question.

She cocked her head and looked at him again. "Have you been reading my mail, or are you a practicing warlock?"

His lips quirked. "It would take a warlock to pet a red-haired cougar, wouldn't it?" His smile widened as he looked down at her. "Actually, I'm a pirate."

"A pirate." She looked at his profile, beard luminous with the last light, teeth a slash of white beneath an arrogant nose. An uncompromising face, quintessentially male, fully suited for a pirate. "I'll buy that," she said. "A southern pirate."

"Southern?" he asked, mounting the stairs at the far right of the beach. "How did you guess?"

"The name. And the sexy drawl. East Texas?"

"Guilty."

Cat realized that she was being carried up the wrong stairway. "I'm the next stairway to the left."

"I'm not."

Suddenly Cat remembered the man she had seen for the last eight dawns, when he dove into the waves and swam out beyond the cove, his body as sleek and powerful as a dolphin's.

"I didn't recognize you with your clothes on," she said whimsically, thinking of the brief black trunks that were all he wore at dawn.

He stopped at a midpoint on the stairs and stared down at her.

"Your dawn raids," she explained, laughing, revealing the white shine of teeth against the tip of her pink tongue.

He glanced from her face to the multilevel redwood and glass house that was one stairway to the left, then at her again. He smiled. "And I didn't recognize you with your clothes *off*." He looked from the thick auburn braids piled on her head to the soaking halter and cut-off jeans, and then to the smooth curve of legs draped over his arm. His eyes moved back up to the taut halter top. "A definite improvement."

Cat followed his glance. She saw herself for an instant as he was seeing her, a slender woman whose breasts were perfectly revealed by the thin, wet cloth of her halter, every curve, every swell, nipples hardened by cold, everything. She had never seen herself through a man's eyes. The experience was both shocking and intriguing.

"Do I embarrass you, Cat?" he asked, his voice gentle, the drawl caressing her.

"I don't know."

He smiled. "Honest little cat, aren't you?"

"Always." There was no laughter in her voice. Then, "I keep feeling we've met before." She groaned. "God, you've reduced me to clichés."

"I know the feeling." He bent his head. His lips brushed across her forehead. His short, crisp beard smelled of sun and salt and man. She closed her eyes, accepting his caress as easily as he had given it.

"For the last three days I've seen you at dawn," he said, "stealing down your stairs like a shadow. You're all but hidden by equipment. Are the jeans and sweatshirt a disguise to keep off predatory males?"

"It's cold at dawn."

"Not if you're in the right bed."

The flooding crimson sunset concealed his expression, but she could feel him waiting for an answer to a question he hadn't asked. "I'm always in the right bed, Travis. Mine." She wondered whether that had been the answer he wanted. His expression told her nothing.

He continued walking up the stairs, breathing evenly, carrying her with ease. She appreciated his strength on more than a simple feminine level. Her own career—and pride—demanded that she keep the flexibility and stamina that she had had as a teenager. At twenty-nine, that wasn't easy. She guessed that Travis was at least five years older than she was. She respected anyone who had the discipline to stay fit on the other side of thirty.

She smiled wryly. She knew several men who got breathless just climbing up her steps. In fact, she had worn out more than one avid male simply by walking down to the beach, swimming for several hours and walking back up. It was . . . piquant to realize that it would take more than mild exercise to wear out the man called Travis.

"Now that looks like a good memory. Or at least," he amended, taking the last step and walking onto a cantilevered wooden deck, "not a bad one."

"It's a new one. Fully worth cutting my foot for. In fact—" Her words stopped as he turned, giving her a view of the sun balanced on the edge of a

shimmering magenta sea. The whole world was gold
and tone on tone of purple. There were no clouds,
nothing to interrupt the razor clarity of the horizon.

And then she saw the sailing ship sweeping before
the wind like a great black bird. Soon it would fly
across the incandescent eye of the sun.

"Put me down," she said urgently, struggling
without realizing it, her whole being intent on the
image that was forming in her mind.

She didn't see his surprised look, the instant of
anger that rapidly became bafflement. Once she felt
the deck beneath her feet, she forgot her wet
clothes, her cut foot, even the disturbingly sensual
presence of the man watching her. Her hands flew
over the camera case. She found the empty camera
body with one hand and the high-speed color film
with the other. She loaded the camera, secured it to
the Novaflex and focused on the sailboat. Less than a
minute after Travis put her down she was taking the
first picture.

She worked rapidly, with a precision that reflected
the years she had spent looking through a lens. The
long Novaflex was sensitive, well balanced, easy to
use. It also felt unreasonably heavy after a day of
photography. A part of her mind cursed the relentless schedule of work that had eroded her reserves of
strength over the last year, leaving her weak when
she desperately wanted to be as strong as the superb
ship skimming over the burning sea. The rest of her
mind ignored regrets and emotions, focusing entirely
in the moment. She poured herself into the camera,
forcing her weary body to obey her commands.

The ship cut the incandescent wake of the sun. In
silhouette the purity of the ship's lines became
breathtaking, more work of art than mere transpor-

tation, curve on curve singing of speed and distance, flight and waiting, power and silence endlessly poised on the edge of creation.

The last frame of film whirred past the aperture. The motor drive fell silent. Cat looked quickly at the sun and the ship. There was no time to reload and not enough light left even if there had been time. With an expression of yearning, she lowered the camera and watched the elegant ship sail into the condensing night.

When the ship vanished she realized that her foot throbbed, her arms were shaking with fatigue, and Travis was bracing her with one hand and holding her Novaflex with the other. She leaned tiredly against his strength, her eyes searching the darkness beyond the setting sun, looking for a ship and finding nothing but colors draining into night.

"It's gone," she breathed, her voice barely more than a sigh, melancholy as the descending night. "Oh, God, what it must be like to sail that ship over the curve of the world, into the soul of beauty. . . ." She shook herself out of the spell the ship had cast and looked up at Travis. His expression was enigmatic, his eyes unreadable. "Didn't you see it, Travis? It was the most perfect ship ever made." Her eyes were luminous, intense. "Some day I'll take a photo as perfect as that ship. Then I'll smash my cameras and never take another picture again."

She heard her own words and laughed self-consciously. "Sorry," she said. "Not everyone feels the way I do about light and shadow and the shape of freedom." She smiled slightly, trying to understand the expression on his face. "I'm not really crazy, Travis. Not all the time. I've just never seen anything quite that beautiful before."

Travis said nothing. His eyes had taken on the

aspect of the night sky: mystery and darkness and something she could not name.

"Travis . . . ?"

"Just what kind of game are you playing?" he asked, his voice rough, his fingers tightening on her arm until they left bands of white.

Chapter 2

CAT STARED UP AT TRAVIS. SHE SHIVERED AS MUCH from the forbidding expression on his face as from the cool wind lifting off the darkened sea. Suddenly she felt so tired she could hardly stand. She swayed with a weakness that frightened her. She couldn't be this tired. Not yet. Not for four more months. Her reserves of strength had to last until January. In January she would crawl into bed and pull the covers over her eyes and sleep for a year.

"No game, Travis. I'm too tired for games. I saw something extraordinary and for once there was someone worth sharing it with." She looked at his hard face. "My mistake."

"What's my last name, Cat?"

"I said I was too tired for games." She tried to release herself from his grasp but his fingers were like iron, caging her. She turned on him with narrowed eyes and a mouth that no longer smiled. "Smith," she suggested acidly. "Johnson? Or Jones, perhaps." She tugged once. His fingers hadn't loosened. "Those are the three most common names in the English language," she said. "The odds on guessing right go down dramatically from here."

She shivered again. Warmth had drained out of the evening as surely as color. She moved, but remained imprisoned by his grip.

"I suppose you don't know the name of the ship, either," he said sardonically.

"The Novaflex is powerful," she snapped, "but it can't read print a half mile away against the sun."

Travis stared at her for the space of several breaths. Gradually his expression and his grip on her arm gentled. His fingertips moved over her skin as lightly as a butterfly sipping nectar. "If the ship were yours," he said softly, "what would you call her?"

"Freedom," she whispered, shivering beneath his touch.

"Is your world a jail, Cat?"

She looked up at his face. His expression was intent yet kind, reassuring. She gave him the honesty his waiting silence demanded. "Not always. The next few months are going to be confining, though."

He pried a key out of his wet pocket and unlocked the door to the gleaming white house. "Tell me about it while I take care of your foot," he said, picking up her camera bag and gesturing her inside with a sweep of the hand holding her Novaflex.

Cat hesitated, then followed, deciding that his shifts in mood were no worse than her babbling about freedom and the soul of beauty.

The unglazed terra-cotta tile of the entryway felt cool beneath Cat's sore foot. Sand grated as she and

Travis walked side-by-side into the luxurious house. Her remaining canvas shoe squeaked with each shift of her weight.

"We're going to ruin your carpet," she said, looking at their sandy feet and the deep maroon carpet that bordered the tile.

"Linda assured me that I can't do anything to it that her parties haven't done already. Twice."

Cat smiled wryly. "I'll take her word for it."

"Have you been to my cousin's parties?"

She shook her head as she looked around the glass-walled, lushly carpeted living room. Modern crystal and mirrors and beveled glass, maroon suede couches and startling minimalist art. "I've only lived next door for six months, but your . . . cousin's . . . parties are legend in Laguna."

Travis waited for her glance to come back to him. "Linda has been in London for the last six months, I think." He caught Cat's quietly cynical smile. "She really is my cousin, Cat. My mother's sister's daughter."

Cat studied him for a moment, then nodded slowly. "Cousin it is, Travis. You have no more reason to lie to me than I have to lie to you."

"You act as though men never lie to women, and vice versa."

"*Men* don't."

He smiled crookedly. "I take it that your definition of 'man' has little to do with age."

"It has nothing to do with age."

He set aside her camera gear, picked her up and carried her through the room. Glass doors slid open to reveal an interior garden. A hot tub steamed invitingly among the greenery and concealed lights. Somewhat cynically, Cat waited for him to suggest that she'd be more comfortable if she took off her cold, wet clothes.

"Do you have a special definition of woman, too?" he asked, setting her on the broad lip of the tub.

The question was not what she had expected. It slipped past her defenses. A memory went through her like black lightning, darkening everything it touched. Billy had been very cruel on the subject of her womanhood. But then, he had been very disappointed. He had wanted to found a dynasty. "No," she said, trying not to let her memories color her voice. "No special definition. Honesty. Warmth. Intelligence. Endurance. The usual things. . . ."

"Usual?" Tawny eyebrows lifted. "The usual things are bust, waist and hip measurements."

"Which, added together, invariably exceed the IQ of the boy doing the measuring."

Travis smiled. "Wise little cat, aren't you."

He pulled off his wet shirt and tossed it aside. The hair on his chest gleamed wetly. She half expected him to take off his jeans, but he didn't. He simply slipped into the tub and pulled her in after. At no time did he so much as hint that she would be more comfortable without her clothes.

Cat relaxed. The heat of the water went through her like a benediction. She sighed with pleasure. "I didn't know how cold I was."

"You mean your lips aren't usually that interesting shade of blue?" he drawled.

She sank down on the bench that circled the interior of the tub. With a groan, she rested her head on the lip of the tub and let heat seep into muscles knotted with the tension and fatigue that had become part of her life in the last few years, especially in the last six months. She was working herself into the ground, and she knew it. But only until January. Then she would cut her work load in half and take proper care of herself again. Until then, though, life was going to be a jail of sorts, with each bar carefully chosen and placed by her own hands.

"Tell me about your jail, Cat."

Her eyes widened, revealing her surprise at his parallel thoughts. No wonder he seemed so familiar. With a lopsided smile, she closed her eyes and enjoyed the warmth seeping into her bones. "I work for myself. That means when I have time, I don't have money, and when I have money, I don't have time."

He watched her with peculiar intensity but she didn't notice. She had given herself over to the luxury of heat after a time of cold.

"Is money so important to you?" he asked with a lazy drawl that did not match the metallic sheen of his eyes.

Cat thought of her brother and sister, twins six years younger than herself, both enrolled in medical school, neither able to work enough to earn more than pocket money. And her dear, gently crazy mother, who had never written a check in her life until her husband died . . . and then she had written too many, for all the wrong reasons, until all the money was gone.

Then there was the redwood and glass house Cat had fallen in love with. She had a lease-option she couldn't afford until she made the last two payments on the twins' education. Yet if she had done the prudent thing and waited, the house she had wanted for six years would have been sold and she would have been reduced to photographing it from afar again. The rent was ferocious, but the thought of losing the house was unbearable. So she had simply increased her work day from twelve to fifteen hours.

Yes, in the last few years money had become very important to her. She earned a good living as a freelance photographer, but she was supporting four people. Soon the twins would be able to support themselves. January. Her mother was also getting married then. January.

Freedom.

She realized she hadn't answered Travis's question. She opened her eyes and saw the mingling of irritation and anger and disappointment on his face. He was a composition in hard angular shadows and savage gold lights glinting through his hair. His lips were flat, almost invisible beneath his thick moustache. Between his lips a thin line of white gleamed.

"Put a knife in those teeth and you'd be Bluebeard incarnate," she said.

"You haven't answered my question."

"Of course money is important," she snapped. "The only people it isn't important to already have it."

"Some people are quite happy without money."

"They don't have to pay my bills."

"And you would be so grateful if someone paid your bills for you, right?" he drawled, his lips curling in disdain.

"Don't worry, Travie-boy. I'm not going to hit you for a loan."

Cat pulled herself out of the water with the same supple twist that she had used to jump out of his arms earlier. The motion was quick, unexpected. She ran through the house, swept up her camera equipment and opened the door to the beach—but the door was slammed shut again before she could get outside. She looked at the tanned, dripping, powerful arms that had shot over her shoulders to hold the door shut.

"You're shivering," said Travis, so close to her that his breath felt hot. "Come back to the tub."

"It's warmer outside," she said without turning around.

"Cat—"

"Open the door."

"I'm not used to women like you," he said, oblique apology.

"I'll bet you aren't used to *women* at all," Cat said coolly. "With your manners you must have to rent company by the hour. The door, Travis."

She expected anything but the laughter that sent an entirely different variety of shiver through her body.

"Do you always draw blood with your claws, Cat?"

She shifted her weight, wincing as her foot complained. The hot tub had taken away most of the sand, but it had done little else except make her realize how exhausted she was. And how cold. "Game's over, Travis—whatever game you were playing."

"I wasn't—"

"Sure you were," she interrupted rudely. "You found the cat, you found the cage, and then you started shoving sharp things through the bars just so you could watch the cat scratch and howl. That makes you feel powerful, and the cat"—she shrugged—"well, who cares how the cat feels?"

There was a long silence. She realized that his hands were no longer flat against the door; they were fists, solid and heavy. Muscles coiled and slid beneath tanned skin, telling more clearly than words of the emotions seething in the man behind her. Yet he wasn't angry with her for trying to leave; she sensed that as surely as she had sensed that her cameras would be safe in his hands. His anger was directed at whoever had caused her pain in the past.

Gradually, his hands relaxed. She noticed fine scars crisscrossing his fingers. Some of the scars were new, some were so old they had all but faded beneath the sun-browned skin. She wondered what kind of work he did that left such spidery marks on him.

And she wondered what kind of female had left invisible, much deeper marks on him.

"Was he really that bad?"

"Who?"

"The boy who put you in a cage and tormented you."

"Probably no worse than the female who soured you on half the world's population."

"Are you so sure it was a woman?"

"A female," she corrected evenly. "And yes, I'm sure. Most people have to be taught to hate."

"Were you?"

Cat did not have the strength to fight Travis and her memories, too. She stopped trying to pull open the door. She looked down at her feet and realized she was standing in a spreading pool of pink-tinged water. He realized it too. He didn't ask if he could pick her up again. He simply did.

"Don't bother fighting me. All I'm going to do is bandage your foot. If you want to leave afterward, I won't stop you."

This time he set her down in a bathroom done in shades of lavender and lemon and pale fuchsia. His brown, powerful back looked so incongruous amid the pastel splendors that she could not help smiling. When he touched her foot, however, the smile became a gasp.

"Hurt?" he asked mildly.

Cat gritted her teeth against an unladylike answer.

"It will get worse," he assured her. "The sand has to be scrubbed out." He looked up. "Do you want me to do it?"

With a grimace Cat propped her camera equipment against the shower and pulled her right foot into her lap to inspect it. There was more than one cut. None was deep enough to require stitches. All the cuts began on her sole and then wrapped around the outside of her foot, almost impossible for her to reach. And he was right; there was sand in all of them. Even if she soaked the foot thoroughly, some sand would remain. It was the nature of sand and barnacle cuts to stick together.

Making a disgusted sound, she thrust her foot back into his hands.

Travis put warm water and disinfectant in a basin, set her foot in it and disappeared. He returned almost immediately, bringing a thick indigo bathrobe. Without a word he wrapped it around her, then settled cross-legged on the floor.

His hands were deft, gentle, quick. With a minimum of pain and no wasted time he cleaned her cuts, put on salve and wrapped her foot with gauze. When he was done he held her foot in one hand and kneaded her calf almost absently with the other. His eyes were unfocused, looking at things only he could see. His hands were warm on her cool skin, his fingers strong and sure as he rubbed away the cramps that had come as she tensed her muscles against pain.

She looked down at his bent head, the tawny hair

alive with every possible shade of brown and gold,
the sensual movement of light through his short
beard, the subtle difference in the texture of his skin
against hers, his fingers curved around the arch of
her foot . . . fluid lines and light and shadow. She
would love to photograph him, as compelling in his
own way as the great black ship had been.

"What are you thinking?" he asked quietly, his
hands warm on her skin, soothing her.

"That I would like to photograph you."

His eyes widened, revealing their brilliant tourmaline depths. He laughed softly, shaking his head.
"Will you always surprise me, Cat?"

"Depends on what your preconceptions are,
doesn't it?" she asked quietly.

"I hearby abandon all my preconceptions," he
said, no longer smiling. "And you—will you abandon yours?"

"I don't have any where men are concerned. Only
boys. I've never known a man."

She felt his large hands caressing the curve of her
foot and calf, warming her cold skin, and regretted
her honesty with him. She had just met him, she had
always known him, she didn't know what to do with
him, and she didn't want him to go away. She waited
while he studied her in turn, visibly weighing her
words against his previous experiences, deciding
whether or not to take her the same way the sailing
ship had taken the night—openly, with nothing held
back.

"May I call you Cat?"

"Haven't you always?" she said lightly.

He rubbed his beard along her calf. "Yes, I think I
have."

In silence he bandaged her foot.

When he was finished he asked her to have dinner

with him. She insisted on cooking it for him at her
home. He was reluctant to let her go but in the end
agreed to meet her in an hour. As she walked home
she felt his eyes watching her. The feeling persisted
even when she was inside. She found herself glanc-
ing at the clock, waiting for an unreasonably long
hour to pass.

Travis knocked on her back door—the beach
door—well before the hour was up.

"I would have cooked dinner for you," he said,
handing over the two swordfish steaks he had
brought from his house.

"You've done enough for me already," she said,
her smile slipping as she looked at him.

No man had ever attracted her more than he did at
that moment. He was freshly showered, wearing a
navy T-shirt and white cotton beach slacks. His
tawny hair gleamed like skeins of rough silk. She
wanted to run her fingers over his beard and the
subtle swells of muscle beneath his shirt. She wanted
to make him stay just as he was, his eyes transforming light into jeweled tones of blue and green. She
wanted to grab her camera and capture him forever,
an image of sensuality to warm the cold center of her
nights.

She took the swordfish steaks from his hand,
noting again the long, tanned fingers carrying their
hair-fine scars. "Have a seat somewhere. I'll just be
a minute."

Travis went to the modern bay window that
overlooked the water. The shelf of the window was
filled with a pile of local shells. He ran his fingers
through them idly as he watched her working in the
open kitchen, which also overlooked the water. His
eyes followed her as she worked. Her hair
shimmered and blazed, making all other colors look

pale. She was wearing a forest green shirt tucked into a pair of sand-colored slacks. The white bandage on her foot made her skin look like honey. Despite the sore foot she moved with a grace and economy that was pleasing to watch.

"Sure I can't help?" he asked in the drawl that sounded so lazy and concealed so much power.

"You've carried me enough for one day."

"But I like carrying you," he said reasonably.

She saw his crooked grin, as familiar to her as her own hands, and felt both warmed and chilled. She didn't need any more complications in her life . . . yet it felt so good to laugh, to look up and see his blue-green eyes approving of her every movement, to watch his hands and remember their gentleness on her skin. She knew she should send him away. And she knew she wasn't going to. Even in the short time she had spent with him, he had filled spaces in her that she hadn't even known were empty, as though he knew her better than she knew herself.

She smiled and shook her head. "Travis, you're—"

"Impossible?" he suggested hopefully.

"Incredible," she said, her voice revealing too much. "Really incredible," she added briskly.

She wielded the chopper over the mushrooms with casual skill. Firm white slices piled neatly to one side of the chopper's large honed blade. With a deft motion, she gathered the slices onto the blade and dropped them in a bowl which already held thinly sliced scallions, nearly transparent rounds of radishes and circles of carrot as thin as gold coins. She squeezed a lemon over everything, crumbled in a bit of basil, ground fresh pepper generously, added garlic salt, stirred and set the bowl in the refrigerator.

"You look like you've done that once or twice," drawled Travis.

"I cooked my way from the Virgin Islands to California."

Though her voice was neutral, something in her manner made him look at her sharply. "Do you do it often?"

"Cook?"

"Go from the Virgin Islands to California."

"Just once."

"You sound like you didn't enjoy it. Seasick?"

Cat pulled the core out of the iceberg lettuce, turned on the tap and held the lettuce underneath. "No, I wasn't seasick," she said, turning off the water and holding the lettuce so that excess water could drain out. Methodically she began pulling off leaves and patting them dry on clean cotton towels. Part of her wanted to tell Travis why she hadn't enjoyed the trip. The rest of her wanted to forget. "I love the ocean," she said finally. "It just wasn't the best time of my life."

He waited, but she said nothing more. "I'm glad you don't get seasick," he said finally. "I'd like to take you sailing."

"Does a boat come with your cousin's house?" she asked, wrapping up the leaves in a damp towel and putting them in the refrigerator.

"No. I came with the boat."

Cat stood on tiptoe and peered out the kitchen window to check the progress of the coals in the small grill on the deck. Not ready yet. She began cutting butter and flour together in a bowl. Sensing his intent look, she glanced up.

Travis smiled. "Aren't you going to ask me what kind of boat?"

"What kind of boat, Travis?" she asked dutifully.

He laughed. "Are you sure you like sailing?"

"I love the ocean. I don't know a damn thing about sailing, except that cooking for thirty in a storm is a real challenge. If you expect me to launch into a discussion of sloops and catamarans, jibs and the six hundred boring shapes of canvas you can hang from masts, you're going to be one disappointed man."

Travis laughed and shook his head. He picked up a handful of shells from the pile by the window and let them pour back down. The shells made a strangely musical sound, counterpoint to his warm male laughter. He looked back at her. She was watching his hands and the liquid fall of shells. Her gray eyes were soft, luminous. Wisps of hair burned around her face in the lamplight. When the last shell had fallen she glanced up to his face, his eyes, and was caught.

"Jason likes those shells, too," she said, the first thing to cross her mind, anything but the feeling of having jumped off her solid world to float in his tourmaline eyes.

"Jason?" The drawl vanished, leaving his voice as smooth and cool as a wave-polished shell.

"My neighbor on the other side. Most of those shells are his. He found me photographing a shell one day, and the next thing I knew he had given me his whole collection." She smiled slightly. "It's just an excuse to visit me. He's a cunning rascal, all big blue eyes and earnest conversation. It would go to my head, but I know I'm just a stand-in for his mother."

"I thought you didn't like boys," said Travis, sorting through the shells as though he had dropped something valuable among them.

"I make exceptions for the seven-year-old variety," Cat said dryly. "Especially when he finds himself the not-so-proud older brother of newborn twins who take up every second of his mother's time. We have a breakfast date whenever he can sneak out." Her lips curved as she turned out the dough and began kneading it on the breadboard. "Sharon, his mother, has threatened to put a collar and leash on him if he doesn't stop bothering me. But he's just lonely."

"You don't mind?" Travis said, absently sorting shells into piles based on size and shape and color.

"He's an excuse for me to relax."

Travis measured her with narrowed eyes. "You need an excuse for that?"

His hard tone made her glance up. "I must have pushed the button marked preconceptions. What are you really asking, Travis?"

"Are you so busy chasing money that you need an excuse to be human?"

She stopped kneading for a moment, feeling tiredness like sand where muscles should be. Four months. January. She could do anything for a hundred days without breaking down. All she had to do was take them as they came—one at a time. She drew a deep breath and attacked the dough again, kneading deftly, counting the strokes even as she talked. "You could say that, I suppose. There's enough truth in it for most purposes."

She didn't need to look at him to sense his disappointment. "Why does that bother you?" she asked casually, glad that she had something to do to conceal the fine tremor in her hands that was caused by fatigue and emotion.

"Money is such a shallow thing to spend your time on."

"No exceptions?" she asked, cutting circles out of the dough and placing them on a cookie sheet.

"Not one." The words were implacable, the tone utterly certain.

Absurdly, Cat felt her throat tighten around tears. She hadn't cried in seven years. That, more than the ache in her back and arms and legs, told her how very tired she was. Anger came finally, giving her the temporary strength of adrenaline.

"Are you finished?" she asked with deceptive calm, tucking the cookie sheet into the oven and setting the timer.

"Finished doing what?"

"Passing judgment on me."

"Cat—"

"No. It's my turn. I don't know what paragon of womanhood you're measuring me against. I do know that I'm damn tired of coming up short. Two choices, Travis. Take me as I am, or take a hike."

"What if I told you I was rich?" he asked cynically. "Would you still want me to leave?"

"Why is it that boys seem to feel money excuses all manner of shortcomings?" she asked in a too-sweet tone.

"Because girls tell them so as soon as they're old enough to know the difference between pennies and dimes," shot back Travis.

"Your choices have just narrowed," said Cat. "Take a hike."

"But what if I'm very rich?" he asked, smiling coldly.

"That would explain everything except my stupidity. I thought I was a fast learner, but I guess some things just have to be gone through twice."

"You lost me."

"That's the way it goes," she said flippantly. "Win some, lose some, some never had a chance. If you're rich, we fall into the third category."

"Cat, you're not making sense," he said, impatience and something more in his voice. Something urgent. Something uncertain.

"Read my lips. Good-bye."

"You don't believe I'm rich," he said flatly.

"Travie-boy, you could spit diamonds and still not impress me."

"I doubt it. Women like you don't—"

"You don't know squat about women like me." She wanted to stop there, but anger and an irrational sense of betrayal forced words past her stiff lips. "I once swam two miles at midnight through the open sea just to get away from more money than you'll ever count. *Rich*," she snarled. "Sweet God above, preserve me from rich boys!"

For a moment there was only silence and the echo of her rage quivering in the room.

"Who is he?" asked Travis finally.

She stared out the kitchen window where coals burned hotly inside a cast-iron trough. When she looked back, her eyes were the color of winter ice. She said nothing.

He left the shells and walked over to her with the easy stride of a man who has spent his life balancing on the deck of a ship. She watched him approach and wondered if that was why he seemed so familiar to her, because he walked like a man who had been to sea, like her dead father, like the man she had thought her husband was . . . Billy, the worst mistake she had ever made.

"Who is he?" asked Travis again, his voice coaxing. "Do you still love him?"

She looked through Travis to seven years ago, memories pouring over her despite her efforts to forget. . . .

She and her husband had been anchored in the Virgin Islands with a group of her husband's friends. She and he had been arguing, as usual. He had been drinking, also as usual. The smell of rum and pineapple turned her stomach. He was yelling at her and waving a piece of paper.

"It's your fault! You lied to me!" he shouted, his perfectly formed face twisted in anger. "I never should have married you! You're not good for anything!"

Cat felt a combination of impatience and despair. The past few months with Billy had been impossible. The days were bad enough, his petulance increasing as the sun rose and not declining at all. The nights were worse. Sex for him was a simple exercise of male prerogative. As she'd never had any other man, she assumed that sex was like that for everyone. Dull, when it wasn't outright uncomfortable.

Billy didn't seem to mind, though. Whenever she tried to do something a bit different, if only to shift her weight slightly, he berated her for being clumsy or overly aggressive. At twenty-two, she had never known more than occasional mild pleasure at her husband's touch. As a result, her natural sensuality was buried inside her like a tightly sealed bud, waiting only for the right conditions to flower.

"What is it this time?" she asked tightly. "Too much rum in your drink or not enough in the bar? Or did they starch your white ducks again? Is it too hot or too cold? Too calm or too windy? Or are all the movies in subtitles and all the food fit only for dogs?" She paused, thinking of her husband's grievances in the last two days. Small things, all of them; but they added up to an endless list of complaints.

Billy hesitated, surprised by his young wife's words. Lately she had been harder and harder to get along with. He thrust the paper under her nose. "This is what's wrong. You lied to me, you useless bitch."

"Names again, Billy?" she said, her voice cold. Suddenly she looked and sounded older than she was, certainly older than *he* was. "No more. I've ignored your moods and name-calling too long, hoping that you'd outgrow it. You haven't. I have."

She turned to go below, only to have her arm grabbed with a force that bruised her to the bone.

"Listen to me, *bitch,*" he said, his voice high and his blue eyes narrowed until she could barely see the black shine of pupil. "It's your fault. All of it. This paper says so. You're lucky that all I do is call you a few names. It'd serve you right if I kicked you overboard to drown!"

Slowly, Cat focused on the paper he was holding in front of her face. She read it through several times before she made any sense out of the words. It was a laboratory report stating that her husband's sample had a low but adequate count of viable sperm. "Adequate for conception" was scrawled across the bottom, followed by an indecipherable signature.

"It's your fault I can't have sons," he said, flipping the paper across her face with each word. The paper didn't hurt her, but the barely veiled intent did; he wanted to slap her but he lacked the nerve. "Your. Fault. You're no good as a wife, no good in bed, and you're sterile. What the hell good are you, Kitten? Huh? You tell me that. How are you going to earn your keep? You can't run home to mommy because she's broke now, and you never went to school. All you were good for was having babies, and it turns out you can't even do that! You're no damn good, Kitten. No damn good at all."

He turned away, swearing violently, and went in search of another drink. Cat leaned against the boat's railing, trembling. Sterile. No good at all. Earn your keep. Sterile. No damn good.

She had stayed out of his way. He had made it easy for her by drinking ashore that night, leaving her to her own uncomfortable thoughts. She knew that eventually he would sober up. Then it would be possible to talk, to decide what their future should be—if they had a future at all. She shut herself in their cabin and lay staring at the ceiling. Sterile. Earn your keep. Sterile.

Finally she fell asleep. When she awoke it was dark, warm, smelling of stale rum. She steeled herself for Billy's unwelcome embrace but the hand that closed around her arm was not her husband's.

"Billy?"

The light came on, revealing a half-naked girl with smeared lipstick and dyed hair. Billy stood behind the girl and shoved her into bed.

"What—?" said Cat, sitting up, staring at her husband's bloodshot eyes. Then she realized that he had decided to bed his most recent playmate on board the boat instead of ashore as had been his habit. With a sound of disgust, she started to get out of bed. He shoved her back with enough force to crack her head against the bulkhead.

"Don't be such a stick. You'd think you had something better to do with your useless body. But we know better, don't we?" He smiled drunkenly

and leaned toward her. "S'okay, Kitten. I thought of
a way for you to earn your keep."

He laughed, sending a rush of rum-staled breath
over her. She realized that he wasn't joking, that he
expected her to stay, to join him and his cheap
playmate in bed.

"No," she said, pushing the girl aside and coming
out of the bed in a rush.

Billy grabbed Cat. She jerked away with a force
that shredded her nightgown, leaving her naked.
The drunken girl giggled and called encouragements
that Cat cringed to hear. Billy laughed and grabbed
for Cat again, trapping her against the bulkhead.
She kicked and scratched and clawed in a silent fury,
determined to be free. Her hand touched the glass
globe of a wall lamp. Without thinking, she jerked
the globe free and smashed it into Billy's head.
Blood welled suddenly over his cheek.

It was a shallow cut, more startling than painful,
but it gave Cat a chance to twist out of Billy's grasp
as his hand went to his face. She ran up the stairs
onto the deck, her mind racing more furiously than
her heart. She could expect no help from the boats
anchored nearby; most of them held a full comple-
ment of Billy's drinking buddies. She knew no one
ashore. Besides, that was where he would expect her
to go. She had to do something unexpected, give
herself time to swim beyond the reach of his drunken
anger.

She left the anchored boat in a clean dive that
made little noise. She swam toward the darkness,
the open sea, where only a single light bobbed up
and down a long way off. Behind her she heard Billy
calling, but his voice was directed away, toward the
shore. By the time she heard the little outboard

motor on the skiff start up, she knew she was safe. He would spend the rest of the time searching his friends' boats and the shoreline. He wouldn't find her.

Only after she had been swimming for a long time did she realize that she had been foolish to head out to sea with only a tiny, lone light as a beacon. The light was much further off than she had thought. What she had believed to be a small boat was actually an enormous power cruiser strung with lights. By the time she reached the boat she was nearly spent. Fortunately, there was a sea ladder down.

Naked, bruised, half-wild, she had climbed up the ladder into Rodney Harrington's life. She would never forget his startled face, brown eyes slanting down in an attitude of perpetual—and deceptive— vulnerability, looking for all the world like a teddy bear misplaced by a forgetful child. She had been nearly incoherent. He had been utterly calm, acting as though he received naked sea nymphs twice daily. He had wrapped her in a blanket, listened, then ordered his crew to weigh anchor.

He had been a miracle of kindness, sailing her into a new life, asking nothing in return. . . .

"Cat?" Travis's hands kneaded her shoulders and rigid neck. He looked at her gray eyes, dilated with memories and pain.

Her eyes focused slowly on him. For a moment she succumbed to the strength of his touch, letting his warmth seep into her. Then she realized what she was doing and pulled away. She wondered if she would be this vulnerable to him in January, when she no longer would feel like a woman being pulled to pieces by too many demands, all of them utterly necessary. He looked so strong, so competent, so capable of love . . . but that was always how the masculine trap was baited.

Billy had looked strong and competent too. Capable of love? No, not even before he knew she couldn't be the source of his dynasty. Boys only love themselves. How many times did she have to be hurt before she learned that simple lesson? And why was she so damned weak that she wanted to believe that Travis was different? A man, not a boy.

"Why are you still here?" she asked, her voice calm. But she could not mask the tremor that began beneath the warmth of his hands on her shoulders and radiated through her body.

His head came down. She felt the heat of his breath on her cheek, the rough silk of his moustache on her mouth, then his lips, sweet and firm and knowing, moving over hers. He demanded nothing, gave everything, warmth and the taste of him slowly filling her senses until she sighed his name. She had never been kissed like that, had never even dreamed such gentleness and caring was possible. Tears stood like crystal at the ends of her lashes. He caught each drop on the tip of his tongue, then bent and kissed her again, sharing the taste of tears.

"Why are you doing this to me, Travis?" she whispered, trembling between his hands. "I'm not strong enough to lose again. Not now. . . ."

"You won't lose, Cat. I promise you." His hands framed her face, then slid into the long, unbraided fire of her hair. He closed his eyes against the confusion and fear he saw in hers. "Don't look at me like a cat with her paw in a trap. Trust me."

"But you don't trust me."

His eyes opened. A trick of light made them

nearly black. "I was twenty when I married her. She was eighteen, pregnant, and very much in love with me, she said. I thought I was in love with her. I knew I wanted the child she carried. Two weeks after we were married she had an abortion."

Cat froze, but he didn't notice. This time he was the one seeing the past.

"She told me it was a miscarriage. I believed her. Later, I found out the truth. Thank God the second baby she got rid of wasn't mine or I'd have—" He stopped abruptly. His hands flexed, pulling Cat's hair almost painfully. He didn't notice. Nor did she. Both were caught in the past, his past. "I paid her off. One million dollars. Being shed of that bitch was one of the few things money could buy that was worth having." His eyes focused on Cat again. His voice was harsh. "What about him? Do you still love him?"

Cat reeled beneath the brutality of his revelations. She had accused him of not trusting her, and he had told her something she was certain he had never told anyone else. Now he was asking the same of her. She didn't want to talk about Billy. But then, Travis hadn't wanted to talk about his past failure, either.

She studied his face intently, weighing her instinct to trust him against the lessons of a past that had almost destroyed her. If she was wrong about Travis, if he was more boy than man, trusting him would be the worst mistake she could make. She would lose more than she could regain by a midnight swim, more than she could regain at all. She would lose herself.

Closing her eyes, she tried to shut out the familiar stranger in front of her. Maybe if she couldn't see him, she wouldn't soar or drown in his compelling eyes, eyes that offered her the sensual release and the freedom of a great black ship skimming the edge of creation.

"I married him when I was nineteen," she said, her voice sounding thin, distant. The words were rough, forced past her unwillingness to remember, memories choking her. "My father had just died; my mother had all she could do to take care of my brother and sister. I needed love. I thought Billy loved me."

She shuddered, remembering, but no words came. She couldn't speak about exactly what had happened. Not yet. Maybe not ever. "I was very, very wrong," she said at last. "Money had spoiled Billy. He didn't know the difference between a woman and a whore. He didn't even care." She closed her eyes, knowing she owed Travis more but unable even to form the thoughts that would lead to words. "No, I don't love Billy. Most of the time I don't even hate him."

Travis kissed her eyelids, then rocked her against his chest, comforting both of them. It was a closeness that demanded nothing, two people holding each other, creating warmth where there had been only chill before, a simple moment of peace.

Chapter 3

DAWN CAME TO THE SEA LIKE A MAGENTA DREAM. CAT stood by the bay window, a cup of tea steaming in her hand, and watched the water beyond the rocks that lined the cove. When she saw a dark, powerful shape cut across the shimmering swells, she set aside her tea, grabbed her camera and ran out on the deck. Through the thousand-millimeter lens she saw Travis almost as clearly as she would have if he were across the room.

She had difficulty keeping him in focus; the long lens had a very shallow depth of field. She had to hold utterly still. Normally that wasn't a problem. This morning, though, her heart was beating so strongly that she had to fasten the camera on a tripod.

She stared through the lens with the pleasure of a miser counting gold. Travis's arms and legs moved rhythmically, tirelessly, propelling him through a dawning world where colors gathered and ran and glimmered with each shift of body and wave.

Seeing him like this she could believe that yesterday had been real, that this man had kissed her, held her, then gently let her go and not touched her again. She had been reassured by both the holding and the letting go. They had eaten dinner like old friends, speaking casually or not at all, until there had come a time of silence. He had brushed her cheek with his fingertips and had left without a word. She had not protested. Each of them needed time to absorb what had happened since they had held each other. Each needed to find anew where self ended and other began . . . because for a single, simple moment there had been no difference. It was a moment neither he nor she had been prepared for.

Cat let out her breath and followed Travis with the lens, tracking him as she triggered the camera. The motor drive beat as quickly as her heart, trying to capture the man and the moment. It was delicate work, probably impossible, but she had to try. She wanted to show him as he was to her, half-shadow, half-dawn, power and mystery and fascination to equal the radiant sea. And like the sea, he could change between heartbeats—gentle, savage, serene, turbulent—shaking the certainties of anyone who dared his depths. Caught in the shimmering, ecstatic light, she could believe anything, even that she had met him yesterday and known him forever.

The phone rang, not for the first time. Reluctantly, Cat put away her dreams and ran inside. There was only one person who would call her at this hour. Rodney Harrington, her New York "angel." It had been on his yacht that she had cooked her way to California. He was also her agent, the man who had nagged and flattered her into her career as a photographer at a time when she had no self-confidence and less self-respect.

"Hello?" she said breathlessly.

"Morning, Cochran. Catch you sleeping for once?"

"Not this year, Angel. Maybe in January. I was taking pictures on the deck."

Harrington sighed. "Swear to God, Cochran, you work too hard."

"Tell me something I don't know."

"You're sexy."

Cat laughed. Harrington was the only man she had ever met who could say such things, mean them, and never crowd the No Trespassing signs she had set out against the male world.

"Well," said Harrington smugly, "you told me to tell you something you didn't know. How are you coming with Ashcroft?"

She was glad he couldn't see the expression on her face. Blake Ashcroft was a very trendy poet. She had been assigned to do the art for a collection of his poems. The book would be oversized, beautifully made, very expensive—in short, a photographer's dream. She was grateful to Harrington for getting her the assignment. She just wished that Ashcroft were something other than a drawing-room octopus.

"Didn't he call you?" asked Cat.

"Was he supposed to?"

"The last time I told him no, he said if I didn't play he'd get another photographer."

"Oh, that." Harrington sighed. "Yes, he mentioned that."

"And?" Cat's hand tightened on the phone. She needed the work, needed the money—but she didn't need the harassment.

"I told him you had herpes."

There was a stunned silence, then Cat choked on laughter.

Harrington cleared his throat. "Don't know that it will do you much good," he admitted after a moment. "Ashcroft said that it was okay, he had it too."

Cat groaned. "Thanks a lot, Angel."

"Yeah. Ready for the good news?"

"Should I sit down?" she asked dryly.

"You remember that Danvers book I talked about last year?"

Cat frowned. Last year seemed like a lifetime ago. She had crowded in so many assignments. "Nope."

"T. H. Danvers, the ship designer. The man whose hull designs win every race they're entered in. It's so bad that the handicappers are talking about making an entirely new category for Danvers hulls."

"Is that good?"

"Good? It's flat incredible! He's revolutionized hull dynamics. Swear to God, the man's a genius, and the most private man since Howard Hughes. Danvers is also a friend of mine. I've been after him to do a book for years, but he never stayed in one place for more than a few weeks. He's on your coast now, and has found something interesting enough to make him change his plans. He's going to stick around for a few weeks, maybe even a few months. I know you're busy—I got most of the assignments for you!—but this is too good to pass up. Can you do it?"

"What, exactly, am I supposed to do?"

"Shoot images for a book called *The Danvers Touch.* Danvers thinks the book is going to be about designing hulls, particularly the Danvers racing hull. Well, that's part of it. But it's also going to be about the man. I want people to see him as the complex artist he is. I want them to read the book, look at your images, and *know* what it's like to design and sail a Danvers hull."

"Swear to God," she said sardonically, "that shouldn't take more than an afternoon."

Harrington laughed. "The money's not bad, Cochran. Ten thousand up front, the same in back, and a matching bonus if the work is really good." He waited. "You're awfully quiet."

"I'm thinking."

"Think out loud."

"I'm about finished with Ashcroft's art. He hasn't seen most of it yet, but it's good. That show you set up in L.A. for late November is crowding me a bit. I haven't picked out more than three of the thirty images they want, much less done anything about the printing, matting and framing."

"Do all that when it's too dark to take pictures," he advised. "If it gets tight, I'll find someone to do it for you. If it gets down to the short strokes, I'll do it myself."

"Ummm."

"Yeah, I know. If you can't do it yourself, you damn well won't let anyone else do it. Independent as a hog on ice."

"Your midwestern roots are showing."

"Soybean money is as good as other kinds and better than most. Take Energystics, for instance."

"I'd love to. Have they sent my check yet?"

Harrington sighed. "Sorry, Cochran. I've camped on their carpet, and all they give me is some variation of 'Your check is in the mail.'"

Cat swore under her breath. She had spent ten weeks on the Energystics assignment, gone all over hell and back shooting art for a massive, full-color report on energy systems of the twenty-first century. They had loved her work, praised her endlessly to Harrington—and had yet to pay a single cent of the thirty thousand dollars they owed her. They hadn't even gotten around to reimbursing her for three thousand dollars of her own money that had gone toward renting a helicopter. No matter how Harrington threatened or pleaded, the Big Check from Energystics eluded her.

"Why is it that I'm expected to pay my bills on time and the rest of the world isn't?" She sighed. "How soon would I get money from the Danvers book?"

"As soon as you sign the contract."

"Translation: As soon as you can pry out money after I've signed the contract."

Harrington laughed. "Not this time, Cochran. The publisher is a friend of mine."

"I'd feel better if your friend was the accountant."

"Accountants don't have friends. Two weeks after you sign you'll get the money. Swear to God."

"You're on, Angel. And you *are* an angel. I'd been counting on that Energystics check."

"I'll call you and set up a meeting with Danvers."

"I suppose he's an octopus, too," she said grimly.

"Not to worry. He likes ships better than skirts. If he wants a woman, he buys her for a while."

"Female."

"What?"

"You buy females, not women."

Harrington laughed. "Is that how it works? Well, whatever you call them, they're standing in line for Danvers. I'll talk to you soon, Cochran. And turn on your answering machine this time, okay?"

Smiling, Cat hung up, flicked on the answering machine and went quickly back to the deck. Travis was no longer in sight. She was tempted to wait until he came back on the return leg of his morning swim, but she didn't have time. If she was going to do the Danvers book, she didn't even have time to sleep. She set a watch alarm to remind her of her doctor's appointment in two hours, stuffed the watch in her camera case and set off for the beach.

Even with the alarm she was late for her appointment. As she rushed into the doctor's office, she acknowledged the apprehension that lay beneath her haste—she was afraid of what the tests she had taken two weeks ago might have uncovered, afraid that her unpredictable periods were caused by something unthinkable.

"Dr. Stone will see you in her office," said the nurse.

Cat followed the nurse back to the doctor's office. She had never met anyone more unlike her name; Dr. Stone was a warm woman of about fifty-five, rather than the grim male gynecologist Cat had expected on her first visit eight months ago. Since then, she and the doctor had become friends.

"Sit down, Catherine," said the doctor, smiling up from a pile of papers. "All your tests came back negative, which is good news for you and bad news for me. There's no obvious organic reason for your menstrual cycle to be as erratic as it has been in the last year."

Cat let out a long sigh. "Happy days," she murmured. "But I'd like to know why my period is so late."

"You still haven't gotten it?" said Dr. Stone, looking at her sharply.

"Oh, it came two days after I had the tests." Cat smiled wryly. "Scared me into it, I guess."

Dr. Stone scanned Cat's file with professional

speed. "Your cycle is highly unpredictable. Six weeks, three weeks, seven weeks, sixteen days . . . Mmmm. Spotting?"

"Sometimes. No pattern."

"Of course not," said Dr. Stone. "That would be too easy. Cramps?"

"Rarely. Nothing aspirin doesn't take care of."

"And according to the tests everything is in the right place, nothing missing and no extras. . . . Mmmm. How do you feel?"

"Tired."

"Taking the vitamins and iron I prescribed?"

"Religiously. There are days I think that's all that keeps me going."

Dr. Stone set aside the file and leaned back in her chair. "Tell me about your days, Catherine."

"I get up, I work, I go to bed."

The doctor's lips curved. "Take me through an average day."

"Up an hour before dawn. Exercise, shower, breakfast, and out the door. The poet I'm working for has a thing about 'rosy-fingered dawn.'"

"So did Homer."

"Homer did it better," said Cat with a grimace. "Blake Ashcroft is a bit soft for my taste." She shrugged. "Anyway, I shoot the Ashcroft assignment for a few hours, then I do a few hours on various small details—bookkeeping, query letters and the like. Then I edit and file slides until the light starts slanting again. Or I go argue with the processor who loused up the color on my prints, or argue with the framer who can't cut a right angle on the mat, or I argue with accountants who can't seem to write out checks paying me for work I've already done."

"I thought your agent did that."

"Only on the assignments he gets for me. The smaller stuff I handle myself. Where was I?"

"Arguing."

"Right. After two o'clock I go out shooting again. That lasts until dark. Sometimes I have a night shoot, but not often. After dark I spend a little more time on office work—filing, filling orders for particular slides and such. Then I go to bed."

"Mmmm. How much sleep do you get?"

"Five hours. Sometimes six."

Dr. Stone's silver eyebrows lifted. "And on the weekends?"

Cat looked puzzled. "The same, unless I'm traveling. Then I sometimes get the afternoon off if a flight is delayed or the art director doesn't show up."

Dr. Stone shook her head slowly. "Seven days a week, no time off for good behavior?"

"That's the trouble with working for yourself. The hours are lousy."

The doctor's capable hands flipped through Cat's folder again. "Nothing has changed since the first visit? There's still no possibility of pregnancy?"

Cat felt her expression change, saw Dr. Stone's suddenly intent look, and wished the question had never been asked. "No. No possibility of pregnancy," said Cat stiffly.

Dr. Stone sighed. "Catherine, I'm hardly going to be shocked if you tell me you've been sleeping with a man and were either careless or unlucky and ended up pregnant." She waited a moment for her patient to say something, then sighed again. "It helps if you cooperate. Without that I can't do much except doodle in your file."

Cat closed her eyes and said very softly, "I can't get pregnant."

"What?"

"I'm sterile."

The chair creaked as Dr. Stone leaned forward. "From the beginning, please."

When Cat's eyes opened they were haunted. "I was married for three years. I never tried *not* to get pregnant. My husband was certified fertile. Ergo, I'm sterile."

"Were your periods irregular then?"

"No."

Dr. Stone frowned and reviewed Cat's file. "I can't see any reason why you shouldn't become pregnant. None of the ordinary causes of infertility are present. Are you sure that your husband was fertile?"

Cat closed her eyes. She could still see Billy's face as he waved the lab report at her: *adequate for conception.* "Yes. I'm sure."

"What did your tests show?"

"I didn't have any tests. Why bother?"

"Infertility is often curable."

Cat shrugged. "A bad marriage isn't." Then, seeing that Dr. Stone wasn't satisfied, Cat added, "Even if I was as fertile as a frog, pregnancy isn't at the root of my irregular periods. To get pregnant there would have to be a man. There isn't." As she spoke she remembered Travis and wondered what it would be like if he were her man. . . .

"Would you agree to some tests to pin down the cause of infertility? Sometimes it's as simple as bad timing or as subtle as incompatible body chemistries."

"Not unless you think it's causing my cycle to be so damned unpredictable," said Cat.

Dr. Stone snapped shut the file, folded her hands and stared at her stubborn patient. "What's throwing off your cycle, my dear Catherine, is the same thing that's causing those dark bruises beneath your eyes. Overwork. You're a prime candidate for whatever virus comes along. Ease off. Take your weekends and play. Build up your reserves of strength."

"In January, I'll do that," said Cat tiredly. "Just get me through the next fourteen weeks, Dr. Stone."

"What happens in January?"

"Easy Street," said Cat promptly. Then she sighed. "Well, at least Easier Street. The twins' last payment for medical school will be done and mother will be safely married. I just have to get there from here."

"Sounds like quite a jump."

"I'll make it. Besides, I love my work."

"Try loving a man," retorted the doctor. "It's less strenuous."

Again, an image of Travis haunted Cat. She hadn't even known him a day and she couldn't stop thinking about him. She cursed her photographer's awareness of texture and line, light and shadow, tourmaline eyes reflecting her in their depths.

"Here." Dr. Stone's brisk words brought Cat's attention back to the office. "I'm changing your prescription. This one is guaranteed to put color in your cheeks. The nurse will give you a B-complex shot and take a blood sample. Make an appointment for a week from today. If your blood count isn't up by then, I'm giving you iron shots." She smiled slyly. "My patients tell me they're painful."

Cat groaned. "I hate shots," she muttered, getting up to leave.

"Catherine?"

She turned and looked back at the doctor.

"It's just as well you can't get pregnant now. You're in no shape for it."

"My silver lining for the day," said Cat flippantly.

Dr. Stone shook her head. "Get some sleep, Catherine. I'll see you in a week."

The rest of the day fled by in a torrent of letters, files and phone calls until the light changed and she rushed off to meet the poet at the base of a beach cliff.

"Ashcroft," said Cat distinctly, "I've shot this cliff at sunset every day for the last three weeks. What makes you think you'll like it any better this time?"

Blake Ashcroft stepped closer to her, smiling slowly. "Cathy-baby, any time you'd rather shoot the interior of my bedroom, just let me know. Until then you'll shoot rocks at sunset or any other time that pleases me."

Cat looked at the fair-haired, blue-eyed cherub in front of her and wished very sincerely to rearrange Ashcroft's pretty face. She knew he didn't need this shot any more than he had needed any of the others she had done for him in the last two weeks. It was simply his way of making life hell for her because she would not lay down for him.

Deliberately she turned her back on him and measured the cliff face once again. There were many fine images buried in those rocks, but Ashcroft wanted none of them. She shrugged off the broad straps of both camera carrying cases and sighed in relief. As she studied the cliff she absently rubbed her shoulders. It had been a long day, one among many. And then Ashcroft. Why couldn't the fair-haired toad just take one of his many groupies and crawl off under a rock? Why did he have to badger the only unwilling woman west of the Mississippi? She should be home now, fixing dinner. If she were home, she might get to see more of Travis than a glimpse through a thousand-millimeter lens.

Grimly, Cat brought her mind back to the cliff. She shifted her perspective. Suddenly, heavy gold light turned the rock into black velvet. Random plants clinging to the cliff became golden sculptures radiant with life and mystery. The air itself seemed to quiver with imminence, reflecting light as though shot through with diamond dust.

Without looking, she stepped back and reached for a camera case. Her hand bumped into Ashcroft's hip. Before she could recover he grabbed her wrist, holding her hand against his body, moving suggestively. She made a sound of disgust and tried to pull free. She couldn't. Ashcroft's poetry might have been soft, but he wasn't. He was both taller and stronger than she was.

"Cathy-baby," he said, smiling coldly, "I'm going to have you whether you like it or not. I know that *I'll* like it."

Cat felt an instant of fear when she realized that the beach was deserted. They were in a deep trough between water-smoothed rocks, shielded from casual observation. Nearby a stairway twisted up the cliff, but she could see only the middle of the stairs, and they were empty. She was alone with him.

Fear gave way to a surge of raw, hot rage. Whatever happened, she would guarantee that Ashcroft would *not* like it. She bent suddenly, grabbing a handful of sand. Before she could fling sand in the poet's smiling face, Travis appeared between the boulders that hid the bottom of the stairway. Long, powerful fingers wrapped around Ashcroft's wrist, found the nerves between the wristbones, and squeezed. The pain was so quick, so paralyzing, that Ashcroft's only response was a gasp as his hand went numb.

Cat jerked free and looked at Ashcroft with hard

gray eyes. It was all she could do to keep from slapping the stunned expression off his face.

"Is he someone I should know?" drawled Travis.

"No," she said harshly. "If I had a choice, I wouldn't know him either."

She looked at Travis for the first time—and had to overcome an impulse to step backward. Violence seethed behind eyes that were more black than green; violence waited in the unyielding planes of his cheeks; violence begged to be free in the purposeful coiling of muscle and sinew. After a final measured squeeze, Travis released the other man's wrist.

"This specimen," said Cat, "is Blake Ashcroft, wunderkind of American poetry. He's also a spoiled little boy. I'm doing the art for his latest book."

"You *were* doing the art, you frigid bitch," snarled Ashcroft, then he flinched at the expression that came to Travis's face.

"I *am* doing the art," shot back Cat. "If you don't believe me, ask Harrington. You try to dump me and I'll sue you for everything from breach of contract to attempted rape." She glanced quickly at Travis. He was watching her with a startled expression that gave way to speculation, followed by a curious satisfaction. "I have a witness, Ashcroft," said Cat.

"An overgrown beach bum," scoffed the poet, looking at the big, barefoot man wearing cut-off jeans and a faded blue T-shirt. "Who will believe his word against mine? You're through, Cathy-baby. Finis. Kaput. The End."

Travis leaned over and spoke so softly to Ashcroft that Cat couldn't hear him. The poet went as pale as his hair, stared in disbelief at Travis, and tried unsuccessfully to speak. Travis waited with the patience of a predator at a water hole.

"For God's sake," said Ashcroft in a hoarse voice, glaring at Cat. "You can do the damned book. But the pictures had better be great or I'll—" He looked sideways at Travis and shut up. Then, almost desperately, "Why the hell didn't you tell me you had a famous, jealous maniac for a lover?"

Cat's eyes widened and laughter tugged at her lips as she turned to Travis. "Are you a famous jealous maniac, Travis, er, *lover?*"

Travis smiled lazily. As he shifted to face her, sunlight transformed his eyes into brilliant blue-green jewels. She stared, forgetting everything but his compelling male presence. His eyes narrowed as though he were reading thoughts that she wasn't even aware of yet. The same fingertips that had brought such agony to Ashcroft caressed the slanting lines of her cheekbones and the curve of her mouth.

"I'm jealous as hell of everything that touches you," Travis said, "even the sunlight. Especially the sunlight pouring over your smooth skin."

Her lips parted in surprise. Slowly, his fingertip slid over the small serrations of her teeth. She shivered at the intimacy of the gesture. Without thinking, she closed her teeth delicately around his finger, wanting only to prolong the tantalizing, unexpected caress. His expression changed again as he focused in the moment with a consuming sensuality that was as exciting as the feel of him between her lips.

Ashcroft said something crude and decidedly unpoetic. Then, "I can see that she isn't going to have her mind on photography. Tomorrow, Cathy-baby. Same time, same place. I don't care who your lover is, you'll get that cliff the way I want it or the deal is off."

"She'll be there," said Travis, not looking up from Cat's smoky gray eyes. "And so will I."

Ashcroft wanted to object but thought better of it. He stalked off without another word.

Cat blinked as though emerging from a deep sleep. Slowly she released his fingertip. When Travis did not withdraw she moved her tongue over his finger with feline deliberation, tasting him. Then she realized what she was doing and flushed to the roots of her russet hair. She turned her face quickly, ending the contact.

"I'm sorry," she whispered, too ashamed to look at him. Her ex-husband had taught her quite well what men thought of women who were aggressive. "Whore" was the most polite word Billy had used. "I wasn't thinking."

Travis caught her face between his hands. His grip was both gentle and inexorable. After a few seconds, she did not fight it. She turned back and looked at him—and her breath went ragged at the desire burning in the depths of his eyes.

"There's nothing to be sorry for," he said, bending down to taste her mouth with his own.

The kiss began as gently as dawn, a simple flow of warmth. Then the tip of his tongue teased the outer line of her lips, burrowed into the corners of her smile, slid between her teeth to taste and cherish the soft heat of her mouth. Though he held her far more gently than Ashcroft had, she could not move. She was too stunned by the sensuality of the man whose taste spread across her tongue like wine. She was nearly thirty, divorced . . . and learning for the first time what it was like to be well and truly kissed.

When he finally lifted his mouth from hers, she was trembling. And then she realized that he, too, had tremors running through his strong body.

"Travis . . . ?" she breathed, sigh and question at once.

He kissed the heat that bloomed across her cheekbones. "I feel like throwing you over my shoulder and sailing off into the sunset. But"—he smiled wickedly—"I'm too old to make love with a woman who doesn't know my full name."

Cat looked at him for a long moment. She realized that beneath his humor he was as hungry to taste her again as she was to be tasted. "You don't know my full name, either," she said in a husky voice.

"I think I do. You mentioned a man called Harrington. Is that Rodney "Swear-To-God" Harrington, promoter extraordinaire, the best friend and most devious man God ever made?"

She smiled despite her surprise. "That's the man." She cocked her head and looked up at Travis. "But he never mentioned you."

"He never mentions anyone by the first name. Only the last. Or by title, as in Ashcroft, the Crown Prince of Treacle."

Cat snickered. "You must know Harrington very well. He's careful who he shares his titles with."

"Like Fire-And-Ice Cochran?" asked Travis.

Cat drew her breath in sharply. That was Harrington's pet name for her, one he had coined in the Virgin Islands the night she'd climbed up his yacht's ladder and walked naked into his lounge, dripping rage and salt water. "Who *are* you?"

"Has he ever mentioned anyone with the title In The Wind?"

She frowned. "Yes, but—" She shook her head. "I'm terrible with names," she admitted.

He brushed his lips over hers. "T. H. Danvers," he said in a husky drawl, "at your service."

Chapter 4

CAT STIFFENED AND STEPPED BACK, HER FINGERS STILL clenched around a handful of sand. "You're Danvers?" Then, quickly, "How long have you known my name?"

"About two minutes," Travis said, looking at her with sudden wariness. "When you threw Harrington at the poet, I guessed you must be Cochran. There can't be too many women photographers in Laguna Beach who have Rodney Harrington for an agent."

She studied him with serious gray eyes, obviously deciding whether or not to believe that he had just found out who she was. After a long moment, she sighed and let sand sift away between her fingers. "I don't like coincidences, but I know they happen all the time."

"I'm not very fond of coincidences myself," he admitted, his lips hard beneath the tawny moustache, sea-colored eyes suddenly distant, measuring. "Did Harrington tell you that I wouldn't guarantee you the job until I saw your work?"

Cat's eyes narrowed slightly. "You think I knew who you were all along, don't you? Well, Mr. T. H. Danvers, you can relax. I'm not one of the females standing in line waiting for a paid vacation with you. If you don't believe me, ask Harrington. He'll tell you the simple truth: I *never* mix men and business."

Travis nodded. "He already told me. In fact, that was the only reason I agreed to trying out a woman photographer. No chance of involvement other than professional." He smiled crookedly. "But then I saw this woman balanced like a cat on the rocks above the waves. She was taking pictures as though there was no tomorrow—and no tide. How was I to know that the beautiful redheaded idiot I rescued would be Harrington's Cochran?" His voice lightly stressed the possessive.

"Three out of five wrong," she said in a clipped voice.

"What?"

"I have red hair, and my name is Cochran." She held up two fingers. "But I'm not beautiful, I'm not an idiot and I most certainly am not Harrington's!"

"He's very fond of you," said Travis, his tone both cool and curious.

"And I'm fond of him," she snapped. "I owe him more than I can repay."

"There's always the usual method."

"Your way?" she said, her mouth thinning to a line of distaste. "Reducing sex to a simple business transaction, so many minutes at so much per groan?" She bent over, picked up her camera bags and shrugged the straps into place on her shoulders.

"I'll call Harrington tomorrow and tell him to find you another photographer."

"No. Not yet."

"Not yet? What are you waiting for? A definite 'go to hell' from me? Fine, I'll make it definite. Go—"

With a swift motion Travis put his mouth over hers, smothering her words. His quickness startled her, giving her no chance to withdraw. Nor did she really want to. The feel of him on her lips, his warmth stealing into her bones . . . each time he touched her he made her understand anew how much she had been missing without him. Unknowingly, he had taken her habit of honesty and used it as a weapon to breach her defenses. She could not tell herself that her response came from long abstinence or temporary hunger, that she would react the same to any man. She responded because he was Travis, unique; and she was Cat, vulnerable to his uniqueness.

"Such a prickly little cat," he said, gently kissing her. "Are you angry because I won't guarantee you the job?"

"No."

"Then what?"

Very carefully, she eased out of his arms. "I'm angry because I don't mix men and business, but"—she made an impatient motion—"suddenly I find I've done just that."

The corner of his mouth turned up in a sardonic smile. "And I don't mix women and emotion, but suddenly I'm doing just that." He looked at her startled expression and laughed. "You can't be that innocent, Cat. Surely you've figured out by now that men want sex and women want money. There's no reason that both can't have what they want. A simple business transaction."

"You're talking about boys and females, not men and women."

"You're dreaming, Cat. Wake up. This is the real world. But"—he bent his head again, traced the sensitive outline of her lips with the tip of his tongue—"the real world has real compensations."

She could not conceal her tremor of response before she jerked her head away. "I'm not a prostitute, Travis."

"Who said anything about prostitutes?"

"You did."

He sighed and straightened. When he spoke, his voice was gentle and oddly sad. "I'm not naive or selfish, Cat. I don't expect a woman to go to bed with me and get nothing in return."

"She's getting the same thing you're getting."

He seemed on the point of saying something, then shrugged. "That's not enough for a woman. Besides, if it's a business transaction, both parties know exactly what to expect. No nasty surprises and no recriminations. And," bluntly, "despite what your expression says, it's not prostitution. The women I've had weren't prostitutes." He smiled slightly. "Mistresses for a time, yes, but never whores."

"Your wife really burned you to the bone, didn't she?" said Cat.

His eyes narrowed until almost no color showed. "She completed my education."

"And just what did you learn—that women are whores?"

"No. I learned that I'll never marry a woman who has less money than I do. And I'm very rich, Cat. Very . . . rich."

Win some. Lose some. Some never had a chance. If you're rich, Travis, we fall into the third category.

Cat's words returned to haunt her. She was appalled at the sadness she felt, and the pain, a razor of regret turning inside her. She realized then just how much Travis had penetrated her defenses and how terribly easy it would be to fall in love with him. And how terribly stupid.

"I'm sorry," she whispered, closing her eyes, not wanting to look at the face of the man she could have loved.

"You've done nothing to be sorry for," said Travis, surprised by the sadness that trembled in her voice.

She laughed a little wildly because it was better than crying.

"Cat? What's wrong?"

"You're rich."

He said nothing, for he didn't understand why "rich" was an epithet on her lips. He tried to gather her against his body and comfort her, but she stepped out of his reach. With a tired sigh she readjusted the weight of her camera gear and faced him.

"Do you want to call Harrington or should I?" she asked. Her voice was flat, giving no clue to her thoughts.

"What for?"

"To tell him to get another photographer."

"You're quitting just like that? Just because I won't guarantee you the job until I've seen some photos of my ship taken by you?"

"Of course not," she said coolly. "You have every right to decide whether my images fit your needs."

"Then why?"

"Simple. You have no right to turn my world inside out, breaking my rules, making me feel—" She stopped abruptly. "I don't mix men and business, period."

"I'm not 'men,' I'm just Travis," he drawled in a reasonable voice that made her want to scream. "And I'll try to make working with me more pleasure than business. I'm not Blake Ashcroft, little Cat. I won't make life hell for you if you don't sleep with me. Besides," he added blandly, "can you afford to turn down work?"

Her lips thinned. She needed money and he knew it. "If I agree to do the book," she said in a clipped voice, "it's the publisher rather than you who pays me. A simple business transaction, Mr. T. H. Danvers, something you should be able to appreciate. Nothing personal at all. Certainly nothing intimate."

"And no possibility of . . . intimacy?"

"We both have our rules, Travis. You don't have a woman unless you buy her and I'm not for sale. What could be clearer than that?"

"The fact that we want each other," he said bluntly.

Cat looked up and saw herself focused in his blue-green eyes. She saw him look at her hair, her lips, the shape of her breasts against her velour pullover, the curve of her legs below her cut off jeans. His desire was almost tangible, as was her response to him.

"No," she said, her voice husky, denying her words even as she spoke them. "It wouldn't work."

"Crap," said Travis politely. His hands snaked out, lifting the camera equipment off her shoulders.

"Travis—"

"We'll argue about it over dinner," he said,

walking toward her house, carrying the heavy bags with an ease she envied. "My treat. Think of it as a business meeting."

She ran until she was ahead of him, then stopped and turned to confront him. "That's exactly what it will be. Business."

His slow smile caressed her. "Whatever you say, Cat."

He took her to a restaurant called Antonello's. There were small leaded-glass windows with frames painted forest green; a thick carpet woven in discreet patterns of deep red, cream and green; red linen tablecloths and fresh flowers, gleaming china, spotless silver, crystal glasses dividing light into rich primary colors; and over all the hushed ambiance of wealth. When she had realized how expensive the restaurant was, she had objected angrily. Only the delectable scents of food had made her give in; she was too tired, too hungry, to argue about how much the food cost.

Cat savored a final bite of buttery scallop, sighed, and sipped her wine. The Chardonnay tasted like sunlight. It had been a while since she had drunk a wine that matched her body chemistry so exactly. She had discovered that wines praised by other people often were bitter to her. At first she had thought it was her untrained palate. Later she had realized that she was simply different.

"Still mad?" asked Travis quietly, his eyes very dark, reflecting only the sinuous dance of candlelight.

She shook her head, making candlelight run like melted rubies through her auburn hair.

"I really didn't choose this restaurant because I thought it was a way to buy you, Cat. I didn't even think about it. If I had . . ." He shrugged. "I'd have taken you somewhere else."

"I know. And you're right—the food here is wonderful." She sighed and looked longingly at the scallops she was too full to eat. "I just wish I could finish it all."

"That good?" he asked, smiling lazily.

"Don't take my word for it," she said, sliding her fork beneath a particularly succulent scallop.

With a skill left over from years of feeding the younger twins, she popped the scallop into Travis's mouth. It wasn't until too late that she realized the unthinking intimacy of her gesture. She made an exasperated sound and wished that Travis wouldn't seem so very familiar to her. She had to keep reminding herself that she had known him only one day, and that what she had learned about him was a clear warning not to become involved. Rich men just didn't know how to love. If she knew that and was fooled by him anyway, then she was indeed a fool.

As her father had always told her: fool me once, damn you; fool me twice, damn *me.*

Travis's tongue licked up a stray bit of sauce from his lower lip. "Mmm. Again." He opened his mouth slightly, waiting.

She hesitated, then deftly fed him another scallop.

"You're very good at that," he said, eyes watching her, blue-green mystery. "Do you have children?"

Her fork made a ringing sound against the china plate. She took a sip of wine, ignoring his question.

"Cat?"

"No." Her voice was low, almost savage. "No children." She looked up at him with pale eyes. "More scallops?"

He hesitated, curious but cautious. He knew his

question had hurt her, but he didn't know why. "Yes, please," he said finally.

Instead of feeding him as he had hoped she would, she switched plates with him. She watched in silence while he finished her dinner, eating from her plate, sipping from her glass because his own wine was too assertive to drink with scallops, using her fork, licking the silver tines clean. The feeling of intimacy was as warm and graceful as the flame dancing at the tip of the scented candle.

"Dessert?" he asked quietly, pouring more wine in her glass before the waiter could, sipping, returning the glass to her.

She shook her head. He smiled. The waiter appeared as though conjured out of candlelight.

"Something chocolate," said Travis.

The waiter returned with a mousse that was light, creamy and just sweet enough to offset the rich natural bitterness of the chocolate. Travis took a bite and nodded his approval. The waiter vanished. Travis filled the fork and held it out to her.

"Open up."

They were sitting side-by-side, well within reach, but he had no experience with the gentle art of spoon-feeding. Part of the mousse ended up just below her lip.

"Damn," he muttered, leaning forward and neatly licking up the evidence of his bad aim. He was so quick, so casual, that she had no time to object. "You can tell that I haven't spent a lot of time doing this," he said, turning her chin with his fingertip to make sure that he hadn't missed any mousse.

"No wonder you asked for a private table," she said dryly.

Travis, his mouth full of another bite of mousse,

simply smiled, scooped and held out another forkful of dessert to her.

"How did you know that chocolate is one of my weaknesses?" groaned Cat, opening her mouth.

"Because it's one of mine."

She savored the mousse. He swore softly.

"What's wrong?" she asked. "You did it perfectly that time. Not a speck out of place."

"I know." He looked regretfully at her clean lower lip. "Maybe next time . . ." He held out another bite.

"You really are a buccaneer, aren't you?" she said as her lips closed around the silver tines.

"Because I like licking chocolate off you?" he asked with a lazy smile.

Cat swallowed and shook her head. "Because you do what you damn well please when it damn well pleases you."

"Are you saying this doesn't please you?" he asked, taking her hand and kissing her palm. With melting gentleness his teeth closed over the pad of flesh at the base of her thumb.

Her breath caught, then resumed, but he had heard the ragged sound. He smiled and rubbed her palm against his beard. For an instant she enjoyed the warmth and silky roughness of his hair. Then she withdrew her hand.

"Last bite," said Travis, holding out a fork heaped with mousse.

"I've had more than my share already."

Travis's eyes narrowed slightly, as though he suspected she was refusing more than a bite of chocolate. She wished he were less perceptive or she were less vulnerable. But she was too honest—or foolish—to wish that she hadn't met him. Though she knew she would burn herself if she came too close to his fire, she also knew it was wonderful to be warm again.

She refused cognac, then ended up sipping the amber liquid from his warm snifter. He watched her with an intensity that would have unnerved her had she not been watching him in just the same way. A primal curiosity consumed them, a mutual fascination that was both sensual and mental, a silent recognition of the other's unique *rightness*.

It wasn't until Travis tucked Cat into the front seat of his gunmetal Lotus that she realized how sleepy she was. Headlights on the opposite side of the freeway moved by in a dazzling hypnotic silver river. Ahead, a ribbon of taillights glowed with ruby fire. The car's throaty growl was oddly soothing, redolent of restrained power.

The fine food, the wine, the cognac uncurling in her mind, all combined to gently overwhelm Cat. She curled against the seat and slept, silently proclaiming her trust in the utterly familiar stranger called Travis.

He looked over at her and smiled, understanding more than she did about her declaration of trust. He drove quickly, skillfully, not disturbing her even when the Lotus's powerful engine consumed the night, making a mockery of miles and darkness and the twisting Laguna Canyon road.

The only time he hesitated was at his own driveway. He looked at the sleeping woman and knew that she would resent waking up in his bed. He parked in her driveway, used her key to open the front door, turned on the lights and looked for her bedroom. The first room he opened had a view of the midnight ocean, a slightly oversized single bed, an antique oak rocking chair and a matching dresser with a beveled mirror. The sunrise colors of the bed quilt were repeated in a thick wool rug. The combination of polished wood and glowing colors pleased him. It was a room that a man as well as a woman could be at home in.

He turned away, assuming from the size of the bed that this was a spare bedroom. Only after he had opened every door in the house without finding another bed did he realize that the room with the single bed in it was Cat's.

He stood for a long time in the center of her room, looking at the bed. After a moment of curious hesitancy he turned down the crisp sheets, stroking them with sensitive fingers. The sunrise colors of the quilt were matched in the sheets. The delicate scent of her perfume rose from the bed, pervading his senses.

"Cat," he murmured, "I should grab you before you wake up and sail over the edge of the world." He smiled, eyes narrowed, temptation plain in the piratical lines of his face.

She was still asleep when he got back to the car. As he lifted her out and shut the door, she murmured sleepily.

"It's all right," he said softly. "Go back to sleep."

She half opened her eyes, saw his familiar smile and sighed, letting herself slide back into the sleep her tired body craved. His lips rested for a moment on her hair before he carried her inside. He laid her on her bed and began undressing her. As he removed her sandals he stacked them to one side and gently rubbed away the small marks the straps had left on her arch. Then he took out the silver clasp that had held her hair in a disciplined coil on top of her head. Strands as soft and warm as dawn spilled into his hands. He buried his face in the untamed silk of her hair, inhaling deeply.

He knew he should stop there, pull the blanket over her and leave. He knew, but he ignored it. He began unbuttoning the teal blue jumpsuit, which followed her curves so tantalizingly. The silky folds of cloth fell away beneath his hand. He paused for a moment, looking at her creamy body, glad that she wasn't awake to see the fine trembling of his hands.

"Do you know what you do to me, little Cat?" he whispered.

There was no answer. He hadn't expected one. He slipped off her panty hose, careful not to hurt the foot she had scraped on the rocks yesterday. As his fingers reached for her lacy bra and panties, he hesitated.

"You wouldn't like that, would you?" he said very softly. "Prickly little Cat . . . I know I should leave you now. But I can't."

With the ingrained neatness of a man who had spent a long time at sea, Travis folded her clothes and his own and set them on the antique rocking chair. Though he had stopped short of fully undressing her, he had no scruples about his own nightwear or lack of it. He was blissfully nude when he lay down beside her in the small bed, gathered her into his arms and eased the covers over both of them.

She moved slightly, neither awake nor fully asleep, sensing his presence. "Travis . . . ?" she asked, her voice slurred with sleep.

"Shhh," he said, stroking her hair soothingly. "Go back to sleep, Cat. Everything is all right."

She sighed and relaxed into his warmth as though she had slept with him every night of her life.

They slept until dawn shimmered over the ocean, mauve and gold, lavender and cream, a glowing fantasy of colors that invaded Cat's bedroom with a soundless rush of light. Her inner alarm clock prodded her, telling her it was time to be up. She stirred in silent protest—and realized that she was moving against something warm and solid. Beneath her cheek a heart beat in the slow rhythms of relaxation. Eyes closed, barely awake, she realized that she was lying half on top of a man, breathing as he breathed, her arm thrown across his powerful torso, her leg wedged between his.

She didn't have to open her eyes to be utterly certain who shared her intimate sprawl. It wasn't so much the vague memories of being carried inside and tucked in bed by Travis; it was the simple fact that only Travis could have slipped through her defenses to the point that she would not only fall asleep on him but would not awaken even when he got in bed beside her.

She opened her eyes slowly, reluctant to wake up. It was deliciously warm against him, and the dawn was usually so cold. Then she felt the change in his heartbeat, in his body, in the tension of the arm wrapped around her waist, and knew that Travis had awakened. In the same instant she realized that he was naked and she was not. Not quite.

How had he known that she would resent being completely undressed by him when she was asleep? And how could she defend herself against a man who knew her so well?

A large hand stroked her hair slowly. "Don't be angry, Cat," he said softly.

She hesitated, then let herself relax along his length, enjoying the feel of his hand moving over her head and shoulders, down her back. "If you weren't bigger than me," she murmured, "I'd throw you over the deck into the surf."

His body moved in silent laughter. "But I *am* bigger, so what are you going to do?"

"I'm thinking about it."

His hand slid beneath her hair and rubbed down to the small of her back. "May I offer a suggestion?" he said, letting his nails scrape very lightly over the base of her spine.

She shivered and arched against him with a feline movement. She felt his breath catch, then deepen. She lifted her head and looked at him. Dawn had transformed the arrogant lines of his face into velvet shadows and luminous planes. His eyes were such a deep green they were almost black, yet light turned in their depths, light and gentleness and laughter. Beneath his thick moustache his lips shaped a pirate's smile.

"Let me guess what you're going to suggest," said Cat, returning his smile.

"Mmm?" His hand slid up to her hair, fingers rubbing over her scalp until she sighed and relaxed against him again. "What am I going to suggest?" he asked in a carefully neutral voice.

"That I get to work."

"On me," he amended smoothly.

"Oh? I didn't know that you needed work," she said, propping herself up on her elbow and looking at him curiously. "You look all together to me."

"I'm just half together." His hands framed her face. "Looking for the other half." He pulled her gently down to his lips, tasted her. "We'll fit together very well . . . two halves finally whole." His mouth moved over hers before she could answer or protest.

"Don't say anything yet," he whispered. "Just kiss me, that's all I ask, a single kiss. Just one. You know you can trust me. Say you trust me, sweet Cat, show that you trust me. A kiss. Just one kiss for the well-behaved pirate who wanted to steal you and sail over the edge of the world but brought you back to your own room instead."

Cat felt herself succumb to the gentle power of his words, pulled like a bright leaf into the whirlpool of his desire. No man had ever wanted her like this. His need was as irresistible as dawn. Slowly she bent her head until her lips touched his.

His fingers tightened very slightly, speaking eloquently of strength and need held in check. She relaxed even more, trusting his restraint. Her lips moved lightly on his. She felt his body shift, felt sensual tension ripple through him, telling her how desirable she was. Shivers of awareness went through her, a feeling of power that was new, as heady as the cognac she had sipped from his glass. Her ex-husband had rarely permitted her to take the lead sexually, and then only for a few moments.

Part of her expected the gentle prelude to end very quickly in a sudden assertion of male prerogatives. When Travis showed no signs of impatience she slowly increased the pressure of her kiss until she could savor the firmness of his lips, sense the smooth hardness of his teeth, feel the warmth of his breath blending with hers.

His fingers flexed in her hair, encouraging her without caging her, coaxing rather than demanding. With a ragged sigh she opened her lips. Unthinkingly she traced the line of his mouth as he had once traced hers. Then she froze, waiting for the angry withdrawal that had always followed any sensual aggression on her part; Billy had been clear to the point of cruelty as to his expectations of her. Wives were passive. Whores cooperated. Sluts enjoyed.

Travis held her head so that her lips never fully left his. He waited, working his fingers through her hair, caressing her, unwilling for the kiss to end before he had even felt the moving warmth of her tongue over his. Just when he was ready to give in and release his gentle restraint, the sweet pressure of her tongue returned.

"You don't mind?" she breathed, allowing herself the unprecedented luxury of teasing the corners of a man's mouth with her tongue.

"Mind what?" he whispered against her lips, his hands kneading lightly down her back, so lightly that she didn't notice their fine trembling.

"This," she said, licking his lips with catlike neatness. "Or this." Her tongue probed inside his lower lip, delicately touched the serrations of his teeth. "Or this . . ." With a shiver of pleasure, she let her tongue find his.

She moved her lips and tongue over his mouth, instinctively seeking the points of greatest mingling, most intense pleasure. She forgot Billy's harsh teachings, forgot that she hadn't known Travis long, forgot everything but the heat and restrained power of the man who was confident enough to let her test herself on him. The kiss became a timeless sensual awakening, a warm sunrise ending Cat's long night of ignorance and misunderstanding of a woman's essential nature.

Before the kiss ended she was lying between his legs, her flushed body responding to him with sinuous movements that both echoed and increased his hunger. He groaned deep in his chest and moved his hips against her in sensuous questing. His heat and hardness sent a shudder of desire through her, making her cry out against his mouth. His hands moved surely over her body, removing the scraps of midnight lace that he had left in place last night. She didn't object, wanting only to be closer to him, to burn away a lifetime of chill in his unique fire.

"Are you sure, Cat?" he asked, lifting her face until he could see her eyes, smoky with passion, and her lips, bruised with the kisses she had given and taken.

She trembled against him, trying to understand his question. "I've never wanted—like this," she said, her breath ragged. "Is that—what you mean?"

Desire ripped through him, an electric response to her words. He pulled her down and kissed her hungrily, achingly, slipping the leash on his control for just an instant, telling her without words what her admission meant to him. Then he held her away again and fought to control himself.

"That's more than I asked," he said thickly. "I just wanted to know if you're protected against pregnancy."

She stiffened, thinking how very well she was "protected" against such an event. Reflexively, she turned away from him, not wanting to see his eyes change when he knew that she wasn't a whole woman, not wanting to know the exact moment when he would no longer desire her.

"Ah, Cat," he said, moving swiftly onto his side, holding her, pinning her gently beneath one strong leg. "Don't be angry with your blunt pirate."

She let her breath out slowly. "I'm not angry."

His lips brushed gently over hers. Though he said nothing, she knew he was waiting for an answer to his question, but the words simply wouldn't take shape on her tongue.

"Cat?" he said.

"I won't get pregnant," she said, closing her eyes.

The words sounded flat to her, harsh, but there was nothing she could do to soften them. She had told the truth. She wouldn't get pregnant.

He hesitated, obviously bothered by the change in her voice, by her refusal to meet his eyes. "Look at me, Cat. Are you sure?" he asked, his own voice almost hard.

An irrational anger surged through her. He had the right to ask the question once, but no more. Her eyes opened, the color of winter rain. "I'm sure. But it doesn't matter."

He raised a tawny eyebrow. "It does to me. I was caught in the baby trap once. Once was more than enough."

Her smile made him flinch. "Not to worry, T. H. Danvers," she said in a brittle voice. "I'm sterile."

As she spoke the last words she twisted aside, trying to get out from under his weight, out of bed, out of his reach, out of the room . . . *out.*

Chapter 5

THIS TIME CAT'S QUICKNESS DID NOT TAKE TRAVIS BY surprise. He sensed her tension, guessed her intent and pinned her in place with his superior weight.

"Not so fast, little Cat," he said. "Not before you tell me why."

Cat's body twisted violently as she tested his hold. Instantly she realized that Travis not only had position on her, he also had more sheer muscle than she had guessed. That didn't frighten her as she had been frightened when she realized Ashcroft's strength. The difference between the two men was both simple and devastating—she trusted Travis not to force her.

That did not mean, however, that she was pleased to be his captive at the moment.

"Why what?" she asked in a stranger's voice. "Why I'm sterile? Or don't you believe that I am?

Would you like a note from my gynecologist certifying my defect?"

His breath came in sharply. "Don't, Cat. Please don't." He bent to kiss her gently, realizing too late how much the subject hurt her. "I believe you."

She turned her head sharply, evading him. "Then if your curiosity is satisfied, get out of my bed."

"Try to understand," he murmured against her hair, his tongue delicately tracing the contours of her ear. "After my divorce, I swore I'd never be caught in the baby trap again. I'd be a regular Boy Scout, always prepared." He laughed humorlessly. "And I have been. If I'd taken you to my own bed, this never would have happened. But I saw your single bed and knew that Harrington was right, fire and ice, and I couldn't leave you, Cat. I had to stay, warm myself with your sweet fire."

"Stop it!" she hissed, shaking with anger and the desire he could call out of her with a look, a touch, a word.

"Why?" he whispered, his breath stirring her hair, his hips sliding invitingly over hers.

Her body went rigid. *"No."*

Gently he turned her face toward his, forcing her to look at him. "Why?"

"I don't feel like celebrating my defect right now," she said bitterly.

"It isn't a defect," he said, his voice certain.

"That depends on your point of view, doesn't it? Billy wanted a dynasty. You want a roll in the hay."

"And what do you want, Cat?" he asked, touching her hair with fingers that trembled very slightly, afraid that he had lost before either of them even had a chance to win.

She said nothing at all. Her face was framed in a cloud of hair that shimmered and burned with each breath she took. Her eyes were pale as ice, looking through him. She was proud and distant, quivering like a racing sloop under full sail, heeled over perilously far, pursued by a storm.

"I can't change the past," he whispered, watching her with eyes that shared her pain. "But I can give you a chance to run before the storm, to feel ecstasy in every motion, every touch, and when the storm sweeps down, I'll be there. . . . Let me love you, Cat."

Like a soft wind his lips brushed over her cheek, her shoulder, her breast, stealing away her anger while the gentle warmth of his hands gave her back the gift of passion. Slowly her rigid body relaxed, softening beneath him, her breath trembling out. His weight no longer confined her, yet she was held more securely by the pleasure he gave her than she had been by his superior strength.

When his tongue teased her for a moment before drawing the tip of her breast into the heat and pressure of his mouth, she shivered at the unexpected sensations that consumed her. His hand surrounded her with warmth as his fingers slowly kneaded her firm breast. When his teeth caressed the hardened nipple she arched against him, her fingernails sinking into his shoulders. He lifted his mouth and she cried out, not wanting him to stop. Her hands slid into his hair, holding his head against her breast as she twisted beneath him. He rewarded her with a biting caress that made her gasp.

He shifted suddenly, his body moving over her with the smooth power of a breaking wave. His tongue probed her lips with increasing pressure, demanding that she share the kiss. When her lips opened he asked for more, tongue sliding between her teeth, taking possession of every soft bit of her mouth. She responded with a heat that equaled his, invading his mouth with her tongue, trying to consume him even as he consumed her. Her hands moved down his back, glorying in the rippling strength of his body, digging into the tensed muscles of his buttocks, seeking the special heat and hardness of his desire, touching him intimately.

His breath stopped, then came out in a hoarse groan. Instantly she snatched back her hands, remembering too late all that her ex-husband had taught her.

"I'm sorry," she said quickly.

"For what?" he asked, his voice husky with pleasure, his hands seeking her.

"Billy—my husband didn't want—he told me men didn't like aggressive women." Her words jerked out, hurting her with humiliating memories.

Travis pulled her hands back down his body, shivered when her fingers brushed against him. "Billy was a fool," said Travis harshly. "You're passionate, not aggressive. That might frighten a boy, but it's exciting as hell to a man. I'm not afraid of you," he said, moving between her hands, letting her feel his pleasure. "I want my woman to touch me all over, everywhere, any and every way she wants to." He smiled lazily, contradicting the blue-green fire in his eyes. "And that's only fair, Cat, because that's just the way I'm going to touch you."

She shivered at the sensual promise that radiated from him, the certainty of ecstasy burning in his eyes, the intense pleasure that shuddered through him when she curled her fingers around him. Suddenly she found the feel of him almost unbearably exciting. With a small sound she buried her face in his neck, caressing his skin with her tongue, biting the hard tendons, then kissing away the tiny marks her teeth left in his flesh.

"Yes, Cat," he said, laughing softly, his arms closing around her, "test me. See how hard I am and"—his fingers moved between her thighs, sliding into her as he groaned—"how soft you are."

His hand moved, seeking the point of greatest pleasure for her, finding it, stroking her until she felt as though she had been caught up in a storm wave that crested endlessly, sweeping toward an unknown shore. She closed her eyes, giving herself over to him, living only where he touched her until he touched her everywhere. She took his heat and hardness into her body, moving to his powerful rhythms as they raced before the storm they had created.

And when the storm broke he was there, surrounding her, sheltering her while ecstasy shattered her world, holding her while her world slowly reformed again . . . a different world, for he was part of her now.

They awoke to sunlight pouring in golden cataracts across the bed. Cat stretched with feline thoroughness, smiling at the memories unfolding inside her, memories warmer than sunshine. When she opened her eyes Travis was there, as she had known he would be. He smiled and ran a lazy, possessive fingertip from her nose to her knees and back again.

"You don't get enough sleep, do you?" he asked, tracing the dark smudges beneath her eyes.

She blinked and patted back a yawn. "Whose fault is that?" she asked, catching his wandering fingertip between her teeth.

"I'll take the credit—er, blame—for this morning," he said, smiling. "But what's to blame for all the other mornings that left marks under your eyes?"

"Work."

"Not men?" he teased, sure of the answer.

"You're the only man I've found who will put up with this bed," she said, yawning again.

"I've been meaning to bring that up. . . ."

"Other men?"

"Your bed. I was delighted"—his eyes caressed her—"to find that you slept single, but—" He dangled his feet over the end of the bed and at the same time bumped his head against the wall. "Do you think we could give my bed a try?"

"For sleeping?"

"Eventually." He moved his body slightly, all but crowding her off the mattress. Only the fact that his arms were around her kept her from falling off the bed. "You're at my mercy, you know," he pointed out. "I'm not only bigger than you are, I'm bigger than you and this damn bed put to-gether."

Cat wrapped her arms around him, measuring his length with her own supple body. "You're right. I'm at your mercy," she said in a low voice, sliding against him, smiling with pure pleasure when he approved rather than reproved her sensuality.

Travis laughed and moved again, pinning her beneath him. "I was going to offer you lunch," he murmured between her breasts, "but I think I'll just devour you instead."

"Lunch?" she said, startled. "What time is it?"

Travis looked at the angle of the sun with a sailor's measuring eye. "Nearly noon. Why?"

"It can't be!"

"All right," he said agreeably. "It can't be." He

nibbled on the swell of her breast. "Maybe dinner is the best idea of all."

"Travis?"

"Mmmm."

"Is it really almost noon?"

"Afraid so."

Cat swore softly, then her breath caught as he kissed the tip of her breast. "Travis, I was supposed to be somewhere at nine."

"I know. Jason's mother called at eight to tell you that he has a slight fever. I assured her that you'd be glad to reschedule."

Cat stared at him. She hadn't even heard the phone.

"You aren't glad to reschedule?" asked Travis.

She frowned and juggled her schedule aloud. "I'd reserved tomorrow for meeting T. H. Danvers." She smiled distractedly at him. "Except for dawn and sunset, of course. They belong to Ashcroft."

"The hell they do," Travis said emphatically. "Dawn is definitely *mine*."

"But I have to shoot Jason for the Laguna realtors."

Travis waited with an expression of patient curiosity that didn't quite suit his pirate's face. "That sounds rather extreme, shooting a child."

"Film, not bullets," she said with a smile. "It's for the 'Laguna, A Fine Place to Raise Children' campaign," she added, as though that explained everything.

"Of course," said Travis solemnly, laughter turning in the depths of his eyes.

"The light is best in the early morning and late afternoon," added Cat, "unless there's a nice lively storm with lots of broken clouds and wind." She frowned and looked out the window.

"Not a chance," he said. "Fair weather and smooth sailing, world without end, Amen. Or until the weekend, whichever comes sooner," he amended whimsically.

"Then I'm afraid it's Jason at dawn and Ashcroft in the evening."

"And T. H. Danvers?" he said, his voice light, his eyes intent.

"I'll fit him in every chance I get," she said, adding hastily as his hands began caressing her, "but this isn't the time." Her breath caught. "Travis, I— Oh!"

"You'll at least promise to see my ship, won't you?" he said, his hand sliding in slow circles down her body, coming to rest between her thighs.

"I can't—think when you—" She shuddered and let her nails sink into the strong muscles of his shoulder.

"Don't think. Just say, 'Yes, Travis, I'll go with you to see your ship.'"

"Yes, Travis, I'll—*oh*—do whatever you—" She made a small sound and gave up trying to think or speak.

"I think I like your version better," he said, laughing against her breast until her hand slid between his legs and he forgot to breathe. "Cat," he said in a husky voice, "if you're planning on getting out of bed today, one of us has to be sensible about this."

"Let me know when it's my turn," she said in a voice that was almost as husky as his. "Besides, it's all your fault."

"What is?" he murmured, closing his eyes, savoring the feel of her hands cherishing his body.

"This." Her nails ran lightly from his neck to his hips. Her fingertips ruffled the tawny hair on his chest, traced the subtle ridges of muscle down his abdomen, tangled again in darker hair, then teased him without quite touching him. "If you hadn't told me that you like being touched, I'd be sweetly passive and you'd be—"

"—bored as Lucifer in church," he finished, laughing. He caught her wandering hand, bit her palm with restrained ferocity, then smoothed her hand back down the length of his body. "How anyone as sensual as you is still running around loose is more than I can understand," he muttered, shaking his head.

"I could say the same of you," she pointed out. "While I won't claim great experience, I can guarantee that the other men I've met didn't make me want to touch them. You, though . . ." She closed her eyes, tracing the strength and changing textures of his body. "You make me *want*."

"Want what?" he asked softly. He opened his eyes, and his breath caught as he saw the intense pleasure she took in him reflected in her expression.

"I want to pull you around me like a warm velvet blanket," she whispered, eyes closed, seeing him only with her sensitive fingertips. "To feel you change as I touch you. To cover you like sunlight covers the sea, to sink into you until neither one of us knows who is being touched and who is touching . . ." She laughed raggedly. "I can't explain."

"You don't have to," he said, lifting her onto his body with a single powerful motion. "You make me *want* in the same way, Cat. And that's as new to me as it is to you."

Her eyes opened, revealing depths of surprise and desire. Before she could speak he rolled over slowly, languidly, taking her with him as he turned. Then he was over her, surrounding her, sinking into her as she made small sounds of welcome, sounds he echoed with hungry kisses. They spoke to each other without words, their bodies riding a cresting wave of mutual need, teaching each other pleasures that neither alone had believed possible. And when the need could be no greater, they held each other, riding a breaking wave of ecstasy to a distant, quiet shore.

It was midafternoon before Cat made good on her promise to see Travis's ship.

As they drove toward the harbor, she curled against the Lotus's door, watching Travis as he drove. His strong hands controlled the car with an ease and precision that she admired. The muscles in his right arm flexed slightly as he downshifted; the movement made sunlight run like gold water over the tawny hair on his arm. As he transferred his grip from gearshift to the steering wheel, the tendons on the back of his hand moved beneath tanned, supple skin. His fingers closed firmly over the leather-sheathed wheel. She watched, remembering the intense pleasure his fingers could evoke. Desire coursed through her, leaving her weak.

"If you keep looking at me like that," said Travis with a drawl that did nothing to cool her desire, "I'll pull over to the side of the road and do things to you that will get us arrested."

She looked away from his hands to his lips smiling beneath his tawny moustache. She remembered the feel of his beard sliding down her body, the exciting silky roughness against her stomach, her thighs.

With a small groan she closed her eyes. "Travis, what am I going to do with you?"

"I don't know," he said with a wicked smile, "but I'm looking forward to every second of it."

She shook her head and laughed helplessly. "Spoken like a true buccaneer."

When Travis slowed to turn off the Pacific Coast Highway, the Lotus growled throatily. The sound deepened as the car accelerated along the winding road into Dana Point Harbor. To the right rose a deeply eroded bluff bearing the skeleton of a failed hotel. To the left were two yacht basins holding row upon row of pleasure craft—thousands of boats tied side-by-side, creating a forest of white masts with seagulls turning and crying overhead.

"Close your eyes," said Travis.

Cat looked at him, startled. Then she closed her eyes and was rewarded by a light touch on her cheek.

"Now keep them closed until I tell you to open them."

"Yessir," she said, her smile mocking her agreement. But she knew she would do as he asked, and so did he.

The car growled through a few more turns, then slowed. Travis pulled into a parking lot next to the bluff, which had been named after Richard Henry Dana.

"Stay put," said Travis.

She grumbled softly.

He laughed, got out of the car and came around to her side. "I can lead you or carry you, little Cat," he whispered against her ear, making her shiver. "Your choice."

"Lead on. But I should make you carry me and eat your words," she added. "At five feet seven inches, I'm hardly little."

He opened the car door and lifted her out. "Never threaten a pirate," he said, shifting her in his arms.

"Travis—"

He kissed her slowly, thoroughly, then let her

slide down his body until she was standing. "Remember. Eyes closed." He took a firm grip on her upper arm, supporting and reassuring her at the same time. "Parking lot, then a pier. Ready?"

"A pier? Aren't you tied up with the other boats?"

"No questions," he said, tracing the line of her lips with his knuckle.

Travis led her carefully through the parking lot toward the small pier, describing obstacles as he went. "Big car to your left, and one backing out—wait—okay. Left about three steps, then right. Good. There's a curb, then a ramp going to the pier, a kid riding a skateboard and carrying a surfboard, and—ah, the hell with it."

He picked her up and strode the length of the pier, ignoring her muffled laughter. There was no one on the end of the pier. He set Cat on her feet, put her hands on the railing, and put his hands on her shoulders. "All right, Cat, open your eyes."

She looked out over the yacht basin. There, beyond the other boats, riding alone at anchor, was the great black bird she had seen flying across the face of the dying sun.

Even with its dark maroon sails furled, the ship was superb. The bold masts and rigging lines made elegant patterns against the empty sky. The ship's graceful ebony hull rippled with the dance of light on water. Gold letters glowed along the side: *Wind Warrior*. Although wholly at rest, the ship was alive, potent, a tangible consummation of wind and wave and one man's extraordinary vision.

Cat turned and looked at Travis as though she had never seen him before. And in one way, that was true: she had never before seen T. H. Danvers, designer and builder of the most beautiful ship ever to fly the seas of Earth.

"I'm dreaming," she said. "First you, then that ship." Her words ended in an odd laugh. "Don't wake me up, Travis, not yet." She quickly looked back over the water and then at him, as though expecting both the ship and the man to vanish before her eyes, leaving her as empty as the sky. "No wonder you wanted to wait and see my work before you agreed to let me do the book. Don't worry." She touched his lips with her finger, silencing the words she saw forming. "The ability to shape beauty out of nothing is one of the few things I respect. I won't belittle your creation with cute, safe pictures. And," she added softly, honestly, "it is a rare, rare pleasure to meet a man like you, T. H. Danvers."

For a long moment Travis stared down at her, drinking her appreciation and wonder until she thought she would drown in the depths of his sea-colored eyes. Then he gathered her in his arms, holding her as though she were sunrise after a lifetime of night. "Thank you." He kissed her gently. "Thank you for seeing the *Wind Warrior* as I do. Most people"—he smiled crookedly—"most people say, 'Oh, what an unusual boat,' and then they turn away, not really liking what they see."

"You make them see too much," she said quietly. "You make them see that beauty is fierce, not soft, that it has the power to turn your soul inside out, forcing you to think again about the world and your place in it. Your *Wind Warrior* makes people afraid."

"But not you," he said, statement rather than question. "You're like me, a wild creature caught in a civilized world." Warm, strong hands framed her face. "Come away with me," he said, low-voiced, intense. "Avalon. Ensenada. Or further. Hawaii. Papeete. The Seychelles or Tasmania or the China Sea. Anywhere in the world the wind blows; and it blows everywhere, Cat. *Come with me.*"

Wanderlust went through her like lightning, shaking her, bringing memories like thunder in its wake. The scent and feel and sound of the sea, the long reaches where only a ship moved beneath the silent dance of stars. Free. No one to worry about, no obligations to meet. Free to photograph the fierce images that haunted her without being concerned about their commercial appeal, free of worries about the Big Check and the little ones, too. Free to be a woman with her man. As free as a great black bird skimming a sunset sea.

Cat sighed raggedly. She had known since she dove over the railing of her husband's ship that nothing was free. She couldn't run out on the twins who depended on her for their education. Nor could she abandon her mother, a woman never made for the rigors of independence. "I can't, Travis," she said, her voice rich with longing and regret.

Anger drew Travis's face into harsh lines. His hands tightened almost painfully around her face. Abruptly he released her.

"Travis?" she said, putting her hand on his arm as he turned away from her.

He spun back toward her, and for an instant she saw again the barely leashed violence that had made Ashcroft turn as white as his hair. Travis saw her expression and stopped as though she had struck him.

"I'm sorry," he said, holding out his hand. "I didn't realize how much I wanted to sail away with you until you said no." He tried to smile. "Don't say no to me, Cat." Then, quickly, "If you can't say yes, don't say anything. Not yet."

"In January," she said, taking his hand, "ask me again in January. By then I'll have paid all my debts that matter." His expression changed again. She could not read his emotions, but she could sense . . . something. "You'll be gone by then, won't you?" she whispered.

"Cat," he said softly. He moved to hold her but she let go of his hand, evading his arms with a smile that was worse than tears would have been.

"I'd like to go aboard the *Wind Warrior*," she said, looking at the ship because she couldn't bear to look at Travis. Not yet. "It's hard to judge camera angles from here. Would it be possible to row around the ship?"

There was a long silence. She felt the pressure of his will reaching out to her, demanding that she turn back to his arms. He was a wealthy, ruthless brigand unaccustomed to the word *no*. And she was an independent cat accustomed to going her own way. She turned to face him, waiting with a patience that equaled his.

"Is that the way you want it, Cat?" he asked finally.

"It's the way it has to be," she said in a voice that had no emotions, certainly not sadness or regret. "I can't leave until January, and you'll be long gone by then. Wanting doesn't have a damned thing to do with it."

"But—"

"I don't expect you to understand," she added.

"Why?"

"You're rich," she said simply. "You've done

whatever you wanted whenever you wanted to.
You've forgotten that for most people, wanting and
getting are rarely the same thing."

"You judge me very easily." His voice was cold,
his eyes narrow.

"I know what it's like to be rich."

Surprise widened Travis's eyes, revealing their
unique color.

"I was born rich, and I married richer," she said
with a thin smile.

"And?"

"I learned that there really are some things money
can't buy."

"Such as?"

"Self-respect. That shouldn't surprise you," she
added. "If money automatically bought self-respect,
you would never have designed your ship."

Travis looked beyond her to the *Wind Warrior*
riding at anchor in the tranquil water. A man was
walking along the deck toward the stern to check the
anchor cable. In the slanting light he threw a long
shadow over the water, like a black finger pointing
toward shore.

Travis's hands shot out and covered Cat's ears. He
whistled through his teeth, a shrill, ascending sound
that carried like a siren over the water. The man on
the *Wind Warrior*'s stern straightened and shielded
his eyes against the glare of the sun. When he saw
them standing on the pier, he returned the questing
whistle. Travis waved, covered Cat's ears again and
whistled, two short and one long. The man whistled
once, waved and vanished over the railing on the far
side in a single coordinated motion.

Cat looked at Travis, her clear gray eyes silently
asking what was going on.

"Diego will bring the Zodiac around to the pier,"

explained Travis after he took his hands off her ears. Then, as though there had been no interruption, he continued talking on the subject of wealth. "You're right about me and ship designing and self-respect. I was born rich, like you, and like you I rebelled."

"You did?"

He smiled ruefully at the surprise in her voice. "When I was sixteen I left home to work on international freighters. It was very . . . different from what I'd known before. The men, the women, the fights." He smiled and shook his head at the speculations he saw narrowing her gray eyes. "I grew up fast. One of the things I learned was how much I missed true sailing. I knew I could go home and step into the life my father had made for me. He was waiting for me to grow up, to accept the responsibilities of my family name. Once I'd done that I could have a sailing ship again. Hell, I could have a hundred of them."

He looked beyond her for a moment, his blue-green eyes absorbing the beauty of the *Wind Warrior*. "The thought of sitting on the boards of sixteen corporations and being listed on thirty select committees left me cold. I didn't want to juggle figures and people. The only power I hungered for was the pull of a clean sailing ship in a good wind. Since I couldn't afford to buy a sailing ship and was damned if I'd give up my freedom just to own one, I decided to build a ship of my own. I apprenticed myself to an English ship builder. He was a big, hard old man who knew more about ships and the sea than he did about anything else. Especially people. His granddaughter became my wife, but that was later."

He frowned, remembering, and veered away from the distasteful subject of his ex-wife. "The day I finished my first ship my father died. I couldn't believe how much it hurt. I suppose I'd had some childish dream about sailing my ship alone across the Atlantic and tying up at his dock to say, 'See, you aren't the only one in the world who can do something special. There's more to me than my family name and money.'

"But he was dead and couldn't hear me, and I wasn't a child anymore. I sold my ship and flew home because I'd grown up enough to know that I couldn't turn my back on my family when they needed me. Sylvia—the old man's granddaughter—followed me." He shrugged. "I realize now that it was my money she wanted. When she found out I was the son of *the* Thomas Danvers, she was determined to marry me. She did, for a time. I was determined to fill my father's boots. I did. The family fortune increased several times under my management.

"Yet I dreamed of the sea and a great black ship. If all my money couldn't buy me that, what the hell good was it? So I found men and women I trusted, trained them and stepped into the wind."

He was silent for a long time. Cat looked from him to the great ship with its wings folded calmly, floating on a quiet blue sea.

Then, "What happened between you and money, Cat? Why do you tighten every time you realize I'm rich?"

She closed her eyes but could not close the eyes of her memory. "Billy," she said curtly, turning away and looking over the railing, her back to Travis. "When I left him he was one of the hundred richest men in the world. *Rich.*" Her lip curled. "So rich he kept score with people instead of balance sheets."

"What did he do to you?" coaxed Travis, yet there

was the hardness of demand just beneath his velvet drawl.

She realized Travis had silently moved closer until he was a warm presence from her shoulders to her heels. Abruptly, she knew she was going to tell him. "It wasn't the love match of the century," she said thinly. "I wanted the security of a husband, and Billy wanted enough sons to make him feel like a man." She paused and added, "I don't think there are that many sons in the world, but I didn't know that then. Anyway"—she shrugged—"so long as I was his wife, the question was academic."

In calm, precise tones, she told Travis about the paper certifying her husband's fertility and, by implication, her own infertility. She told him about Billy's rage, his need to punish her, his cruelty. Sterile. No damn good. Sterile. And the white paper slapping her face while his fingers ground her flesh against bone.

Arms came around her, wrapping her in warmth, pulling her against Travis's strong body. She accepted it gratefully, putting her hands over his.

"The worst of it was that I believed him. When he—" Her voice tightened until it broke.

"Cat, you don't have to tell me any more," Travis said, his voice as tight as hers, as tight as the arms holding her, wanting to protect her from her own memories.

"I want to. I've never told anyone, not even Harrington, but I want to tell you. I want you to understand why I can't just put my hand in yours and step into the wind with you for a day or a week or a month."

She took a breath as though preparing to dive into cold water. "Like I said, it wasn't much of a marriage to begin with. It's not that I minded his other women." Her lips twisted down. "Sex with him wasn't so special that I wanted to keep it all to myself. But one night—one night." She swallowed and fought to keep her voice level. "One night he brought his latest bar girl on board. I was asleep. When I woke up, he was shoving her into bed with me. He had a little *ménage à trois* in mind. After all, I had to be good for something, right?"

Travis's breath came in sharply. "Cat—"

"When I tried to get out of bed," she continued, ignoring his interruption, ignoring the nearly painful strength of his arms surrounding her, "Billy started slapping me and tearing off my nightgown, yelling at me that since I was a washout as a wife, I could *earn my keep* as a slut. I don't remember exactly what happened after that. I guess I went a little crazy."

The muscles in Travis's arms were like steel, but Cat didn't notice the fierce tension of his body. She was held in the poisonous coil of memories that still made her nauseated and enraged at once.

"I remember grabbing something cold and smooth. I hit him. Glass flew. His cheek was cut. There was blood dripping and that slut screaming with laughter and Billy cursing and kicking me. Somehow I got onto the deck and over the railing. I swam a long time before I saw Harrington's yacht hove to beyond the harbor. I thought I was going to drown. But I didn't. I'm a good swimmer."

She realized she was trembling all over. "Poor Harrington. He was entertaining a lady when I came up the sea ladder wearing only a few bruises. I've always wondered how he explained it to her." She laughed strangely. "Maybe he didn't. Women of all kinds are attracted to him. Those sad brown eyes, I guess."

Travis held Cat as he had the first night, rocking slowly, comforting her without words. After a time, she continued her story. Her voice was steady now, almost calm. The worst of the memories were behind her, words spoken aloud, poison draining away into the past where it belonged. And Travis held her.

"Harrington left the Virgin Islands before dawn. His lady was about my size, and very sympathetic. I shared her clothes. She even taught me how to cook at sea. When we docked in Acapulco I sold my wedding rings to buy a Mexican divorce. Then I went back on board Harrington's yacht and worked my way to California as a cook."

"A good one, if the dinner you fixed me was any measure," Travis said, kissing her hair gently. "You're good at so many things, do you know that?"

"I wasn't that good at first," she said, smiling with lips that wanted to turn down. "I learned a lot that trip. Some of the passengers asked me to take a picture of them with their Polaroid. They showed me what to do, I did it, and when I saw the image condensing out of nothing on that little piece of cardboard, the hair on my neck lifted. I knew I had found something miraculous."

She looked up at him intently, trying to see if he understood. "Putting a camera in my hands was like putting a fish in water. I *earned my keep* cooking, saved until I could buy my own camera, and then worked my tail off until Harrington insisted that I let him represent me. I'm good at what I do, Travis," she said, her voice smooth and certain. "I'm a washout in the baby department, but no man can say I don't *earn my keep* as a photographer."

As she spoke, the Zodiac approached, its small outboard sounding like a power saw. The engine cut off, letting the black inflatable boat coast smoothly to the stairs beneath the pier. In the sudden silence, Travis's words sounded harsh, almost brutal.

"You didn't keep Billy's last name."

It was a statement, not a question, but she answered it anyway.

"No, I didn't keep anything of his. Not his name, not his rings, not one dime of his vast wealth. Nothing but my freedom and a few bruises."

"What is Billy's last name?"

Travis's voice was like a stranger's. Startled, she looked up. His expression was distant, savage. Yet his arms were very gentle around her.

"Nelson. Why?"

"I sail everywhere, Cat," he said, bending down to take her lips. "Someday I'll meet him. I promise you."

Chapter 6

CAT WAS TOO SURPRISED TO SAY ANYTHING, NOR DID she know what she would say if she could speak. Travis's combination of leashed violence and gentle protectiveness was new to her; it left her feeling confused and, oddly, safe. Before she recovered, Travis led her down the stairs to the water and handed her into the *Zodiac*.

"This is Diego," he said, gesturing toward the compact, dark-haired man at the stern. "Diego, meet Catherine Cochran. If you behave you may call her Cathy," added Travis in an amused drawl.

Cat smiled and held out her hand. Instead of shaking it as she had expected, Diego stood gracefully and bowed over her hand.

"I always behave," said Diego in a clear tenor voice, "and most especially I behave for beautiful women." He smiled, transforming his looks. He had a Mediterranean beauty in his face that only smiling revealed. "And you are very beautiful, *señorita. Muy hermosa,* like a rose in winter."

"*Gracias,* Diego," murmured Cat, wishing her Spanish were up to returning the compliment. The corner of her mouth curled in a slight smile. "Why is it that I look at you and see a string of broken hearts circling the world?"

Diego's dark eyes lit with laughter. He looked over at Travis and nodded approval. Travis put his hand on Cat's hip in a reflexive gesture of possessiveness that Diego noted and immediately understood.

"You see broken hearts," drawled Travis, leaning down to put his lips on Cat's auburn hair, "because Diego is a heartbreaker. If you listen carefully, you can hear girls crying, too."

Cat cocked her head, pretending to listen but actually enjoying the play of light in Travis's hair. When she spoke it was without thinking.

"They don't cry for you, do they?" she asked Travis in a low voice. "They don't cry because tears come from hope, and when you go you leave nothing behind, not even the hope that you'll return. No hope . . . no tears."

The expression on his face changed, anger and regret, and then nothing at all but distance and restraint. She realized what she had said and tried to make a joke of it.

"Ah, my secret is out. Your great-grandfather might have been a pirate, Travis, but I come from a long line of Scots witches. Second sight and third as well." She winked at Diego. "So be on your best behavior, *hombres,* or I'll turn you into toads and gingerbread cookies."

Diego smiled brilliantly, ignoring the grim lines of

Travis's face. "I'm warned, *señorita*. Only the best for you." He turned his attention to the engine.

"Wait," said Travis.

Diego stopped, his hand on the switch. Cat looked at Travis and wondered if he had changed his mind about taking her aboard his ship. Not that she blamed him; it had been a thoughtless, almost cruel thing for her to say. The fact that it was true made it worse, not better.

"Your cameras," said Travis.

"What?"

"Your cameras are locked in the trunk of my Lotus."

"I know. They'll be safe there, won't they?"

"Cat," patiently, "don't you want to take pictures of my ship? That's why we're here, isn't it?"

"If it makes you feel better, I'll get my cameras," she said. "But I'll just throw away whatever I take today." She looked beyond him to the elegant, powerful ship floating at rest on the water. "Something like the *Wind Warrior* can't be taken by storm," she said slowly. "I'll need time to absorb her presence, her lines, her silence." Cat's mouth turned down in a self-mocking line. "I know it sounds crazy, but . . ." She shrugged.

"Seduction rather than force?" suggested Travis softly, his expression no longer grim.

"Exactly."

His finger followed the line of her chin. "Whatever you say, my Scots witch."

Cat was too startled by his use of the possessive "my" to reply. She concentrated on the ebony ship that loomed larger with each second as Diego guided the Zodiac across the small harbor. She followed Travis aboard, barely hearing as he described the ship's dimensions and attributes. She was lost in the feel of the ship, the glow of polished brass and new paint, dark rigging and black masts, the muscular bulge of sails furled along the booms. Traditionally ships were referred to as "her," but there was a masculine potency to *Wind Warrior* that reminded Cat of the man who walked beside her.

". . . fathoms," said Travis. He stopped, took Cat's chin in his hand and forced her to look at him. "You haven't heard a damn thing I've said."

Cat blinked, called out of her private thoughts concerning the nature and reality of the ship called *Wind Warrior.* "Sure I have," she said. "Two masts, schooner rigged, thirty meters long . . ." She gave him a guilty smile when her memory failed her. "You're right. But I'm not going to photograph her keel or her bilge or her exact speed in a twenty-knot wind with following seas, so what's the point of remembering all that?"

"What are you going to photograph?"

A man's soul.

But she couldn't say that; she'd already said more than her share of foolish things to him. She simply shook her head and said nothing.

Travis led her below, saying little about the ship's construction and inner dimensions. It was just as well. She wasn't listening again. She was running her fingers over hardwoods from every part of the world, rare woods inlaid and polished to make a table or frame a door, hardwoods gleaming, their lives and histories laid out grain by grain in swirling patterns. T. H. Danvers designed and built state-of-the-art racing hulls, poured and formed and polished them to exact computer specifications . . . but his cabin was filled with exquisite textures of wood and brass; the sheets on his oversized bunk were made of smooth linen; a beveled mirror was set like a diamond in the hull, and the overhead light shone through a carved crystal globe.

Cat looked around the room again, seeing with a photographer's eyes, missing nothing. She realized that there was no contradiction between the modern hull and the textured richness of the cabin. Both were the culmination of long traditions, both were essentially sensual, both were powerful rather than meek in their beauty. And besides, where was it written that an engineer can't be a pirate too?

She smiled to herself as she watched the play of light through carved crystal.

"The cat that licked up all the cream," murmured Travis. He put his hand behind her head, burying his fingers in the auburn hair that fell to her shoulders. "Share some with me."

Her lips parted even as she felt his fingers kneading her scalp. Warmth uncurled along her nerves, the heat that always came when he looked at her with blue-green fire in his eyes. She gave herself to his kiss with an abandon that made hunger leap deep inside him. His hands moved over her almost harshly, molding her to the hard lines of his body as though he were going to take her into his very bones.

After a long time he lifted his mouth from hers. He started to say something, but the temptation of her lips was too great. He groaned deep in his throat and kissed her again, not stopping until she melted against him and her eyes were nearly black with passion.

"Go back on deck," he said, touching her cheek with a hand that trembled.

"What?"

"Go before I take off your clothes and taste every bit of you until you're hot and wet and crying for me and—" He saw passion quiver through her at his words. Swearing softly, he reached for her again.

"Captain?" called Diego, descending from the deck.

Travis swore, but not softly. He stepped in front of Cat, concealing her flushed face before Diego could see her. "What is it?" asked Travis curtly.

"Some official wants to know how much longer we'll be anchored here," said Diego, stopping just outside the open cabin door.

"Does it matter?"

Diego grinned. "Not to me. I think the man just wants a guided tour of the *Wind Warrior.*"

"So give it to him."

"When?"

"For the love of God!" exploded Travis. "Now, Diego! Give it to him right now!"

Diego raised his eyebrows and left.

Travis swore again and looked ruefully at Cat. "The things you do to me, Miss Cochran—little Cat, Scots witch, woman. That most of all. Woman." Then, softly, "Go topside, woman. I'll be along shortly."

Cat hesitated, not wanting to leave him. Then she slipped by him without touching him, watching him with eyes that were still very dark. The rest of the time aboard the ship they were careful not to touch each other, for hunger burned between them at the slightest look. He took her home, made her promise to take a nap before dinner and reluctantly released her.

A few minutes later the back door—the one leading down to the beach—opened. A small boy's head appeared.

"Cathy?"

"Come on in, Jason," she called, leaving her slides

and light table. "Does your mother know you're here?"

Jason hesitated. Very blue eyes peered out at her beneath a fringe of black lashes. Black hair fell in unruly waves over his forehead. His skin was deeply tanned, making his lips appear quite pink in contrast. He was saved from mere prettiness by the precocious maturity of his expression and the intelligence that gave depth to his eyes.

"I'll call her," said Cat with a resigned, amused smile, holding out her hand.

Jason smiled and ran to her. "The twins were hollering and she was trying to change both of them at once and daddy's coming home late and I dropped my juice and—"

"—you sneaked out the back way," finished Cat, reaching for the phone to call Jason's mother. She hesitated as she remembered that Jason was supposed to be ill. "Are you feeling okay?"

"Sure."

"No fever?"

"Nah," said Jason with a grand gesture. "Only babies get fevers."

"Baloney."

"Sliced and diced?" asked Jason.

Cat laughed and shook her head. Sliced and diced baloney was Jason's favorite "madword." She put her cheek against the boy's forehead. He didn't feel hot, nor did he look ill. She dialed Jason's mother and waited for seven rings. A breathless voice finally answered.

"Sharon? Cathy."

"Oh Lord. Jason?"

"Right. Bedtime?"

"You're sure?" asked Sharon anxiously.

"I'm sure. Eight o'clock." Cat hung up and

smiled. She and Sharon had exchanged so many calls on the subject of Jason that they had it down to a code.

Jason whooped and did a restrained dance. "Can we go shell hunting, Cathy, huh? Can we, huh?"

"Maybe," she said, stacking and putting away the slides she had been sorting. The surface she was working on glowed softly, illuminating the slides from below. The light table made sorting slides easier and was much better for the delicate color emulsion than running slides through a hot projector. "First we'll do some pictures like we agreed on, okay?" She smiled down at him. "It was nice of your mom to dress you in a red T-shirt, new jeans and red sneakers."

He smiled proudly. "Wasn't my mom, it was me. I remembered you said red was good for pictures."

"It's the best," she said, hugging Jason. "And you're very smart to remember."

Jason returned her hug. "Where are we going this time?"

"Bluebird Park. Then Main Beach, then back here for sunset."

She frowned, remembering all the futile sunsets she'd taken for Ashcroft. At least he'd called off the shoot today. Which reminded her—she'd better leave a message for Travis. She called his cousin's home, but not even a machine answered. She grabbed a piece of paper, wrote quickly, stuffed it into an envelope and put his name in block letters on the outside. As she closed the front door behind herself and Jason, she wedged in the envelope. When Travis came to pick her up for dinner he couldn't miss it.

Jason watched with ill-concealed impatience. "Who's that for?"

"Travis. A friend of mine. He might meet us later. You'll like him."

The boy's face settled into different, stubborn lines. "Won't."

There was a world of loneliness and jealousy in the single word. Cat, remembering her own feelings when her twin siblings had preempted her mother's attention, knelt next to Jason. "Probably not," she agreed. "Most people don't like pirates."

"He's a pirate?" said Jason, interest leaping in his eyes. "A really for sure pirate?"

"Yup."

"How can you tell?"

"He sails a black ship."

"A really for sure pirate!" crowed Jason, convinced. "And I get to meet him! Boy, that's something baby twins can't do!" He stopped, struck by a thought. "Does he steal kids, I mean really little kids, like babies?" he asked hopefully.

Cat fought not to smile. "I don't think so, but we can ask."

She followed Jason up the outside stairs to the garage, which was above the house but still below street level. She strapped him into the front seat of her Toyota and backed up the steep driveway, planning her first shots as she drove and listened to Jason tell her about the twins' latest disasters. He kept talking as she parked the car, led him to the playground and turned him loose.

After his initial excitement wore off she gradually structured the shots to achieve the lighting and textures she wanted. Jason obeyed her without argument, for she gave as few instructions as possible. She didn't need to. Jason was not only a handsome child, he had a total unselfconsciousness that made him a natural model.

By the time they were finished with the park and Main Beach, the sun was low. Santa Ana winds had blown all day, bringing the warmth of the Mojave Desert to Laguna Beach. Jason's shoes and socks had been peeled off, wadded in a ball with his T-shirt and left on the steps leading up to his house. He was prowling the tidepools like a small black panther, pawing the sun-warmed water and then emerging triumphantly with a bit of wildlife wriggling in his palm.

Cat caught it all with her camera: his intensity and intelligence, his curiosity and laughter, his endless delight in the scent and sound and feel of the world around him. She forgot how tired she was, forgot her promise to Travis that she would take a nap before dinner, forgot everything. The camera was her third eye, a mystical window that allowed her to see the universe condensed into a child's smile.

Jason brought her shell after shell, piling them at her feet, pale offerings against the radiance of his smile. She took photos until the light was gone, then she lifted the sandy, delighted boy in her arms and hugged him soundly.

"You've earned yourself a hamburger, fries, *and* a milkshake."

"A milkshake too?" he asked, throwing grubby arms around her neck. "Chocolate?"

"Is there another kind?" She shifted his weight, setting him on his feet in the sand, wishing she weren't so tired. "If you gain another ounce I'll need a crane to lift you."

"That's because I'm seven," he said proudly. Then he sighed. "Mom says I'm a little man now."

Kneeling, Cat smoothed back the boy's black curls, revealing the wistful depths of his blue eyes. He liked the idea of being grown up, but he wasn't quite ready to let go of being his mother's baby. The arrival of the twins didn't leave any choice, however. Cat understood the paradox of Jason's eagerness to grow up and his hurt at no longer being a baby. She had felt the same way at his age, and for the same reason. Eventually she had come to love her twin siblings, but not right away. Not for several years.

"Tell you what," she said, dropping a kiss on his short nose, "you can be a little man for your mother and a little boy for me. Deal?"

"Deal." He became very serious for a moment, then asked hesitantly, "Does your pirate like chocolate milkshakes?"

Cat blinked. She was used to Jason's non sequiturs, but this one was more outrageous than most. "My pirate?"

"He looks like a pirate," said Jason, staring over her shoulder. "Do you sail a black ship?"

"That boy knows a pirate when he sees one," drawled a deep voice behind Cat's back. Travis knelt next to her. "And," he continued, looking at Jason, "this pirate loves chocolate milkshakes." He held out his hand to Jason. "I'm Travis. Are you the boy who gave Cat all those shells?"

"Yeah." Jason shook hands in a manner his mother would have approved, little man to big. "She's too busy taking pictures to find good shells, so I do it for her."

"It's a shame that someone can't sleep for you," muttered Travis, looking meaningfully at the darkness beneath her eyes. "I thought you were going to take a nap."

"Ashcroft canceled, Jason appeared, the light was good." She smiled and shrugged. "No nap, but lots of fine shots."

He seemed on the point of saying something, then

looked at Jason's eager face and sighed. "Did I hear dinner mentioned?"

She smiled apologetically. "Jason's favorite scarf-and-barf is just down the highway."

Travis winced. "I hope the food isn't as bad as the name."

"It isn't," Cat assured him, picking up her camera cases. "It's worse."

The food was as bad as expected, but they endured it for Jason's sake. After they dropped him off at home they went to Travis's house. Wordlessly they peeled off their clothes and sank into the hot tub. Naked, relaxed, Cat lounged chin deep in the gently steaming water and tried to stay awake. She clenched her jaws against a yawn but didn't fool Travis. No matter how discreet she was, his eyes assessed her tiredness with unflinching precision.

"Bedtime for you," said Travis, turning her so that she faced away from him. Strong fingers rubbed her shoulders and back, easing muscles knotted by balancing heavy lenses hour after hour.

She relaxed against his strength, letting herself drift. "It's not even nine," she murmured.

"You're yawning."

"I yawn every night."

"Try sleeping."

"I do. Midnight to five."

His hands stopped. "Five hours? That's all?"

Cat's only answer was swallowed by a yawn.

"If you weren't here," said Travis, "what would you be doing?"

"Sorting slides. Duplicating slides. Mailing slides to photo agents. Writing dunning letters." She yawned and stretched luxuriously. "Choosing mats and frames for the L.A. gallery." She sat up. "I've got to choose images for that show!"

"Tonight?" asked Travis, his voice and face unreadable.

"Yes." Cat wavered, then settled back into his strong hands. "But not right this minute. Later."

For a time there was only silence and the small sounds she made as his hands soothed aching muscles.

"When are your days off, Cat?" he asked finally.

"No such animals," she said, fighting a yawn and losing.

"No weekends?"

"No. Price of being self-employed."

"Do you always work this hard?"

Cat shook her head. "You just had the bad luck to meet me during a cash crunch." She felt his hands stop and remembered his contempt the first time she had mentioned that she had money difficulties. She leaned forward and reached for a towel. "But that's my problem."

His hand closed over her arm. "It's mine, too, if it keeps you away from me."

"So lean on Energystics," she said flippantly, looking at him over her shoulder. "They owe me thirty-three thousand." She saw surprise flicker over his face. "Yes," she said coolly, "I do rather well for myself, all things considered. *I earn my keep.*"

The last words were an echo of her ex-husband's cruelty. Travis heard the echo and understood some of what drove Cat, yet he still wasn't satisfied. "Self-respect is very cold comfort. It took me years to learn that. Let's see if you're smarter than I was."

He turned her in his arms, holding her with a strength that made a joke of her attempt to pull away. His mouth closed over hers in an angry demand that she resisted but finally couldn't deny, not when his tongue began to tease her lips gently and his breath was sweet in her mouth. She sighed and let herself melt into him, enjoying the sensations caused by her breasts rubbing across his bare chest.

A shudder went through him. "Cat, witch, woman, sail with me, just two days, Catalina Island and back. You can spare two days for me, for yourself, us. . . ."

His husky whisper shimmered over her nerves, making her breath stop and then come back in a ragged surge. "When?"

"Tomorrow."

She closed her eyes and felt her nails digging into the palms of her hands. "I can't, Travis. I . . . can't."

"You mean you *won't*." His voice was different, hard. "All you care about is measuring your self-respect by the amount of money you make." He lifted her off his lap and grabbed a towel. "Well, I sure as hell won't get in your way."

Her eyes opened, too bright, blinking back exhaustion and frustration and tears. "That isn't true," she whispered, because a whisper was all she could force past the tightness of her throat.

Travis climbed out of the hot tub and began drying himself. He didn't look at her, yet she couldn't look away from him, each muscle and sinew outlined in honey-colored light, water drops sparkling and sliding down his strong body. He was the most beautiful, most powerful thing she had ever known . . . and she would lose him.

"Oh, Travis," she whispered, "why couldn't I have met you in January, when we might have had a chance to love?"

She heard her words and realized what she had said, what she had revealed. Anger finally came, driving out exhaustion, giving her strength. She reached blindly for a towel, stood, and fumbled with the thick cloth, unable to control her fingers long enough to tie a simple knot. She did not look at him again, could not, because if she did, she knew she would cry. She hadn't cried for seven years and had no intention of starting now. Certainly not for another rich bastard.

"Cat," softly, "you're so tired that you're coming apart, but you won't even let me hold you together."

She put her hands over her ears, not wanting to hear his words melting her anger, his concern making her want to run to him, trust his strength, love him. . . . "No, oh God *no,*" she whispered to herself. "Not that. Not now!"

"Not what, Cat?"

She looked at him wildly, then put her face in her hands. Her body shook with the force of her attempt to control her emotions. Instinctively he wrapped her in his arms, feeling her tension in every line of her body. He cursed himself for pushing her too hard, too soon.

"Tell me," he said, his voice coaxing her, his body warming her cold flesh. "No matter what you say, I won't get angry." He kissed her eyelids lightly, warmly. "Tell me, little Cat."

"No," she said, turning her face away from him. *"I don't want to love you."*

There was such desperation in her words that it took a moment for Travis to comprehend their meaning. When he understood, he bent and kissed her trembling lips, murmuring words of comfort and caring, kissing her until she had to cling to him just to stand. And then she held him fiercely, wanting him and at the same time afraid that if he made love to her again she wouldn't be able to keep from loving him.

His hands slid from her face to the towel wrapped around her breasts. He hesitated. "Cat . . . ?"

She shivered, cold and hot at once. And then she knew that it didn't matter; she couldn't lose more of herself to him than she already had.

"Yes," she whispered, "yes."

Without another word he lifted her in his arms, carrying her into his bedroom. He unwrapped the damp towel around her, replacing it with a silk comforter. She shivered continuously as he lay next to her, covering both of them with the quilt. He held her until he felt warmth return to her skin. She gave a shaky sigh and relaxed against him. He saw the dark hollows beneath her eyes, the paleness beneath her tan, the bones pressing against her skin.

"Sleep," he whispered, kissing her cheek.

Her arms slid around his waist. She kissed the hard muscles of his chest, lingered to tease his flat nipples into tiny hard buttons.

"You're too tired," he said regretfully. "You wouldn't be able to enjoy making love."

"Try me," she whispered, her hand trailing down his body.

Travis caught his breath. "On one condition."

She smiled. "Name it."

"Stay with me. No more work, not tonight."

He saw her reservations in her frown and knew that she had been planning to sort more slides when she got home tonight. Gently he caught the tip of her breast between his fingers and squeezed. Her back arched in response.

"No fair," she said breathlessly.

"Sue me." He bent over her, rubbing his bearded cheek between her breasts. Her hands slid down to his hips. He caught her wrists in his fingers. "I take that as an unqualified yes," he said, searching her face.

"Yes," she sighed, closing her eyes.

His mouth caressed her breasts until she moaned and moved blindly. He smiled and traced the flush spreading across her body. "Now, the second condition—"

Cat groaned. "Unfair. You said just one."

Travis laughed and nibbled down her body until he felt the smooth curve of her thighs beneath his lips. He sank his teeth lightly into her flesh, then shifted his weight in a fluid movement, sliding down her like warm water until his hands held her hips in a hard embrace.

"Travis . . . ?" said Cat in the instant before her breath caught in her throat.

"It may shock you, my red-haired Scots witch," he said in a husky voice, "but I've wanted to do this since I carried you off that rock, and I'm damned if I'm going to wait any longer."

Sensations radiated up through her body: heat and lightning and the changing pressure of his lips, his tongue, his teeth. Whatever shock she might have felt at the caress vanished in wave after wave of pleasure exploding through her. Making a choked sound she opened herself to his intimate kiss without reservation, and he rewarded her with a heat and hunger that made her cry aloud.

She tried to say his name, to tell him the extraordinary pleasure he was giving her; but she had no words, only her body twisting and melting, needing him. When she thought she could stand it no longer he came to her in a rush of power, filling her, answering her with his own savage need until neither he nor she knew who gave and who took, for giving and taking were inseparable from the ecstasy that consumed them.

When she woke up she was alone in his bed. A note was pinned to the pillow next to hers.

Gone sailing.
I wanted to take you with me.

Travis

Chapter 7

Dr. Stone studied the results of Cat's most recent blood tests and sighed. She looked at Cat over the rim of her reading glasses.

"Your blood count is too low," she said flatly. "You're strong, child, but you haven't learned the working woman's truth: You can do *anything*, but you can't do *everything*."

Cat grimaced. "I'm not crazy, Doctor. I know I can't do everything."

Dr. Stone smiled, taking years off her age. "But do you practice what you know?"

Cat looked at her hands and said nothing. In the five days Travis had been gone she had worked herself mercilessly. She had spent the long night hours sorting and resorting slides, choosing images for her Los Angeles show until her eyes refused to focus on the dancing colors. Then she had tried to sleep. If sleep wouldn't come or came only for a few hours, she got up and began the endless round of bookkeeping that went with running her own business.

When each dawn finally came she looked over the ocean and remembered and tried not to ask herself why she had thought Travis was different, why even now her body longed for him, why the sound of his laughter haunted her sleepless hours, why she could not forget the first time he had held her and taught her that peace as well as pleasure could flow between a man and a woman.

And with each night came the worst question of all. Why had he left?

The only good thing that had happened was that Blake Ashcroft had stopped trying to crowd her into his bed. She still shot sunsets for him, but she shot them alone. Tonight he was coming over to examine the work she had done. She wasn't looking forward to having him around, though she doubted that he would revert to caveman tactics. The poet was also a pragmatist, and the pragmatist had a healthy fear of a certain hull designer. If that weren't enough, Cat wouldn't be taken by surprise again. It wouldn't have happened the first time if she hadn't been concentrating on her photography.

She laced her fingers together and wished heartily that Ashcroft hadn't insisted on having her around when he reviewed the slides. On the other hand, he had every right to expect her presence. It was his book, after all, his poetry and his choice of images. He could hardly be expected to explain what he liked and disliked over the phone.

But it would have been very nice just the same.

"Catherine?" asked Dr. Stone.

Cat glanced up from her tightly laced fingers. "What?"

"I asked if you were taking the new vitamins."

"Yes."

"They aren't meant as a food substitute," said the doctor dryly, looking at Cat's finely drawn face.

"I know."

"How many meals a day are you eating?"

Cat shrugged. "Depends on what you call a meal. When Jason comes over at dawn, he makes breakfast for me."

"Mmm?" The doctor waited expectantly.

"Cocoa and peanut butter toast."

Dr. Stone laughed and shook her head. "Well, at least your body can put the carbohydrates to good use. But you might teach him how to make scrambled eggs."

"I tried. Took me two days to get rid of the smell. Besides"—Cat smiled slightly—"I've acquired a taste for peanut butter."

"What about lunch and dinner?"

"Soup. Eggs. Cheese and crackers. Whatever."

"Fruits? Vegetables?"

"They're the 'whatever,'" said Cat, shrugging. "Whatever looks good when I get to the supermarket."

"I want you to keep track of what you eat between now and next week's appointment."

Cat sighed and said nothing. She knew she should eat better meals, but had neither the time nor the ambition to cook for herself. The more tired she became, the less she ate; and the less she ate, the more tired she became.

Dr. Stone called the nurse in and left instructions for B-complex and iron shots. A few minutes later

Cat left the office rubbing her hip. The doctor had been right—iron shots were a literal pain in the rear.

On the way home Cat stopped at the camera store and picked up her latest batch of processed film. The majority of the slides were duplicates of slides in her files. She'd long since given up mailing originals across country to various photo agents. They didn't like getting duplicates, but the quality of the slides was such that they put up with it, knowing that the alternative was no slides at all from the woman called Cochran.

She was, however, careful not to send identical slides to different agents. Each agent had slides that no one else had. It was more expensive that way, but it paid off in the long run because agents could assure clients that the precise slide or slides that they were looking at could be bought nowhere else.

Even so, she flinched at the cost. Including her professional discount but not including the cost of the film, the bill came to $478.93; and it was only the first of several batches of slides she had sent off to be processed. At least the long nights were bearing fruit of a sort, although she would have preferred to catch up on her backlog of work in some other way than out of loneliness and anger.

She carried out the cardboard carton full of Kodak yellow slide boxes to her car and thought gloomily of all the sorting and filing and mailing to various agents that lay ahead of her. It was the sort of work that least appealed to her. It also was vital at this point in her career.

As she pulled into the garage, she heard the phone ringing. Simultaneously, she remembered that she hadn't turned on the answering machine when she left. She ran down the stairs to her tiny front yard, vaulted the little white gate and unlocked the front door. Unfortunately, she'd left the portable phone on the lowest floor of her trilevel house. She raced down the stairs connecting the levels and snatched the receiver out of its cradle, promising herself that as soon as the Big Check from Energystics came she'd buy a phone for every level of the house.

"Hello," she said breathlessly.

"Forgot your machine again, Cochran."

Disappointment went over Cat like winter surf, cold and powerful, almost numbing. Only then did she realize how much she had wanted the voice on the other end to belong to Travis. She swallowed and fought to answer in her normal teasing tones.

"Hi, Harrington. Going to be my green angel again?" she asked, referring to Harrington's gift for getting highly paid assignments for her.

"I'm trying," he sighed, "I'm trying. It'd be a hell of a lot easier if I could talk to you from time to time. Swear to God, Cochran, I'm getting you a beeper for Christmas. Maybe I won't wait that long. Hold it—"

There was a pause. Vaguely, Cat heard one of Harrington's six assistants speak hurriedly to him. His answer was muffled and abrupt.

"Swear to God," he sighed into the phone, "the bigger the boobs, the dumber the booby."

The assistant's response was muffled, creative and explicit.

"They're going to get you for sexual harassment, Angel," said Cat, laughter curling in her voice.

"Jim? Nah. He's been lifting weights. I get out of line, he'll just hammer me into a thin paste, right Jim?"

"The 'booby' in question is a man?" she asked, startled.

"Sure. There isn't a woman here who could give a C-cup bra a run for its money."

There was a chorus of outraged and outrageous responses questioning Harrington's eyesight and more intimate functions. Unperturbed, he continued speaking loudly into the phone, drowning out the comments.

"They've got no sense of humor," Harrington complained. "I hope you do. You're gonna need it. Energystics has stopped returning my calls. Word is that they're in a cash flow crunch."

Cat said something pungent.

"Yeah," said Harrington. "I said about the same thing to them in a registered letter. I mentioned accountants, contracts, lawyers, courts and other obscenities."

She frowned. She couldn't afford the time or expense that a suit would involve. "That bad?"

"Let me put it this way, Cochran. I'm tired of being jerked around by Energystics. I'm so tired of it I'm going to sue their tight asses off unless they pay."

Cat sighed. She trusted Rodney Harrington too much to question his judgment. If he said a suit was necessary, then she somehow would find money to pay the lawyers. "How much do you need and when?"

"How much what?"

"What else? Money. All those obscenities you mentioned cost a lot."

"Nothing right now. If it gets serious, three to five grand should take care of it. Think of it as an investment, because sure as God made little green apples, we'll get every cent of it back out of their corporate hide. But it probably won't come to that. Usually these business types come across when you wave a lawyer at them, especially when you have them by the nuts. And that's where we have Energy-stics, Cochran."

"Then squeeze," said Cat bluntly. "I need that Energystics money, Angel. The twins' next to last school payments aren't very far away. And mother—" She hesitated, not wanting to criticize the very dear, very helpless woman who was her mother. Mrs. Cochran still believed that checks were a magic form of money unrelated to dollars and common sense. "Well, you know mother."

"Lovely lady," murmured Harrington. "A real old-fashioned woman. Wouldn't know a balance sheet if it walked up and introduced itself."

"January," said Cat, code word for freedom.

"I'll drink to that," agreed Harrington, under-standing the pressures Cat was under. It was he who had introduced Cat's mother to her future husband. Privately, Harrington had been heard to say that it was the best piece of work he'd ever done for Cochran. "I have some good news, too. Well, it could be good, anyway."

"I'm listening."

"Remember that new account of mine, the guy who started a face-goo company?"

"Er, no. Does it matter?"

"He'll pay five thousand dollars per shot for every shot he uses in an ad campaign. He's looking for five good ones."

"What does he want—beach, flowers, hills, skin?"

"Just pretty, Cochran. Whatever you have that would go well on a gooey greeting card or a post-card. You know, the kind of shot that makes people say, 'Ohhh, isn't that pret-ty.' Not your usual style, but you must have some little cuties hiding away in that wall of filing drawers."

"Boxes and boxes," agreed Cat. "There's a lot of

demand for pret-ties. Photo banks love them. Most common denominator and all that. Like Ashcroft's poetry."

Harrington laughed. "How has the octopus been behaving? Did the herpes gambit work?"

"No. He tried to get physical—" Cat flinched and held the phone away from her ear for a moment. "It's okay, Angel. Travis happened to be near. He cut off most of Ashcroft's arms and tied the rest in knots."

"Danvers? As in T. H.?"

"The same. He has chivalrous instincts and the strength to enforce them. Ashcroft has been very well behaved."

"Chivalrous?" said Harrington in an ascending tone. "Cochran, are we talking about T. H. Danvers, the ship designer? About six foot two, odd-colored eyes, hard-faced and meaner than a junkyard dog?"

"Hard-faced?" said Cat, unaware that her voice had softened as she remembered Travis's face close to hers, Travis smiling with pleasure as she lifted her lips to his. "Mean?" Memories of laughter and gentleness, his sensitive fingertips bringing warmth to her, his body sharing with her the gift of passion and shimmering release. She laughed softly. "Must be talking about two different men."

"Cathy."

Harrington's quiet use of her first name shocked Cat. He had called her Cathy only once before, when she had comforted him after his youngest child had died.

"Are you listening?" he asked gently.

"Yes," she breathed, wishing she wasn't, knowing she wasn't going to like what she heard.

"I'd give my life for Travis and consider it well

spent," said Harrington, his voice calm and absolutely sure. "He'd do the same for me. He's unique, brilliant. A man couldn't ask for a better friend to share a bottle or a fight or a dark night of the soul." He paused. "But Cathy—"

"Yes?"

"That man is hell on women."

"What do you mean?" she asked, her voice flat, afraid that she knew the answer before she heard it.

"They fall for him and he gets in the wind. Something to do with his ex-wife, I think."

"Yes. He told me."

"He did?" said Harrington, startled. "Then you're the only person other than the two of them who knows what burned him. He never told me a damn thing except that he was divorced." There was a long silence. He sighed. "Oh, hell, Cochran. You're a woman grown and all that. But be careful. For women, Danvers is like one of the big storm waves at Oahu—glorious and fascinating as hell until you get caught in it. Then it's damned terrifying. I care about you too much to want to pick up the pieces after the wave goes out again."

"I know," softly. Then, "I'm a good swimmer, Angel," she said, succeeding in keeping her voice light. "Remember? But thanks. I care a lot about you, too."

"Send the pretties," he said gruffly. "Turn on your machine. And Cochran—"

"Yes?"

"Take care of yourself."

He hung up before she could answer. Cat stared at the phone for a long time. *They fall for him and then he gets in the wind.* Is that what had happened? Because there was no doubt about it. She had fallen like a breaking wave, curling over and tumbling until she was little more than spindrift glittering on a sandy shore.

But she thought he had been with her, riding the crest of the wave.

She closed her eyes, angry that she missed Travis the way she had never expected to miss anything. It was futile to care about him. Rich men didn't know how to care about anyone but themselves. Surely she should have learned that by now.

Yet his great black ship flew across her mind, as indelible and compelling as the memory of his touch. How could the man who created such wild, fierce beauty be as shallow as her ex-husband?

With a dispirited curse, Cat went to her cluttered desk, drew out boxes labeled "To be paid," "Overdue," "Owed to me," and began adding columns with the aid of a small calculator. She worked for several hours, writing checks, delaying some bills and paying part of others, trying to make the outgo balance with the income. She worked until her jaw ached from the tension of her clenched teeth.

No matter how many times she juggled the figures, they came up dripping red. She rubbed her eyes and the back of her neck and reached for the phone. An hour later she had several small jobs lined up, weddings and company portraits, grinning heads and handshakes around a polished table. It was the type of work she generally avoided. She couldn't afford to be choosy now, not until the Energystics check or the Danvers assignment came through. And the latter seemed as much in doubt as the former.

Pushing away from the desk, she stood and stretched, then kneaded the small of her back. The bills were in different pigeonholes now; that, plus a hip that ached from iron shots, was all she had to show for the morning. She was tired, really tired. But so what? She had learned that if you weren't born wealthy, hard work was the price of freedom.

Besides, the checks always came. Eventually.

With a sigh she sat down at the typewriter, pulled over the box marked "Owed to me," and began writing the daily round of dunning letters. When she finished with them she would have to call the custom color printers and find out if the first round of prints for the L.A. show was ready. If the prints were in, she should pick them up if they were correctly done and argue about them if they weren't. If they were good, she should take them immediately to the framers and spend several hours trying out various combinations of mats and frames.

If the prints weren't ready, there were slides to sort, cover letters to write, slides to file, slides to duplicate. Cat stifled a yawn and thought longingly of a nap. She resisted the temptation. She was having enough trouble sleeping at night as it was. Besides, when she was working she wasn't thinking about Travis "Hell-On-Women" Danvers.

At five o'clock she remembered lunch. Only the thought of having to write down "peanut butter and crackers" for Dr. Stone drove Cat to the stove. She looked in the refrigerator, hesitated, then decided on a cheese-and-whatever omelette. In this case, whatever turned out to be scallions and two limp mushrooms. She assembled the ingredients, cooked and ate the omelette without enthusiasm. Fuel, not food. Food was something you prepared with pleasure and shared with friends.

Cat wrote out a grocery list on the pad hanging next to the refrigerator, cleaned up the kitchen and decided to treat herself to a hot, lazy bath. It was therapy, not a waste of time, she told herself as she

headed for the bathroom. It was either that or a glass
of wine. Maybe both. She had to be more relaxed
than she was now if she hoped to cope successfully
with the Crown Prince of Treacle. At the very least
she had to stop listening for Travis's laughter, stop
straining to see the *Wind Warrior* flying across the
evening sea.

When Cat finally dragged herself out of the tub
her skin was flushed pink and steam claimed every
corner of the bathroom. She took a long time drying
her hair, enjoying the thick, silky feel of it as it
tumbled in auburn waves to her shoulder blades.
Subdued fire licked through her hair, gold and
bronze, flame and orange, hot colors burning beneath the darker mass.

Out of habit she lifted her hair and sprayed a
subtle perfume on the back of her neck. She looked
at her face, pale underneath the honey tan that was
all her fair skin allowed. She reached for some
makeup, then made an impatient sound. She didn't
care if she looked—or smelled—like three-day-old
fish for Blake Ashcroft. With quick motions she
twisted her hair into a coil on top of her head,
pinning the slippery mass in place with an ebony
comb. Black underwear, black jeans and a high-
necked, long-sleeved black pullover sweater
completed her outfit. She measured the image in the
mirror and nodded her satisfaction. No man could
mistake her somber clothes for a come-on, not even
a man as self-absorbed as Ashcroft.

What she didn't understand was the effect of her
hair quietly burning above an unsmiling face. Her
translucent skin was drawn tightly over high cheekbones, leaving intriguing hollows beneath, hollows
that tempted a man's lips. Sleepless nights had made

her eyes larger, colder, reflecting the energy seething beneath the pale surface. The sweater and jeans weren't tight; they merely revealed the woman beneath in the same way that her hair revealed fire— with each breath, each movement, aloof and alluring at the same time, a red-haired sorceress with eyes of ice.

In one way she was correct, though. She was a woman to tempt a warrior, not a poet. At least not a poet like Ashcroft.

The doorbell rang, three impatient bursts of sound that told her Ashcroft had arrived. She yanked on black ballet shoes and climbed the three levels to the front door.

"Somebody die?" asked Ashcroft as she opened the door.

"Don't tell me, let me guess," she said. "You prefer pink ruffles."

Ashcroft grimaced and followed her down the twisting stairs without a word. Her workroom was on the second level. She flipped switches until the only illumination in the room came from the light table. She handed him a photographer's magnifying glass that was shaped like a cone without a point. It was about four inches high, wider at the base than the top, and made to be used on slides illuminated by a light table.

"You look at them like this," said Cat, taking a slide from a box, placing the slide on the light table and putting the wide end of the magnifying glass on the cardboard that framed the slide. "Bend over, squint as though it were a microscope or a gunsight, and look. If you like what you see, put the slide in the tray to the right. If not, put it in the one to the left. I'll be on the deck, if you need me."

Ashcroft looked dubiously at the magnifying glass and the boxes of slides and muttered, "A projector would be easier and quicker."

"It would also fade out the slides. It's your book, though. Your choice. I can set up the projector."

"I'll try it your way for a while. Don't be gone long."

"Long enough for a cup of tea."

"Sounds lovely. Brew one for me."

"You'll have to drink it somewhere else," she said crisply. "No food or drink at the light table."

Ashcroft muttered and bent over the first slide. Cat left quickly, made a cup of tea and went out on the deck by her back door. She sat in a chair by the glass-topped patio table and listened to the sea. The deck was cantilevered, jutting out from the steep slope of the bluff. Twenty-five feet below, surf prowled and muttered over rocks hidden by darkness.

A cement stairway zigzagged down to the sea. During the rare autumn storms that whirled up from the south, the cement stairs took the full force of waves two or three times as tall as she was. The stairs were built for it. A cold iron railing as thick as her arm lined both sides of the concrete stairway; but for the last ten feet, the rails were twisted and bent, mute reminder that the sea could be as violent as it was beautiful.

Tonight the sea was quiet, a dark playground where moonlight danced. She looked longingly at the stairs leading diagonally down to the beach. She could tell by the waves' low sounds that the tide was retreating, withdrawing back to the restless body of the ocean. She wanted to steal down the stairs, follow the tide, feel the gentle seething of foam over her feet as she looked up at the moon's tilted smile.

On an impulse she scuffed off her ballet shoes, rolled her pants to her knees and walked down the stairs to the sea, balancing her teacup in one hand. The sand was dense, dark, infused with spent waves. Her footprints gleamed for a few seconds as her weight squeezed water out of the sand. The first touch of the waves was chill, almost cold. She didn't retreat. She stood quietly, letting waves lap her calves and gently bury her feet in sand.

She stared with unfocused eyes into the night, wondering what it would be like to sail a silver moon trail, to see sapphire lights glinting in the crests of black satin waves. She wondered if Travis was out there somewhere, moonlight like a benediction on his hard features, strong hands holding the helm of a huge black ship. Was he looking at the fluid curl of waves and thinking of her?

With an impatient sound Cat forced herself to think of something else. She lifted the teacup to her lips and was startled to find that the tea was colder than the sea washing over her toes. She realized that she had been outside for a long time—long enough for the waves to retreat beyond her feet. She had been lost in the moonlight and night, thinking of many things . . . black waves flexing, sea gleam and moon smile, but most of all she had thought of Travis.

And now she was cold.

Gooseflesh rippled over her arms and legs as she shivered. She knew she should go back inside, but what she really wanted to do was to walk a few feet further down the beach and let the waves wash over her calves again, setting her mind adrift, spindrift gleaming on a distant shore.

Abruptly she realized that she was standing there because somewhere deep in her mind it made her feel closer to Travis, knowing that the same ocean that touched her also touched the *Wind Warrior*. She spun around and ran up the stairs, spilling cold tea at each step.

"Where the hell have you been?" said Ashcroft as she reached the deck. "I've been looking for you."

"Here I am." She set down the nearly empty teacup, washed her feet at an outside faucet and turned to face him. A single look at his face told her that he hadn't liked the slides. Yet she had been counting on the money she would get on completing the assignment for him. "Finished?" she said curtly.

"I've seen enough, if that's what you mean." His full upper lip lifted slightly. "I don't like them."

She walked past him into the house. He hesitated, then followed her. She didn't stop until she was in the workroom. The right-hand tray, the one she had designated for slides he liked, had two slides in it. Two out of the two hundred she was contracted to supply. The left-hand tray was a disorderly mound of slides. Most of the boxes of slides hadn't been opened. Apparently he had indeed seen enough and had decided not to waste his time looking further.

Automatically Cat sorted out the mound of slides, putting them correctly into the tray. She was neither hurt nor surprised that Ashcroft didn't like her images; after all, she didn't like his poetry. She did, however, need his money. And she was a professional. If he could tell her what he wanted, she could deliver it to him. She picked a handful of slides at random from the left tray and put them in a vertical line on the light table. Opposite, she put the two slides he had selected. She straightened and faced Ashcroft.

"Look," he said quickly. "I want you to know that

this has nothing to do with what happened a few days ago. I mean, nothing personal. Hell, Cathy, even if you were sleeping with me, I still wouldn't like those pictures."

Cat watched him with unblinking gray eyes, measuring the emotions in his voice—uneasiness, frustration that had nothing to do with sex, irritation, sincerity. He was telling the truth. He didn't like the work she had done, period. Nothing personal about it. A simple, fundamental difference in taste.

"Cathy, I'm telling you the truth."

"I believe you," she said, turning away and bending over the light table, magnifying glass in hand.

She studied the two slides Ashcroft had selected as suitable to accompany his poetry. The first slide was a breaking wave, a side view that showed many shades of blue fading into creamy foam. The lighting was rather flat for her taste, the image uninteresting after the first glance. Nothing wrong with it technically, simply . . . shallow. Pret-ty. She had included it more for contrast than content.

The second slide was taken on the beach. It showed Jason working over a rather disheveled sand castle. He was smiling, his cheeks and lips deep rose, his blue eyes like cut glass, his black hair curling every which way. He looked cuddly and adorable, everyman's image of the perfect child. Cat sighed. Again, there was nothing technically wrong with the image. Light, focus, composition, everything in place. But after one glance there was nothing more to see.

She had another picture of Jason that she liked much better. He was standing at the edge of the ocean, holding his cupped hands in front of him, watching water drain back into the sea. He was unsmiling, intent. The sidelight picked out his round cheeks and tiny teeth, shadow of the baby he had been; the same light also illuminated the intelligence behind his beautiful eyes and the intensity of his taut body, foreshadow of the man to come. It was a riveting image, one that repaid study.

But it wasn't pret-ty.

She turned to the five slides she had picked at random from Ashcroft's reject pile. The first slide was a close-up of a single shell lying on wave-smoothed sand, sidelit by the setting sun. A thin line of spindrift glittered in an irregular, curving diagonal across the damp sand above the shell, a line echoed by the transparent gleam of a retreating wave below the shell. The shell itself was old, imperfect, its spiral worn by the ceaseless roll of waves, its exterior milky rather than opalescent, matte-finished rather than gleaming. The purity of line and colors appealed to her, the sensuality in the contrasting textures, the feeling of time and completion and peace. But again, not pret-ty.

The next slide was of a rock at the instant a wave broke against it. It was a late afternoon shot, and she had underexposed to silhouette the rock. The wave and spray were molten gold, the rock a sable dragon rising out of the sea, orange blood running from its jagged black mouth. Mystery and power, fire and night, myth and violence, darkness defining light.

No, not pret-ty at all.

But it was an image well worth nearly losing her cameras for, as she would have done were it not for a tall stranger lifting her off the dragon's back and carrying her to shore.

Carefully, Cat set aside the magnifying glass and turned toward Ashcroft. "I think I know what's bothering you about the slides, but I'd rather have you tell me. That way there's no chance of a mistake."

He paused, then shrugged. "There's no nice way to put it, baby. Those pictures are as cold and empty as you are."

Chapter 8

CAT'S FINE-BONED FACE WAS ILLUMINATED FROM below, giving haunting shadows to her eyes. She was alone, staring down at her slides lined up in rows, tiny squares of color gleaming like gems: blues and greens, ebony and cream, silky flesh tones and fiery sunsets. She saw none of the colors, none of the grace, none of the beauty.

They're as cold and empty as you are.

Was that why Travis had stepped into the wind? Had the pleasure he'd given not been returned to him? Had the sweet burning gone no further than her own skin? Had the peace permeated only her own mind, her own dreams?

The questions turned like knives, cutting her until her hands became fists and she fought not to cry out. Gradually she became aware that she wasn't alone in the room. She took a deep breath, realizing that her nails were digging painfully into her hands. She

wondered why Ashcroft had come back, what else
he possibly could have to say to her. Perhaps he had
changed his mind about giving her another chance.
She couldn't allow that. She needed the money too
badly.

With a quiet breath she wiped all expression from
her face and turned around. She only had to turn
partway before she saw him, dressed in clothes as
black as her own, nearly invisible in the dimly lit
room. Yet there was no doubt who stood there.

"Travis."

She hardly recognized her own voice, cool and
remote, as untouchable as a winter halo around the
moon. A voice for Ashcroft, not Travis, but she said
nothing more because she couldn't. So much had
gone wrong that she was afraid even to believe he
was back. And for how long? A night? An hour? A
minute? Not that it mattered. A lifetime was hardly
enough, and he wasn't interested in sharing
lifetimes.

"I knocked. No one answered," said Travis. "The
door was open, so I came in." He shrugged, but the
eyes examining her face weren't casual. "What's
wrong?"

Cat closed her eyes. Hearing his voice again,
seeing him close enough to touch but so very far
away   Her hands clenched again, each nail returning to the livid crescents that hadn't faded from
her palms Against her will her eyes opened again,
hungry to see the angles and shadows of his face.

"Long day," she said, trying for a light voice and
failing badly. "Nothing. Just a long day. One in a
long series." She laughed harshly. "Getting longer
every day." She forced herself to look away from his
eyes, more black than blue or green in the low light,
as sensual and mysterious as a midnight sea.

Abruptly she unclenched her hands and began to gather up the careful ranks of slides. "How was your trip?"

"Lonely."

Her hands shook, spilling slides. She swore once, violently, betrayed by her own body at a time when she most needed strength. Strong hands closed over her arms. Warm hands. She could no more hide the tremor that went through her than she could still the trembling of her body.

"Cat," he whispered, his breath warm on her ear, "I missed you . . . too much."

She was rigid beneath his hands, fighting for control. "It was your choice, Travis, both the leaving and the missing."

He turned her so that she had to face him. As his head bent, light caught in his eyes, transforming them into blue-green gems.

"I wanted you to come with me." His voice was rough, his expression almost cruel.

"Not enough to wait for me, apparently." She stepped out of his hands and turned back to the light table. "But thanks for the invitation, Travis," she whispered, blindly stacking slides. "It helped me feel less . . . cheap."

She heard his sharply indrawn breath and almost regretted her words. Almost. It was the truth, though. It had been brutal to wake up alone in his bed, to walk alone to her own house with the taste and scent and memory of him permeating her body, to know that he had gone, that he had left her so easily when it had cost her so much not to go with him.

He whirled her around so quickly that the slides she was holding flew out of her hands. Little squares fluttered to the floor like brilliant butterflies. She made a small sound of distress and reached to gather up the slides, only to find herself held in an unyielding masculine vise.

"My slides—"

"Screw the slides," he snarled.

"They haven't been duplicated," she said, her voice thin, stretched almost to breaking. "If they're ruined they can't be replaced." She remembered Ashcroft's words suddenly. Strength drained out of her, leaving her nearly limp in Travis's grasp. "It doesn't matter. He won't be using them. They're cold and empty. Like me." She looked at Travis with blank silver eyes. "That's why you left, isn't it?"

Concern replaced anger in his face. His hands moved to her cheeks. Her skin was almost cold to his touch. The shadows below her eyes were deeper, the hollows beneath her cheekbones more pronounced, the bones in her face very close beneath her perfect skin, her eyes as colorless as winter. She looked both fragile and yet strangely powerful, a sorceress caught in a moment of human weakness. He bent and kissed her lips very gently, holding her as though she were made of light.

Before she could respond he released her and began picking up slides. He looked up and saw her expression, puzzled and shaken and bemused, a cat that for once had failed to land on its feet.

"We'll talk as soon as the slides are safe," he said, his voice both soothing and disturbing her. He smiled crookedly. "Neither one of us is making a hell of a lot of sense right now."

Wordlessly Cat helped gather up the slides. As she put the last few on the light table she realized that Travis was studying some of the others. Almost absently his hand closed around the magnifying glass and placed it properly on the slide. For an instant

Cat wanted to snatch away the slides and hide. The feeling appalled her. She was used to criticism; it came with the territory. She knew all about differences in taste as opposed to differences in artistic quality.

Yet seeing Travis look at her slides made her want to crawl into a dark corner and pull the shadows in after her until she was invisible. If he didn't like her work, she would be devastated on a level that had nothing to do with professional pride. Just as the *Wind Warrior* was part of his soul, those slides were part of hers. If he saw them as cold and empty . . .

She rubbed her palms over her arms, trying to drive away the chill that covered her skin more thoroughly than the black sweater. Without looking up, Travis took her hand and moved it slowly against his beard. When he shifted the magnifying glass to another slide he didn't let go of her, working one-handed, staring down at the slides with an intensity that was almost tangible. Finally he straightened and kissed her palm.

"They're brilliant," he said simply, looking at her as though he had never seen her before. It was the way she had looked at him when she'd first realized that he was the designer of the ship that had sailed across the sun.

She drew a ragged breath, realizing that it was the first one she had allowed herself for a long time. "Ashcroft didn't think so. He said they were cold and empty, like me."

"Ashcroft has the esthetics of a manure pile."

Cat's mouth relaxed around a small smile. "But he's the boss. I'm reshooting the lot. Postcards coming up. Boring, superficial and pret-ty," she said, her voice mocking the last word.

"Pretty pictures for pretty boys, hmm?"

She nodded, then looked into his eyes. "I'm very glad you don't feel that way."

His hand tightened on hers. He looked at the slides spread across the light table, colors glowing, tiny realities enclosed in white squares. "You see an extraordinary world," he said huskily. "Things stripped down to their essential curves; colors that reveal, rather than conceal, meaning; as balanced and powerful as a racing hull."

He touched one slide, moving it into a place by itself. She recognized the slide. It was the one she had taken the day he had lifted her off the rocks.

"No wonder I had to drag you away. If I'd seen dragons and gold hiding in rocks and spray, I'd have forgotten the tide, too." He smoothed her palm against his beard, then kissed her wrist swiftly, fiercely. "Thank you for sharing your world with me, Cat. It's so much like you, pure and brilliant, radiating life even in its darkest shadows."

Cat realized she was crying when she felt the hot tears spill over her cheekbones, tears salty on her mouth. She put her arms around him and held on until she ached. She had missed him more than she had admitted or even known until now. She had missed him since she was born.

Travis held her, rocking slowly, letting his warmth seep into her, kissing her temples and eyelids, her eyelashes, murmuring her name. The warmth he gave her returned redoubled, filling him and giving ease to an emptiness that had been part of him for so long that he hadn't even known it was there until she had filled it. And then he had left her and measured the loss.

Finally she drew a long, deep breath and relaxed against his body, softness and strength blending.

"Pack an overnight bag," he said, kissing her lips

slowly. "We're going on board the *Wind Warrior*. No arguments, witch. I'm the boss now, just like Ashcroft."

She lifted her head and looked at him, startled.

He smiled. "You're doing the photos for my book, Cat Cochran. No arguments about that, either. So bring your cameras, too. Bring whatever you need." He bent until his lips were just touching hers. "Bring your warmth, Cat," he whispered. "Bring your fire. It's been so cold without you."

Cat packed in a daze, fitting her few things into a bag no bigger than a purse. Her camera equipment was another matter. Travis shook his head in rueful amusement as he reached to take the five heavy cases from her.

"It's a wonder you can stand up under all that stuff."

She smiled. "I could use a bearer," she admitted. "Are you looking for work?"

He bent swiftly and lifted her, smiling.

"Not me," she said, laughing. "The cameras."

"You carry them. I'll carry you." He started for the door, putting her down only when she realized she had forgotten to turn on her answering machine.

"Harrington," she began, only to be interrupted.

"I know. He's forever chewing on me for being out of reach, too. Serve him right if I just grabbed you and sailed over the edge of the world, leaving no number at all."

Cat's hand hesitated for just an instant while his words kindled her imagination—freedom and Travis and the sea—then she sighed and turned on the machine. He followed her out the front door and waited while she locked it. He took the heavy carrying cases from her and started across the patch of hardy plants that was her front yard.

"Can we take my car?" asked Cat as they climbed the steps to the garage.

He turned and looked at her, surprised. "Sure."

"I have more gear in the trunk," she explained. "It's stuff I rarely use but never know when I'll need. Specialized equipment. Reflectors and tripods, flashes and a change of clothes, hiking boots and—" She stopped, laughing at the expression on his face. "I keep my magic broom there, too."

"I was wondering where you hid it," he said mildly. He opened the garage door. "Back out. I'll lock up for you."

Cat maneuvered the little Toyota out of the narrow garage and up the steep driveway. He lowered the door, snapped shut the padlock and walked toward the car with long strides, illuminated only by moonlight. She watched him with open appreciation, planning how to take a picture that would capture both his animal grace and his intense intelligence. Sidelight, surely. Or perhaps illumination from below as she panned her camera with his movements, freezing him against a blurred background.

"Wake up, Cat. Or do you want me to drive?"

"I'm awake," she said absently, balancing angles and lighting in her mind.

"Convince me."

"I was wondering whether to shoot you in sidelight or up from below, to freeze you against a blurred background or to do a close-up."

"What did you decide?" he asked, sliding into the passenger seat.

A slow smile curved her lips. "To shoot you and then have you stuffed."

He chuckled. "Sounds rather drastic." He waited until she drove the car onto the Pacific Coast Highway and turned right, heading toward Dana Point. Then he began talking quietly. "I didn't mean to be gone so long, Cat. *Wind Warrior*'s rigging is new, not only the lines but the sails as well. I'm doing some experiments, stealing some ideas from parachute designers."

He glanced sideways at her, smiling. "I won't bore you with the details. I'll just say I'm trying out a few new sail designs, and a few new ways of controlling those sails. I had to get used to them under various conditions of wind and wave. It took longer than I thought it would, and it's still not working the way I want it to. If it helps," he added softly, "I was surprised I'd only been gone five days. It felt more like five weeks. I missed you, Cat."

She said nothing, looking only at the highway winding between small shops and beach cottages.

"Still mad?" he asked quietly.

"Suppose I'd made love to you, then left you when you were asleep, and you woke up and found a note that said: 'Gone shooting. Wish you had come with me.' And then I didn't show up for five days. Or five weeks." She turned and looked quickly at him. "It just as easily could have been five weeks, couldn't it? You make your own rules, Travis, your own world." She shrugged. "I can understand that. I live the same way. But how would you have felt if you'd been the one to wake up in my bed and I was gone and you had to walk home alone, wondering why?"

She braked smoothly for a stoplight and watched the red circle with unblinking eyes. His hand caught her chin, turning her face toward him.

"I'd have been mad as hell," he said, his voice deep and certain. "I'd have bought a ship and chased you until I caught you."

"That's the difference between us, Travis," she said, looking at his hard eyes, his unsmiling mouth, his tawny beard almost black in the dim artificial light. "You're used to buying what you want. I'm used to going without. But we're alike in one way. I was as mad as hell."

The light turned green. She accelerated smoothly, coaxing every bit of power from the Toyota's little engine.

"I had to test the rigging, Cat," he said at last. "I couldn't do it in the harbor."

"I'm not arguing that. I'm arguing the way you left."

"If you'd been awake, I couldn't have gone," he said simply.

Startled, she turned to look at him. He was staring ahead, his eyes concealed in shadows, his profile hard beneath the erratic illumination of streetlights.

"I'm not sure I believe that," she said, her voice uncertain.

"Why?"

"I don't think I affect you the way you affect me," she said evenly.

"I agree. If I affected you the way you do me, you wouldn't have sent me to Avalon alone."

"That isn't fair, Travis. I have to work to survive. My choices aren't as easy as yours. In any case I wouldn't have left you hanging for days, not knowing if we'd ever see each other again."

"Is that what you thought?"

"What else was I supposed to think, Mr. In-The-Wind Danvers? Or is it Mr. Hell-On-Women Danvers that I'm with tonight?"

"Damn Harrington!" snarled Travis suddenly, showing his anger for the first time. "What has he told you, Cat?"

"Nothing that I didn't already know. I'm playing with fire. At first I thought I could just enjoy the warmth."

"And now?" he demanded.

"Now," she said grimly, "the only question is how badly I'm going to be burned."

He drew in his breath with a sharp sound. Then, slowly, he relaxed and touched her cheek. "Funny you should mention that. I feel the same way about fire—about you. I almost didn't come back, Cat."

She drove automatically, trying not to cry out in protest at the thought of never seeing him again. After a mile of silence and darkness, she said, "Why did you come back?"

"Why are you here with me now?" he countered softly.

"It's better than the alternative," she said, her voice rich with irony and something softer, almost yearning.

"Yes," he said, his voice as gentle as his fingertips tracing the line of her hand, her arm, her cheek. "Much better."

They finished the drive to the harbor in silence, touching each other from time to time. The touches were more reassuring than provocative, small tactile statements of mutual pleasure at being within reach of each other. It was a kind of undemanding intimacy that she hadn't known since she was a child, a warmth that penetrated all the way to her core.

She pulled into the nearly empty parking lot, switched off the engine and looked across the harbor to the ship rising clean and black and potent out of the moonlit sea. The *Wind Warrior* was both serene and wild, an elemental force drawn in sable lines against a glittering sky.

"I'd give my soul to capture just part of her

strength, her elegance, her savage beauty," she whispered.

"Yes." The word was short, almost harsh. But Travis was looking at her rather than his ship.

Cat turned toward him, wanting to say more. Her words caught in her throat. He was like the ship, fierce and powerful, and he was looking at her as though he wanted to melt through her into her soul. It was more than passion, more than desire; it was a shattering hunger that was as complex and compelling as he was. She would have been frightened by his intensity had it not been so like her own feelings as she looked at him.

The hands that circled her face were warm and very hard, their restraint underscored by the muscles that stood out tautly on his arms.

"I can't believe I didn't dream you," he said, his voice both harsh and wondering.

He took her mouth in a swift, hard kiss, as though to reassure himself of her reality. Her lips softened, opened, invitation and demand, and her hands went to his face, holding him as fiercely as he held her. They kissed each other without reservation, as though a single kiss could say everything, be everything, ensure everything they wanted of each other and themselves.

A kiss wasn't enough. Their hunger went deeper than desire, but only their bodies could say what neither had the words to express. Only by blending together, sinking into each other, could they begin to describe or appease the levels of need they aroused in each other.

"Travis—"

"I know," he breathed against her lips. But still he couldn't bring himself to let go of her. Not yet. He caught her mouth, kissing her with a sweet hunger that made her moan. He swore very softly and released her.

Without speaking they drew apart. She closed her eyes and fought the weakness that curled through her in liquid waves. Travis pulled camera gear out of the back seat, got out and walked around to her side of the car. When he opened her door she slid out and locked up the car with hands that would not stop trembling. She stuffed the keys into her pants pocket, not feeling up to fumbling with the buckle on her purse. Travis took her hand, lacing his fingers through hers with an open sensual pleasure that made her weak all over again.

"It would be easier if you didn't enjoy so much," she said shakily.

"You're the one who taught me how to enjoy," he whispered, rubbing her fingers against his beard as he led her toward the dock.

"Me?" She laughed. "You're the experienced one."

"Pleasure and experience aren't the same thing. That's what you taught me, Cat." Then, so softly that she almost didn't hear, he added, "I hope I won't regret learning it."

His hand tightened painfully in hers, and he looked down at her with eyes as dark as the sea. She understood his fear because it was the same fear she had of him. If she were wrong about him, if he were less than he seemed . . .

In silence they climbed into the *Zodiac*. The engine was loud in the quiet harbor. A lantern bloomed suddenly on the *Wind Warrior*'s stern. A shutter descended once, twice, blocking out light, then returning it in a long flash before the lantern was shuttered completely.

"Diego," said Travis beneath his breath. "He wants to talk to me."

Cat's fingers tightened in Travis's hand, silently protesting the intrusion of another person into their world.

"I wonder what the hell couldn't wait until morning," said Travis fiercely. He helped Cat up onto the ship's deck, handed over her camera equipment and pointed her toward the steps leading below. "It will be quick, I promise you," he muttered.

She watched him stride toward the dark shadow standing discreetly against the helm. Travis's voice floated back, curt and questioning. Diego's tenor responded soothingly. Cat turned and went down the stairs to Travis's cabin. She closed the door and looked longingly at the bed. The luxurious silk and wool blankets smelled vaguely of the soap Travis used. Their soft warmth was too tempting to resist.

After she put away her cameras she pulled a blanket over herself and sighed, relaxing for the first time since she had awakened and found a note pinned to the empty pillow beside her. She stretched and yawned, then lay quietly, thinking of Travis, listening to the soothing bass murmur of his voice drifting down to her. She yawned again, snuggling deeper into the blankets that smelled so reassuringly of him.

Inevitably, sleep claimed her.

She woke to find Travis standing next to the bunk, his hand smoothing a lock of hair away from her eyes as he frowned down at her.

"You've lost weight, haven't you?" he asked softly. "You're working too hard."

"It's only temporary," she said, yawning and rubbing against his hand like a cat. His frown deepened, reminding her how much he disliked her pursuit of money. "What did Diego want?" she asked, changing the subject because she didn't want to argue about money now.

"I sold one of my hulls to a fool. He ran it aground somewhere in Australia. The insurance company wants my estimate of salvage value." Travis peeled off the soft blankets covering her, slid into the bunk and pulled her onto his chest before he covered both of them again.

Cat braced herself on his chest, wanting to see his brilliant, changing eyes. Unconsciously her fingers spread over his chest, savoring both the texture of the cashmere sweater he wore and the resilient muscles beneath. "When are you going?" she asked quietly. Not if. When. She had learned.

His fingers moved up to her head, combing out the silver clasp that held her hair in a twist. Her hair spilled over his hands like sunset. His fingers clenched suddenly, chaining her. His tongue invaded her mouth, claiming her with long, slow strokes that made her bones melt.

Her hands slid beneath his black sweater, along his ribs, over his chest, tangling gently in the tawny, springy hair. Her fingers smoothed and caressed each ridge of tendon, each supple swell of muscle. When her nails brushed over his flat male nipples he shuddered lightly. Instinctively she returned to the sensitive area, wanting to give as much pleasure to him as he gave to her.

The hunger of his kiss increased, making her ache, shortening her breath until it matched his, just as her racing heartbeat matched his. His legs parted until she sank between them and was held in a sensual vise. His eyes were an intense blue-green, narrowed, revealing his desire as surely as the sinuous movement of his hips.

"Come with me, my Cat, my woman," he said huskily, moving against her, coaxing with his hard body as much as with his words. "I know you don't have the time to sail there. We'll fly. It won't take long to see if the hull can be salvaged. When I'm done we can dive along the Great Barrier Reef, drift in diamond waters with fish more brilliant than any jewels. We can love each other and sleep in the sun, and then we can love again beneath a moon as big as the world. *Come with me.*"

For a moment she let his warmth and need overwhelm her. She let him see the temptation to go with him written in the liquid heat of her body flowing against his. For just an instant she allowed herself to think of what a few weeks with him would mean to her. Then reality returned, stealing away the softness of her smiling lips.

"I'm sorry," she breathed, closing her eyes against the hunger in his, concealing her own hunger from him. "I can't."

"Why?" His voice was as blunt and smooth as river stone.

"My work. And—" She hesitated, then said calmly, "There's the fact that we've said nothing about anything, really."

His hands unclenched, letting her hair spill away. His legs loosened, freeing her. "I told you, Cat. I'll never marry a woman less wealthy than I am."

Abruptly she pushed away from him and sat at the far end of the bunk, her face pale and very still. "Who the hell said anything about marriage?"

"What else could you be talking about?" he snapped. He saw the silver blaze of her eyes and said quickly, "Cat, listen. We're so very special together. I've given up fighting it, whatever it is. I want to give you—want to share with you—a simple time of peace, companionship, pleasure, passion. And when the time is over, I won't be so vicious that you have to jump overboard to escape me."

Cat closed her eyes and concentrated on the pain of her nails digging into her hands, hearing five words again and again in her mind. *When the time is over.* Not even *if,* just *when.* She hadn't known how simple and devastating a single word could be.

And the worst part of it was that she still wanted to go with him, even if it was only two weeks, two hours, a minute.

"No," she said tightly. "I can't. There's too much I have to do. Ashcroft's book. Some small jobs I've lined up. My show in L.A. Your book."

"Christ!" he snarled. "Is money all you ever think about? Well, if that's the way you want it, I'll be glad to pay for the pleasure of your company. Two thousand dollars? No, that wouldn't be enough, not for a fancy photographer like you. Ten thousand dollars. How about it, Cat? Ten thousand dollars for two weeks."

Holding herself very carefully, Cat climbed off the bunk. "If you stopped buying women," she said in a thin voice, "you might just find out that there are women who can't be bought."

"Twenty thousand," he said flatly.

She stepped backward and looked at him for a long moment. His face was closed, cruel. His eyes measured her with cynical certainty, sure that she would allow herself to be bought when the price went high enough.

"Forty." His voice was like a whip.

"*No.*" She spun around. In one step she was out of the cabin.

"Running won't do any good, Cat!" he called after her angrily. "I'm not letting you go until we agree on a price!"

She raced up the steps to the deck without looking back. She ran the length of the deck, leaped up on the railing, hung poised for an instant against the shimmering moonlight, then left the *Wind Warrior*'s stern in a long dive that barely disturbed the dark surface of the harbor. She was invisible in her black clothes. To anyone on the ship it would seem that she had vanished into the night.

The water was cold but not numbing. She swam cleanly, her exhaustion counteracted by the shock waves of adrenaline that flooded her system. Very quickly she came to the steps leading up the pier. Dripping, shaking as much with emotion as with cold, she climbed the stairs and ran to the parking lot, grateful that she had left her keys in her pants pocket instead of her purse. As she unlocked the car she heard the snarl of the Zodiac's engine. She was out of the lot and accelerating down the harbor road before the Zodiac reached the dock.

Only when she got home did she remember that she had left her cameras behind.

Chapter 9

CAT AWOKE TO MULTICOLORED DAWN SPILLING OVER her bed. She looked through the open curtains toward the gloaming sea. A man's black figure cut across the shimmering waves, swimming powerfully, leaving a shadowed wake behind. Travis was as at home in the sea as Neptune himself. Was he thinking of her, wondering if she could see him swimming like a god through the heart of dawn?

With an impatient sound she wrenched herself out of bed. The floor was cold beneath her feet. She shivered and rubbed her arms, remembering the chill that even a steaming bath had not erased. It had taken her three hours to get to sleep. Three hours of trying not to think, not to remember. Sleep hadn't been much better. Four hours of fragmented dreams that dragged her to the brink of consciousness only to let go of her at the last instant, sending her tumbling back down into troubled darkness.

Dreams of cameras that didn't work, broken lenses, slides warped and torn . . . hell presided over by a shadow figure whose power was exceeded only by his grace, a voice as compelling as the heat that radiated from him, he was smiling, touching her, and she was burning.

Grimly, Cat yanked on her clothes. She had had enough of her dreams. Anything was preferable, even trying to figure out how she was going to get her cameras off the *Wind Warrior*. Obviously Travis had gotten home somehow, even though she had driven off and left him. At least when she went to retrieve her equipment he wouldn't be on board the ship.

She went to the kitchen, hoping that a cup of tea would make her feel better. The first thing she saw was the blinking light on her answering machine. She wondered who would have left a message for her already; even in New York, the workday hadn't started yet. She flicked on the tape. Diego's clear, apologetic tenor spoke to her.

"Mr. Danvers instructed me to tell you to pick up your cameras at nine o'clock this morning. If that isn't convenient, please call and make an appointment. The number . . ."

Cat barely heard. She stared blindly out the window. Travis was invisible now, a shadow among shadows, colors flowing like wine through the powerful waves. Irrationally, it hurt that he was as eager to avoid her as she was to avoid him. She shook off the feeling with an impatient sound. She should be out shooting now, when the light was best, taking pret-ty pictures for the pret-ty poet with the oatmeal mind; but her cameras were out of reach. It was just as well. She was too angry to take postcards right now. Dunning letters better suited her mood.

At eight thirty-five her timer sounded, reminding her to put away office work and go to the harbor. She drove quickly, feeling her heartbeat increase with each mile closer to the *Wind Warrior*. She wasn't sure whether anxiety or anger was responsible. She avoided thinking of Travis. She avoided thinking of anything at all.

Diego was waiting at the dock. He ferried her to the ship, helped her aboard and conducted her to the cabin below. The camera bags—all five of them—were lined up neatly on the bunk. Next to them were a pen and several sheets of paper covered in angular printing that fairly shouted of T. H. Danvers's male hand moving furiously across the paper. Cat flipped through the papers with a growing sense of disbelief and anger. She turned on Diego, her gray eyes narrow.

"I'm sorry," he said quickly. "I tried to talk him out of it but—" Diego shrugged gracefully. "You don't know him when he's mad. Or"—he looked closely at her pale face—"maybe you do. I'm sorry, but I can't release the equipment to you until you've checked and signed off each piece. The equipment is very valuable, I'm told. I'll be on deck when you're finished."

She stared at Diego's firm, apologetic expression for a long moment, then at the pieces of paper that were headed "Catherine Cochran's Camera Equipment." She was supposed to examine everything and check it off as being present, accounted for and in working order.

Grimly, Cat turned to the first case and began examining the contents. She worked quickly, efficiently, manipulating each lens and camera body with the familiarity that only came from long experience. When she finished each case she closed it and set it aside near the door.

Gradually her anger diminished, soothed away by the cool curves and ebony cases of cameras and lenses. They were old friends, loyal friends, her curved windows on the soul of the universe. And Diego was right; the equipment was valuable. To replace it would cost at least twenty thousand dollars. Yet if she sold it, she'd be lucky to get seven thousand. It was the old story of secondhand not being as valuable as new, even though the pictures were the same irrespective of the age of the camera.

"You know," drawled a voice behind her, "if you need money so damn bad, you could always sell some equipment."

Cat's heart stopped, then beat so hard it made her dizzy. She had not expected to confront Travis. She was not prepared for it or for the casual suggestion that she sell off her very life. She put the last lens in its nest, closed the fifth case and set it aside. She straightened but didn't turn around.

His tanned, strong hand came around her arm and scooped up the papers. His legs brushed past her, stopping only inches from her as he leaned against the bunk. Even now, she wanted to run her palm over his arm, feel his warmth and male strength. The impulse angered her as nothing else could have.

"I'd no more sell my cameras than I'd sell my children," she said distinctly. Her hands froze as she listened to the echo of her own words . . . *my children, my children.* A soft, anguished sound broke through her control. She looked up at him, her eyes blind, her voice shaking. "That's it, isn't it?" she asked. "I'm passionate, poor and *sterile.* That makes me great mistress material but not worth more than a few nights in the sheets, not worth really caring about, certainly not worth loving!"

Wildly she looked toward the door, her desire to flee as clear as the white lines of pain bracketing her mouth. She stood and swayed forward, reaching toward the door with hungry hands.

"If you go overboard again," snarled Travis, "I'll throw your precious goddam cameras after you."

Cat stared at his face and knew that he meant precisely what he said. She had never seen a man so angry, had not even known that such anger existed short of violence. She looked at her cameras, then at the door that had never seemed farther away. Numbly she put her arms at her sides.

"The papers," she said, her voice aching from the strain of not screaming. "I haven't signed them." She held out her hand, not looking at him, not looking at anything except the cameras lined up by the door. "I'll sign, then I'll take my cameras and go."

Hard fingers closed on her chin, snapping her head around to face him.

"You wouldn't stay on board for love or money," he said coldly, "but you'll meekly stay for a few piles of metal and glass. What the hell kind of woman are you?"

She flinched and went white before color returned in a rush of anger and adrenaline. "Tired, beaten and cornered," she said, her voice as ragged as her nerves, "that's what kind of woman I am. My cameras are all that's left since you tried to buy what I'd have given you for a few gentle words, a touch, your warmth in the cold center of night. . . ."

She hated the tears burning behind her eyes, choking her voice, drowning her. "Damn you," she said brokenly, "give me my cameras and let me go!"

"Cat." His voice hurt even more than her unshed tears. "Don't," he murmured, pulling her against his chest, wrapping his arms around her. When she struggled he held her closer, gently showing her the futility of fighting his strength. "I'm sorry," he whispered, kissing her eyes, her cheeks, her hair, rocking her. "I didn't understand. I couldn't believe that there was a woman alive who couldn't be bought. I believe you now. God help me, I believe you. Don't leave me, my woman, my Cat. Stay with me," he whispered, ". . . warmth in the cold center of night."

Hearing her own needs, her own words whispered in his voice, unraveled her anger, leaving her almost too weak to stand, much less fight. She leaned against him and let his presence sink into every pore. With a ragged sigh she gave herself over to his strength, floating on him as though he were a wave curling up out of the sea, carrying her irresistibly to an unknown shore. She didn't object when he lifted her onto the bunk and lay down beside her.

"Hold me," he said, sliding his arms around her. "Just hold me for a minute, then I'll let you go. If you want to go."

She felt the shudder that went through him when her arms circled his body, heard the broken sigh against her hair and knew that he was drinking her presence as hungrily as she had drunk his. The realization went through her like cognac, heady and powerful and very fine, fire spreading through her in expanding waves. She moved her head slightly, found his mouth waiting for her. With a low sound she opened her lips, tasting his heat and sweetness. She kissed him deeply, pouring herself into him until she suddenly realized that she was shaking with need. And so was he.

She made an incoherent sound, telling him of the fire burning inside her. Slim hands moved beneath his dark T-shirt, tugging upward impatiently, hungry for the feel of his naked skin beneath her palms. He shrugged out of the T-shirt with a muscular twist that made her breath shorten. In the half-light of the cabin his body was beautiful, skin rippling over his male strength, tawny hair catching light, his face drawn by need and anticipation, his teeth two hard white lines divided by the tip of his tongue as he pulled her mouth down to his.

Her blouse and bra vanished beneath his fingers. When she felt his hands on her breasts her body changed, liquid waves of pleasure gathering, shimmering, building with each caress. She arched against him, her whole body taut with the need only he had ever been able to create and satisfy in her.

He moved suddenly, turning, pinning her beneath him with one strong leg. With a hoarse sound he tore his mouth from hers. Before she could protest the end of the kiss, she felt his tongue on her breast, his teeth closing around the hardened nipple, then she was taken into the hot, changing textures of his mouth and caressed with a thoroughness that shook her.

She twisted slowly against him, barely able to breathe for wanting him. Her hands raked down his chest to his jeans, seeking to know all of him, his strength and his passion and his need. When her hands found him, stroked him, his body tightened like a bow.

For an instant he thrust against her, eyes closed, lips thinned by the force of the desire raging in him. Then he moved suddenly, peeling off the rest of her clothes with a strength that shocked her. His hands moved almost roughly over her soft skin. His mouth searched hungrily over her, touching every secret of her body, claiming her most intimate warmth with a passionate caress that did not stop until liquid waves of pleasure curled and broke and ecstasy shimmered through her.

"You're mine," he said, his teeth closing delicately on her, sending yet another wave of pleasure breaking over her.

He moved swiftly, one powerful hand stroking up the length of her body, tangling in her rich hair with a claiming as fierce as the passion burning behind his eyes. He held her motionless while his free hand caressed her, fingers sliding into her warmth and moving until she moaned and he smiled, watching her. "You're mine, sweet Cat, my woman; you're mine and I've only begun to touch you. . . ."

The hunger and need in his eyes, his touch, his male heat and arousal sent fire along nerves still quivering with ecstasy. She cried out and reached for him, wanting only to give him a pleasure to equal what he had given her. Her hands kneaded down his body, savoring him with palms and fingertips and delicate raking nails. It wasn't enough. She wanted to taste him, to know him as passionately as he had known her. Futilely she tugged at his belt buckle, her hands trembling too much to unfasten it. He laughed softly and slid out of the rest of his clothes.

"Let me—" she began, then his mouth descended on hers and the world narrowed to the feel of his tongue moving over hers, his fingers echoing the slow rhythms of love.

Waves of pleasure went through her, pleasure she shared with him, melting over him as she made small sounds at the back of her throat. When he finally lifted his head she was covered in a fine mist of heat, her eyes wide and almost wild. She whispered his name, her hands and eyes asking for something she didn't know how to say.

"Yes, my woman?" he said thickly against her throat, his hand still buried in her hair, holding her while her body arched and quivered. "What do you want? Tell me and I'll give it to you. Anything."

"I want—" A shudder moved over her, tightening muscles inside her body in a reflex as old as passion.

He smiled, his teeth a vivid flash of white against his tawny beard. "What is it that you want, little Cat?" he murmured, moving his head until he could lick the mist off her breasts with quick, light strokes. She made a ragged sound and shuddered again. His mouth moved, enjoying her. "Do you know how good you taste?"

"Travis," she said, then her voice broke over a moan. "That's what I want, only—" Her nails dug into his shoulders as another wave of pleasure broke over her.

"Only what?" he said, his blue-green eyes lambent as they watched her taken by the wave.

"I—" She took a deep breath as the wave passed, giving her back her body and her voice until the next wave would come, claiming her. She touched his hardness lightly, longingly. "You once said I could touch you anywhere, any way I wanted to. Did you mean that?"

His lips curved in a smile that took her breath. "Yes."

Her fingers traced the length of his body, lingering over his heat and maleness. "I've never been touched the way you touched me," she said. "I've never wanted to touch a man the way I want to touch you. Let me touch you. Please."

His hand tightened almost savagely in her hair, chaining her for an instant while his lips drank the pulse beating strongly in her neck. Then he released her, letting her slide down his body, a sweet fire licking over him.

She flexed her fingers like a cat, rubbing her palms down his chest and stomach and thighs, teasing him by just avoiding his most sensitive flesh. At the same time she let him feel the sharpness of her nails and the softness of her tongue. She looked up and found him watching her with eyes that burned too vividly to be real. She smiled, not knowing how beautiful she looked to him with her hair tumbling around her naked shoulders, her mouth bruised and her body hot with the pleasure she wanted to share.

With a small sigh she bent forward, letting her hair fall over him in a fiery cloud. Gently she explored his body, running her cheek and mouth over the smooth muscles of his abdomen, enjoying the textures of warm skin, resilient muscles, tawny hair like rough silk, the softer hair of his thighs and calves. She savored him, fascinated by his male body, his strength and potency.

When her tongue tentatively traced his length, the powerful muscles of his thighs contracted. He moved sinuously, telling her without words that he reveled in the intimate caress. Desire shook her as thoroughly as it shook him. To have the freedom of his body, to feel his uninhibited response was as exciting as being touched by him had been. With a small sound she let the rest of the world slide away, forgetting even herself in the pleasure of loving Travis as she had never loved any man.

"Cat—"

His voice was unrecognizable, torn between a groan and a fierce cry of pleasure. She eluded the hands trying to drag her back up his body, wanting only to continue setting fire to him with the changing pressures of her touch, caught as completely as he was in the wildness building between them. For a few moments more she held him with tongue and teeth, then the world tilted crazily and she found herself looking up into hot blue-green eyes and a dark smile, her body imprisoned in the grip of a man whose strength she had only begun to measure.

"Witch," he muttered thickly, his fingers closing over her breasts with sure possession, "I hope you want what you've been asking for, because I'm going to give you every bit of it."

She arched her hips hungrily and dug her nails into his hard buttocks, giving her wildness to him, sure that he could control it. With a deep male sound he took what she offered, filling her, moving with a barely leashed savagery that undid her. Only his mouth over hers prevented her from crying aloud as fierce ecstasy transformed her. She drank his hoarse cry, feeling his powerful body shake as he poured himself into her.

For a long time they held each other, letting the aftershocks of passion shiver through their bodies. When their breathing no longer caught with each movement, Travis gently shifted his weight. She made an inarticulate sound, not wanting to be separate from him. His finely scarred fingers framed her face.

"I didn't hurt you, did I?" he asked, searching her eyes. "I've never lost control like that, even when I was a kid."

She smiled and tightened her body, holding him inside her warmth. She opened her lips to speak, only to have him take her mouth almost hungrily.

"The way you answer my questions could get you in trouble all over again," he said when he finally lifted his head.

She laughed and rubbed her cheek against his beard. Her hands moved slowly over the muscles of his back, enjoying him with an intensity that was reflected in her warm gray eyes. "Insatiable, aren't you?"

"Not usually," he said, his hands stroking languidly over her body, "not like this. This is new, Cat." He buried his head in the fire of her hair. "Everything you bring to me is new. I want to make love until I can't tell who is you and who is me." His fingers rubbed through her hair in sensuous assault even as he moved inside her. "I want to fill you until you'll be empty if I'm not there. *I want you.*"

"Yes," she murmured, fitting herself against his strength. "Yes."

Then her breath caught and she couldn't say anything more, only hold onto him. A potent wave gathered, surging slowly up from the sea of their passion, claiming her, claiming him, joining them until they dissolved into each other, holding back nothing. The wave curled over them, enclosing them in a translucent, shimmering world where nothing existed but the ecstasy that they shared with each other.

By the time Travis and Cat emerged on the deck of the *Wind Warrior*, the sun was halfway across the afternoon. Diego was gone, as was the Zodiac. Travis smiled. "Looks like you're going to have to swim for it again."

Cat yawned and stretched languidly. "I'd go down like a brick. Looks like you're stuck with me."

He tilted her face up, kissing her swiftly. "Remember that, witch. You're mine."

Her eyes widened. She looked up at him through dense lashes that glinted red and gold. His smile was rakish and utterly male. "You really *are* a buccaneer, aren't you?" she murmured.

"Where you're concerned, yes," he admitted, smiling down at her.

In the slanting afternoon light his eyes had a jewel-like purity of color. His skin was taut, deeply bronzed, and his beard was spun from dark gold. Beneath his black sweater his body radiated ease and power.

"Don't move," she breathed. "I'll be right back."

She raced back to the cabin, grabbed the two camera cases she used most often and ran back on deck. While Travis waited quizzically, she pulled out a camera and a small telephoto lens. When she retreated a few feet back along the deck, he moved as though to follow.

"No," she said. "Don't move. You're perfect."

"Cat," indulgently, "what the hell are you doing?"

"Taking pictures of a pirate."

The motor drive surged quickly, pulling frame after frame of film past the aperture.

"You're supposed to be taking pictures of the *Wind Warrior*."

"I am," she said simply. "You're part of the ship, Travis. The most important part. Creator, owner, soul."

She caught the sudden intensity of his expression, an almost startled recognition of her words. The motor drive whirred in response to her command. After a few moments she lowered the camera and smiled. "Get used to it, Travis. It comes with the territory called *The Danvers Touch*."

He laughed and put his arm around her, pulling her snugly against his side. Together they walked the deck of the ship from bow to stern and back again, talking quietly. From time to time Cat would move ahead or behind, taking photos of Travis and the *Wind Warrior* from various angles. She worked with an unfailing attention to nuances of light and texture and composition. He waited patiently, sometimes attending to a detail of rigging, at other times simply standing quietly, appreciating the lithe woman who handled cameras with the same total familiarity that he handled wind and sail.

When Cat concentrated on catching the highlights of rigging brought out by the late afternoon sun, Travis sat cross-legged on the deck and began splicing rope. Cat, sensing his absence, looked around. She found him in a pool of sunlight, his head bent over his task, sunlight running molten over his tawny hair. She set aside her camera and went to him. Without a word she took the rope out of his hands and started pulling off his T-shirt.

After an initial instant of surprise, Travis submitted to her with a pirate's smile of anticipation. She smiled in return, the serene smile of a sorceress, and threw the T-shirt aside. She put rope back into the hands that were reaching for her and took up her camera again. He made a face at the camera, then resumed splicing rope, his disappointment clear. She photographed him as he worked, seated like a god in the center of a golden cataract of light.

He watched her without seeming to, brilliant flashes of blue-green measuring her progress around him as she climbed the rigging and the railing in search of the perfect angle. At one point she miscalculated. Travis rose in a single fluid motion and snatched her off her precarious perch just as she would have fallen. She laughed and let herself slide down his body, her hands savoring his supple, sun-warmed skin. He held her close, breathless, kissing her until she made soft sounds and melted over him like sunlight.

That afternoon set the pattern of the weeks that followed. Travis didn't mention going to Australia or anywhere else again. Nor did Cat ask him when he was going to leave. It was hard enough simply to know that someday he would board the *Wind Warrior* and sail over the curve of the world, never to come back to her again. She didn't want to know the exact date of the last hour they would have together.

When she had to work on other assignments, Travis often was her "bearer," carrying her heavy camera bags. He came to anticipate her needs, handing her a piece of equipment she wanted before she could ask for it. The first time that had happened she had simply stared at him, feeling herself come apart at his slow smile.

"What did I ever do without you?" she asked, trying to make her voice light.

His answer was a kiss as swift as it was fierce. "The same thing I did without you—go through life not knowing what the hell I was missing."

One night she learned how he had gotten the spider-fine scars that crisscrossed his fingers. She was at her light table sorting slides when Travis came in carrying a cardboard carton.

"Dinner?" she asked hopefully.

"Didn't you eat?"

She shook her head. "These slides should have been in the mail weeks ago. Besides, I didn't have time to go to the store."

"I'll bet you haven't eaten since we had peanut butter and cocoa with Jason this morning."

She didn't bother to deny it.

He swore quietly. "Cat, you don't know the first thing about taking care of yourself. You work too damn hard." He stopped abruptly. Her work schedule impinged on the one subject they knew better than to raise: money.

She looked at him quietly, shadows haunting her lovely eyes, shadows lying deeply beneath her high cheekbones. She knew better than he how hard she was pushing herself. And if she hadn't known, her weekly visits to Dr. Stone were a brutal reminder. Her hips were bruised from iron shots, and her ears were burned from the doctor's caustic remarks about endurance and exhaustion.

Yet Cat didn't know what else she could do. She needed the money that came from work, but she could not deny herself time with Travis. Some day he would leave as suddenly as he had come. Until that day she would beg, borrow and steal everything she could from the rest of her life, hoarding seconds and minutes and hours to give to him, her only regret being that there was never enough time.

He kissed her in silent apology. "I'm sorry, Cat. I know I take up too much of your time."

"No," she said quickly, "never that. I'm just . . . greedy. World enough and time." She smiled ironically, rubbing her aching neck. "Not much to ask, is it? Just everything."

His kiss deepened until it was just short of bruising, but he said only, "I'll bring you something to eat."

He reappeared in a few minutes, balancing a plate of spaghetti in one hand and a bowl of salad in the other. "The miracle of take-out pasta," he said, smiling triumphantly.

She eyed the mound of spaghetti, appalled at its size. "My God, Travis, it'll take me a week to eat it all."

He smiled sheepishly. "I remembered that I hadn't eaten, either."

They sat at the small table she had put in the corner of her workroom so that Travis would have a place to work on his hull designs while she sorted or made duplicates of the endless boxes of slides. When she couldn't eat any more food no matter what he threatened, Travis calmly finished the spaghetti, cleared away the dishes and set the carton he had brought on the table.

"What's that?" she asked again.

"Whittling."

She blinked. "Come again?"

"Carving. You know, sharp knives and pieces of wood." As he spoke he pulled out several blocks of wood bigger than his hand. "Do you think Jason would like dark or light wood better?"

She looked at the intelligence and laughter lighting his eyes and felt a familiar weakness wash through her. Her lips quivered slightly as she smiled. "Dark, of course. Like the *Wind Warrior*. Is that what you're going to do—make him a ship?"

Travis discarded all but the piece of nearly black wood. "How did you know?" he asked, touching her cheek with a gentleness that made her ache.

"He worships you," she said, kissing his palm.

"He's very special to me," said Travis, slowly turning over the ebony block in his hand. "I would have liked a son like Jason."

Cat closed her eyes quickly, afraid that he would see the pain scoring through her. He hadn't meant to hurt her with his words. In any case, even if she could have children, they wouldn't be his, and she was both proud and pragmatic enough to realize it. In an odd sense there was nothing personal in his refusal to love her. Love required trust, and Travis required a certain level of wealth before he would trust a woman. Cat did not have that wealth. It was a fact like gravity. Nothing personal at all.

But that didn't make it hurt any less.

Travis turned the dark block of wood over and over in his hands, as lost in thought as she was when she looked through a camera lens. She didn't interrupt, giving him the same undemanding companionship that he gave her when she was absorbed in her own work. Absently he fished a thin, razor-edged knife out of the carton. He turned on and adjusted the gooseneck lamp that hung shoulder high above the table. A shaft of white light poured over the rich wood, picking up hints of chestnut and mahogany in the densely grained block. The wood glowed against the deep tourmaline color of his shirt, a color that enhanced the smooth textures of his skin and highlighted the golden hair along his forearms.

Before he touched blade to wood, Cat knew that she had to photograph him, his concentration, his exquisitely sensitive hands, the flow of light and shadow over his face. He was so accustomed to her cameras that he didn't even look up, perhaps didn't even hear the whirring of the motor drive or notice the occasional flash she used when the existing light didn't please her. She worked with an intensity that equaled his, narrowing her world to the width of a camera lens, trying to capture the essence of the only man she had ever loved.

Minutes blended into hours. Slowly, miraculously, an image of the *Wind Warrior* emerged from the sable wood. It was difficult work, for the wood was almost too hard to be carved. Travis's concentration never wavered when the knife inevitably slipped and knicked the back of his fingers, leaving behind a hairline of red that bled freely. He didn't stop carving until blood threatened to stain the wood.

"Damn," he said, licking the back of his fingers. "One more scar." He stretched the tight muscles across his shoulders and flexed his cut hand ruefully. "I usually have a choppy sea to blame for my clumsiness."

"Blame it on the hour," said Cat, stretching as he had stretched.

He looked at his watch. Two in the morning. He looked at her dark eyes and the litter of empty film canisters scattered on the floor around the table, mute evidence that she had been working as hard as he.

"Ah, Cat," he said, shaking his head and pulling her onto his lap, "I had other plans for the night."

She smiled and rubbed her mouth lightly over his. "It's still night."

"It's late, and you're so damn tired."

"When I'm *that* tired, you can call the undertaker. Besides"—she yawned delicately, closing her teeth on his ear—"I'm going to make you do all the work."

His hands hesitated, then moved knowingly over her body. "Are you sure, little Cat? I can wait."

"I can't."

Lazily she tugged at his shirt, wanting to end this night as she had so many others, deep in his arms. There were times when she didn't know which was the greater pleasure, sharing his mind or sharing his body. She did know that nothing would be the same without him, that he had become as much a part of her as her own skin, her own dreams. She loved him as she had never thought to love any man.

She said nothing of this to Travis, for to say "I love you" is to ask that the love be returned. She would not ask that, because she already knew the answer. He had told her he would never love a woman who had less money than he had. She believed him. They had never lied to each other in the weeks that they had spent together, weeks of relentless work and sweet laughter, days and nights electric with his presence.

She believed she was strong enough to keep her love to herself, to accept what he could give and to give him what she must silently. She never guessed that she would tell him in an instant of shared fury what she had been too wise to tell him in all their times of shared ecstasy.

Chapter 10

AIR THAT SMELLED OF SALT AND SUN FLOWED OVER Cat's face as she leaned on the railing of the *Wind Warrior*. Travis was a warm presence at her back, two strong arms bracketing her body, male laughter in her hair. She rubbed against him with a feline ease and sensuality, enjoying the heat and strength that radiated from him.

"Like this, do you?" he murmured, closing one arm to catch her against his body. "I thought you would. Cats are the only animals other than man that live well at sea."

She laughed softly and lifted her hand until she found the rough silk texture of his beard. Sensitive fingertips moved along the line of his lips, his jaw, the smooth lobe of his ear. "You've made a beautiful world for yourself."

"This is nothing," he said, taking her hand and kissing its palm. "Wait until she spreads her wings."

On either side of the *Wind Warrior* the rocky barriers of man-made jetties rose out of the sea, baffling the smooth-backed waves, creating a tranquil harbor for the myriad pleasure craft sleeping at their white slips. The channel itself was a straight green river leading to the sea. There was no swell yet, simply a subliminal rocking motion that hinted at the immensity of the Pacific waiting beyond the narrow thrust of jetties.

At the farthest reach of the jetties seagulls soared and cried. Ocean swells creamed around the rocks, reaching for *Wind Warrior*'s sable elegance. The ship changed subtly, responding eagerly to the nearness of the unconfined sea. At the edge of Cat's awareness the crew moved in silent concert, preparing the ship. Normally Travis would have worked with the crew, but he had wanted to be with Cat at the exact instant that his ship stepped into the wind.

The *Wind Warrior* rounded the jetty and slid into the sweeping embrace of the sea. Overhead, maroon sails unfurled in a coordinated rush of canvas. The ship quivered, transfixed by wind . . . and then she heeled over and flew like the great black bird she was.

Cat stretched out her hands to the horizon and laughed softly, exultantly. She had been to sea before, but never like this, carried with such grace and elegance and sweeping power. Travis drank her response as totally as his ship drank the wind, and then he turned Cat in his arms and kissed her until they became a single figure swaying to the rhythms of the unbridled ocean.

"Thank you," he said huskily, looking down into her lambent gray eyes.

"For what?" she said, smiling, wanting and loving him in silence.

"For being here, for being alive, for being *you.*"

She blinked back unexpected tears, unable to speak for fear she would say what must not be said: I love you. She stood on tiptoe and kissed him as though for the first time—or the last—and he answered with an intensity to equal hers.

Silently, holding each other, they watched the blue-green ocean divide around the ship's ebony bow. Water seethed and creamed along the *Wind Warrior*'s sensitive hull, wind filled her powerful sails, eagerness vibrated subtly through every sleek centimeter of her. She took the swells cleanly, rising to meet their looming liquid walls with an economy of motion that made her easy to sail despite her experimental rigging.

After a time, though, Cat was forced to admit the growing uneasiness of her stomach. She had been lucky when she was young. Seasickness for her had been something that, if it happened at all, came and went within a few hours. She hoped that hadn't changed. Motion sickness pills made her so sleepy that she usually refused to take them.

She realized that her queasiness might be born of hunger rather than seasickness. She had been so caught up in getting the right camera gear aboard that she had forgotten to eat any breakfast. But the thought of food now made her stomach turn in vivid warning. She swallowed hard and thought of something else besides food, anything else: the cry of gulls and the patterns of white foam curling out from the bow.

The ship swooped down the side of a particularly large wave. She closed her eyes. That was a mistake. She quickly opened her eyes and saw Travis's rueful, sympathetic smile.

"Getting to you?" he asked softly.

She nodded.

"Want something for it?"

"Not yet. It should pass. It always has before."

She breathed deeply through her nose, then let the breath hiss out from between clenched teeth. It was a trick she had learned when she'd first gone to sea, a means of avoiding the transient nausea of *mal de mer.* Usually it worked. When it didn't, there was always the head or a nearby railing.

The nausea didn't pass. She spent the next few hours leaning on the rail, letting the wind blow over her and breathing out through her teeth. When the grip of nausea eased, she tried to take up her cameras and shoot the *Wind Warrior* under sail as she had planned to do. It didn't work. Changing her perspective from normal to through-the-lens, moving the focus and shifting her position nearly undid her. When Travis appeared in front of her with a pale yellow pill and a glass of water, she accepted without argument.

She slept for sixteen hours. When she awoke, the nausea returned, redoubled. She almost didn't make it to the head. Afterward she felt better. The nausea faded even further when she was out on deck. Lassitude, however, claimed her. The slow rhythms of the sea dissolved her ambition. She was supposed to be climbing masts and scooting about in the Zodiac, dangling from the railing and performing all the rest of the contortions a photographer goes through to get the best angle. She tried to work, but the shifting perspectives brought back her nausea.

It was the same with food. As long as she didn't smell or eat food, her stomach behaved. When the men ate breakfast, she was careful to find a spot on the deck upwind. Travis found her there after he had eaten. Her face was tilted up into the wind and her eyes were narrowed against the tiredness that seemed to consume her, leaving behind only an insatiable desire to lie on the bow and let the sea part before her. When Travis sat down behind her, she looked over her shoulder with a sad smile.

"I'm sorry to be such a disappointment," she said. "I don't know what's wrong. I've never been a bad sailor before."

He smiled and pulled her between his legs, settling her weight against his chest. "What could be disappointing about holding you?" he asked softly, burying his face in her subtly burning hair. "Go ahead and curl up in my arms, little Cat. You make me feel like a god bringing you the gift of sleep."

"But I'm supposed to be shooting the ship and the sea," she murmured, relaxing against him despite her words.

"The sea was here before civilization began. It will be here when civilization ends. Sleep, Cat. There's all the time in the world."

She burrowed into his warmth with a sigh and let the world slide away, keeping only him.

She spent the remaining two days of the trip curled in his arms, letting the gentle winter sun wash over her, counting waves, counting heartbeats, sleeping and waking to his gentle smile.

No matter how much Cat slept, her body cried out for more. Though nausea was infrequent, her appetite didn't return. She wasn't surprised. Her appetite had varied from slim to nothing during the last few weeks. It had happened before to her during the times she'd worked too hard and slept too little. When Travis tried to get her to eat more than toast or crackers, she simply smiled and refused, explaining that she was still slightly seasick and would resume eating normally as soon as she was on land again.

Travis took Cat at her word. After they returned to their anchorage in Dana Point Harbor, he drove her back home. When he dropped her off at her house, the last thing he told her was that he would return with a five-course meal and she would eat every bite of it.

Cat stood in the kitchen, watched his lithe descent of her beach stairs, and wished food had never been invented. She leaned on the counter until sunset light sent carmine shadows over her hands. From time to time she wondered what Travis would bring back with him. Every food that occurred to her sounded either uninteresting or outright disgusting.

Even the thought of food made her stomach move warningly. She flattened her palms on the cold tile counter, breathed sharply through her nose, then gritted her teeth and let the breath hiss out. She had forgotten that it took her body as long to get used to motionless land again as it had taken to get used to the shifting sea. Even though she had been off the *Wind Warrior* for several hours, the room still swayed gently when she closed her eyes . . . and her stomach swayed a good deal less gently whether her eyes were open or closed. The idea of coping with dinner defeated her.

Tired. God, she hadn't known what the word meant until now. Too tired even to yawn, despite the last few days lazed away in Travis's arms.

She went to her workroom and slumped into the chair next to the answering machine. She rewound the tape, knowing she had to sort through the calls that had come in while she had sailed on the *Wind Warrior,* sleeping in the arms of a pirate, listening to a deep East Texas drawl that caressed her more warmly than the honey sunlight pouring over the autumn sea.

Resolutely she put Travis out of her mind and began listening to her answering machine's recorded messages.

"Cathy-baby, where the hell are you? Just wanted to say that the pictures are great, baby, really great! Just what I wanted, all soft and warm and creamy. I knew you could do it if someone just showed you—"

Cat stabbed the advance button and said a few pungent words. It was like the arrogant Crown Prince of Treacle not even to identify himself. But then, no one else she knew was insensitive enough to call her "Cathy-baby." At least he was happy with the slides. That meant money, pure and sweet and very much needed. The last half of the advance for Ashcroft's book wouldn't cover her siblings' final tuition payment and her mother's monthly expenses, much less her own photographic expenses; but the money would help her hang on until the Big Check from Energystics came.

And the Big Check had to come. She had already spent fifteen hundred dollars on lawyers to pry out the thirty-three thousand Energystics owed her. Without that check she wouldn't make it to January. In the last few weeks she had borrowed heavily on signature loans, knowing she could pay them off the day the check arrived. She closed her eyes. Her stomach quivered. She forced her eyes open. It would be better in a few hours. It had to be. It couldn't get much worse.

Fumbling, she activated the machine again.

"Stoddard Photographic. Your slides are in."

She sighed. More processing to pay for. More

slides to sort and duplicate, mail and file. Which reminded her—she had to buy film soon. She had only enough for a few days of shooting. Money and more money, dollars disguised as light-sensitive emulsion coated on a perforated ribbon of film. But there was no choice. No film, no slides. No slides, no money.

"Hi Cathy, this is Sue from Custom Framers. When are you going to come in and select mats and frames for the prints Stoddard shipped to us? You did say your show was in December, didn't you?"

Cat took a very deep breath and hissed it out between her teeth. Yes, her show was in a few weeks. Yes, she had to select mats and frames for prints she hadn't paid for yet. Thirty-five images, ten prints of each. Not all of them had to be framed, of course. Just a few of each, and a few more of the ones the gallery owner expected to sell most quickly. Three hundred and fifty prints costing her between $45 and $145 each for the enlargement, depending on size and special instructions. Then the framing. Another $80 to $165 each, depending . . .

Thousands of dollars. Money she didn't have. Money Energystics owed her.

"Damn damn damn!"

Frustration didn't help her nausea one bit. Only the thought that somewhere on the tape there might be a call from her green angel kept her from quitting right there and hanging her head in the toilet.

Sure enough, the next call was from Harrington.

"Hi, Cochran. This is Harrington. Glad to see you have the damn machine on for a change. Energystics is now returning my calls, but they aren't saying anything very interesting. I'll keep you posted on that one. I know tuition and Momma's check are due pretty quick. Ashcroft called to tell me he loves the postcards you took for him. Swear to God. Unfortunately the idiot has developed writer's block. The last section of poetry just isn't coming along. Naturally the publisher won't pay your part of the contract until Ashcroft fulfills his part. Remember that guy who wanted the pret-ties? He decided to redo his image along other lines—chartreuse hair, black fingernails and safety pins in unlikely places. I'm sending the slides back to you. Sorry. Better news next time. Swear to God it can't get worse. Say hi to Danvers for me."

Cat looked at the dial on the machine. One message left. For a second of pure cowardice she almost stopped the tape. She'd had all the bad news she could take for a while. On the other hand, maybe a fairy godmother had died and left her a pile of gold dust. . . . Smiling sardonically, Cat waited for the message to begin.

"Catherine, this is Dr. Stone. I hope you're sitting down, child. This time the reason your period is eight weeks late is that you're pregnant. No, there is no doubt. If you hope to stay pregnant come in and see me immediately."

For a long time the only sound in the room was that of the surf prowling along the beach below. Then, shakily, Cat rewound the tape and played the last message a second time, and a third. She stared at the little turning tape reels in dazed fascination, hearing over and over the impossible word. *Pregnant.* Laughing softly, she pulled herself to her feet and went downstairs to her bedroom and stared at herself in the full-length mirror. Pregnant! A world of possibilities growing inside her, another heartbeat, another mind, another living being. Travis's baby. Her baby. *Their baby.*

She was still laughing softly, hugging herself, when she heard Travis come in.

"Cat?" he called.

"Travis," she said, laughing and running to him as he put his packages onto the kitchen counter, catching him before he could even close the door. "Travis!"

She threw her arms around him and held him, unable to speak for the happiness overflowing her. His arms lifted her high, cradling her in a warm hug that was as familiar as his smile.

"You look like you swallowed the sun, little Cat," he said, kissing her lips, smiling at her because it was impossible to see her joy and not smile.

She smiled in return, her eyes huge and brilliant with emotion, looking at him as though she had never seen him before: Travis H. Danvers, the man she loved, father of her child. "Do you believe in miracles?" she asked breathlessly, then kissed him before he could answer. "I do," she said, kissing him quickly after each word. "I do! I'm pregnant, my love. I'm pregnant!"

Travis's arms tightened until she couldn't breathe. "What did you say?"

She caught his face between her hands. "A baby, Travis, my man, my lover, my love. *Our baby!*" She laughed softly, moving her head to catch his lips again, but she was sliding down his body, her feet hitting the floor with punishing force. She grabbed his arm to steady herself, swaying dizzily. "Travis?"

When she saw his face she instinctively stepped backward, out of reach. Violence and rage burned blackly in the depths of his tourmaline eyes. His body rippled with the involuntary motion of a predator poised for the killing leap, adrenaline pumping, muscles tensed. He closed his eyes, saying more clearly than words that he didn't trust himself to look at her. Like his eyes, his expression was closed, his face as grim and unyielding as the rocks lining the beach. When he spoke, chills coursed over her. His voice belonged to no one she knew, soft and cold, vibrant with rage.

"And your Big Check, Cat," he said, watching her, "did it finally come?"

The unexpected words confused her. She shook her head as much in baffled reaction as in answer to his question. "No, but what does that have to do with me being pregnant?" Her voice was small, quivering, more poignant than tears.

"The voice is very good," he said, reaching into the pocket of his red windbreaker. He brought out a pen and a checkbook. "You're as good an actress as you were a lover. But then, maybe you were acting all the time."

He made a savage gesture, cutting off whatever she might have said. The suddenness of his attack left her defenseless, unable even to speak.

"Actress, mistress, whore, it doesn't matter. Not any more. But hear me, bitch," he said cruelly, "and hear me good. You're going to have that baby, and then it will be *mine*. No running off for an abortion. No holding the child for ransom. You'll have it, and I'll raise it, and you'll never see either one of us again." As he spoke he wrote rapidly in his checkbook, slashing at the paper. He tore out the check and held it out to her. "My attorney will have the papers to you in a few days."

In disbelief she stared at the check quivering in his fingers.

One million dollars.

The price Travis had paid to be free of his wife.

Fire went through Cat, burning her to the bone. When there was nothing left to burn, then would come the time of ice.

"Take it," he said harshly, his emotions finally breaking through his control. "Take it or I'll tear it up and write a smaller one."

Her hand moved with the speed of a striking snake, taking the check so quickly that the edge of the paper sliced through his skin. Blood welled.

"So that was your price," he snarled, flexing his hands as though hungry to feel her neck between his fingers. "*Christ!* You'd think whores would be more original and men would be less gullible!"

With neat, quick motions Cat shredded the check. "You're right, T. H. Danvers. People should be more original. But then, 'I love you' isn't the most original phrase in the universe."

"Whores don't love anything but money," he said, his lip lifting in contempt.

She opened her fingers. Tiny, pale blue pieces of paper fluttered to the floor. Travis slapped his checkbook onto the counter. His pen stabbed across the paper. This time the check he held out to her was for $900,000.

"That little gesture cost you $100,000." Contempt tightened his face, making his sensual mouth a hard line.

Her only answer was the sound of paper ripping and ripping again.

Cold eyes raked over her. "It will cost you $100,000 every time you tear up a check." As he spoke, he began writing again.

"Then write faster and smaller until you reach zero, you bastard," she snarled. "I can't wait to see your back going out that door." She watched him for a few seconds, then snatched the checkbook out from under his pen. "My way is faster!"

With one hand she snapped on a gas burner on the stove. With the other she held the checkbook deep in the fire, feeling nothing, not even heat as flames scorched her. Shock was a powerful biological defense, taking away pain and leaving only numbness. She watched her hand in the flames with a total lack of interest. She was too cold to feel fire. She was buried in ice as old as the world and as thick as time.

"Cat! My God—!" Travis yanked her hand back from the fire and turned off the gas.

She turned on him, eyes empty.

"It's *my* baby now. You can go out and knock up a string of women if you want kids. This one is *mine*. Even if I could get pregnant again, I wouldn't give up this child to be raised by a man who can't see love when it stands in front of him. Like me, now. I love you, Travis," she said, each word calm and cold, falling like snow in the silent room. "But that's my mistake. I should have known better. My husband was such a fine teacher. Rich men just don't know how to love. And we both know how *rich* you are, don't we?"

"So that's it," he said. His lips curled in a travesty of a smile. "A million wasn't enough." He shrugged. "I'll make it two million. You were worth it, lady. Really great. But," he added brutally, almost casually, "if you're holding out for marriage, you can forget it. Marrying a whore is the kind of mistake I don't make twice."

She took the smoldering checkbook and crushed it into his hand, burning him. "Thank you for my child," she said, her voice as soft as it was cold, "even though it was an unwilling gift. I'll take the baby. And you, Travis, you can take your money and go to hell."

She watched fury ripple through him, turning his eyes black. Distantly she wondered if he would lose control now, loosing the violence that seethed visibly in him, shaking his restraint like winter storm waves pounding against a crumbling sea wall.

Abruptly Travis spun away from her and stalked through the open door to the deck. The door shut softly behind him. Too softly. For an instant there was only silence. Then came a thick sound of fury, glass shattering, metal crashing onto rocks below.

T. H. Danvers had finally slipped the leash on his control.

Cat didn't have to look out the window to know what was happening. Her patio chairs and glass-topped table were being smashed and hurled over the railing to the rocks below. Her lips thinned in a cold smile as she listened to the sweet sounds of destruction. She didn't blame him at all. She envied him. It was what she would have done if she had his strength.

Then she shuddered violently, realizing that if she had Travis's strength she might have smashed more than furniture. The thought shocked her out of her unnatural stillness. As the adrenaline storm passed, nausea returned with a wrench. With a small cry she fled to the bathroom.

Even after she threw up and the worst of the nausea faded, her appetite didn't return. Tea and a few soda crackers were the most she could manage to swallow. She kept listening for the phone or the sound of footsteps coming up the stairs from the beach. She heard nothing but the wind and the sea and the silence between breakers.

When it was dark she tried to sort slides, but found herself staring purposelessly at the white cardboard surrounding the squares of film as she arranged the slides in endless random patterns across the light table. Her hands trembled, scattering slides. When she bent to pick them up her fingers were as clumsy as a child's. She straightened, empty-handed, and leaned against the light table. After a long time she realized that she was staring at the clock on the wall across the room. Midnight. Exactly.

The second hand swept on its downward curve, marking out the first instants of the new day.

Wearily Cat pushed away from the light table and went to bed. For a time queasiness kept her awake. Eventually she drifted into a haunted sleep. There wasn't anything particularly menacing in the dream she had, neither monsters nor pursuits nor sleeting colors of terror. There was simply . . . *nothing*. A great black hole in the center of her universe, a place that was no place at all, a horrible expanding emptiness where the sun should have been.

She awoke in a rush, clammy, nauseated, her body rigid. For a few awful moments she didn't know where she was. She reached out automatically, searching for the comfort of his solid warmth next to hers.

"Travis?"

Memories came like ice water. She turned on her side and curled around herself. She lay without sleeping, her eyes fastened to the black rectangle of the window, straining to see the first hint of dawn.

By seven-thirty she was sitting in her car outside Dr. Stone's office, waiting. She knew the office didn't open until nine, but she didn't care. She had taken all the silence she could for a while, silence and listening for sounds that did not come, footsteps and laughter and his voice calling her name.

"Catherine?"

Cat blinked and focused on Dr. Stone's concerned face.

"Are you all right, child?" asked the doctor, opening the car door and leaning in.

Cat felt skilled fingers press against her wrist over her pulse. "I'm fine, Dr. Stone. Just a little—"

"—exhausted," finished Dr. Stone curtly. "I've buried patients who looked better than you do. Can you walk, or should I bring out a wheelchair?"

Cat started to laugh, then realized that the doctor wasn't joking. "Nausea isn't my most becoming color," she said, trying to smile.

"Have you eaten?"

"This morning?"

The doctor's eyes narrowed. "Let me rephrase that. When was the last time you ate?"

"Tea and crackers. Yesterday."

"And before that?"

Cat shrugged. "Travis—" Her voice broke over his name. She swallowed and tried again. "I went sailing for a few days. I was seasick, which hadn't ever happened to me before, not like that. I had a little juice, some tea, toast."

"How many days?"

"Sailing?"

"No. Since you've eaten a decent meal."

Frowning, Cat tried to remember.

"Never mind," said the doctor curtly. "You've told me all I need to know." She pulled the office keys out of a small leather purse. "Stand up."

Under the doctor's critical eyes, Cat climbed out

of the small Toyota. Nausea coiled in her stomach. She let her breath hiss out through her teeth. Dr. Stone's expression softened with rueful sympathy.

"Come on. I'll make you some tea with lots of honey. And you'll drink every bit of it."

When Cat was seated with a steaming mug in her hands, Dr. Stone settled into her comfortable desk chair. Over folded hands she watched Cat sip tentatively at the sweet tea and nibble on the saltines the doctor had provided.

"Better?" asked the doctor after a few minutes.

Cat sighed. She was still queasy, but she thought she could hang on to the meager breakfast. "Yes. Thanks."

"How often are you nauseated?"

"Most of the time, lately."

"How often do you vomit?"

Cat grimaced. "I hate throwing up. But last night, this morning. Yes. Twice."

"Are you still spotting?" asked the doctor casually.

"Yes."

"How often?"

"Every day."

"How much?"

"Not much, usually. This morning, though . . ." Cat's voice faded.

"Cramps?" asked the doctor crisply.

Cat nodded.

Dr. Stone's questions continued in a rapid fire that gave Cat no time to weigh her answers. When the doctor was finished she looked at her short, unpolished fingernails and sighed. "Do you want this pregnancy?"

"Yes."

The doctor looked up, caught by the intensity of Cat's voice. "Then I hope you're stronger than I think you are," said the doctor bluntly. "Obstetrically speaking, you're among the worst risks I've taken on in my career."

Cat's gray eyes widened in her pale face. "What do you mean?"

"Right now, this instant, your body is doing everything in its power to abort this pregnancy. And frankly, Catherine, I don't blame your body one whit. It's a simple survival reflex. You can barely sustain your own physical demands right now. Where on earth will you find the resources to support the additional demands of pregnancy?"

"But—but pregnancy is natural for a woman."

"So is illness. So is death. So is spontaneous abortion. So is birth and health and laughter." She smiled an old, wise smile. "We just like some of those things better than others, so we call them natural."

Cat closed her eyes.

The doctor sighed. "I'll do what I can. All anyone can. But you must understand that your chances of a successful pregnancy are very, very low." She saw the pain on Cat's face. "Would you rather I lied to you?" Dr. Stone asked softly.

"No," whispered Cat.

Dr. Stone leaned forward and took Cat's tightly clenched hands between her own. "You aren't sterile. I suspect your vaginal chemistry was simply too acid for your husband's sperm to survive. It's not an uncommon problem, and one that is easily solved. But"—she smiled—"obviously you're quite chemically compatible with at least one man. There will be other chances for you."

Cat stared at the doctor without seeing her. Other chances, yes; but none she wanted. None with Travis. She didn't want just any man's baby. She wanted a child with tourmaline eyes and tawny hair and a smile to break her heart. . . ."I want *this* baby."

There was a silence followed by a sigh. "All right, Catherine. Let's get you in the stirrups and see what we have to work with."

When the examination was over Dr. Stone took Cat back to the private office. The nurse had arrived, followed shortly by the first of Dr. Stone's appointments. The doctor shut the door, sat, and faced her pale patient.

"If your spotting were just a bit heavier, our previous discussion would have been academic. I'll call the hospital and have them check you in."

"Hospital! Unless it comes with a money-back guarantee, I can't afford it. I'm not insured." Cat's hands clenched again. She closed her eyes, only to sense the presence of the hole that had expanded in her dreams. "Never mind," she said desperately, opening her eyes. "If that's the only way to keep this baby, I'll get the money somehow."

"Relax, child," murmured Dr. Stone, rubbing Cat's hands gently. "That kind of tension doesn't do you or the baby any good."

"Relax?" Cat laughed a little wildly. "How long would I have to stay in the hospital?"

Dr. Stone hesitated, then sighed deeply. "I'm not sure. In fact, I'm not sure that lying in a hospital ward worrying over money wouldn't make things worse. Not to mention exposure to infections in your run-down state. . . ." The doctor frowned and absently tapped her clean nails against Cat's medical folder. "But damn it, child, someone has to take care of you! You need regular meals. You need to get off your feet until the spotting stops. If it stops."

"Could I get up long enough to go to the bathroom or fix a quick meal?" she asked.

"Yes, but who would shop for you? Who would wash your dishes? Who would do your laundry? Who would take care of the house? Who would—"

"I'll find someone."

Frowning, Dr. Stone opened Cat's folder. "You live on the beach, don't you?"

"Yes."

"Stairs?"

"Yes."

"You can't climb them. And don't lift anything heavier than a cup of tea. No work for you, Catherine Cochran. Someone from Home Volunteers will be calling you. They'll bring you one hot meal a day. Drive home and then don't drive again. Go to bed. And understand that no matter what you do, the chances are overwhelming that you'll miscarry before the fourth month." She stroked Cat's hand soothingly. "Next time, child, when you're rested. Then we'll talk about happier things, like cranky babies and diaper rash."

Cat knew that there wouldn't be a next time. She wouldn't trust herself with a man to that extent. Fool me once, damn you. Fool me twice, damn *me*. Somewhere, vulnerability had to stop and survival had to take over. For her that somewhere was here, now.

"I'm giving you antinausea pills for a few weeks," continued the doctor, writing briskly in Cat's file. "You can't build up your strength unless you eat. The nurse will give you some shots before you leave. I'll visit you once a week unless you need me more often. Any questions?"

Cat shook her head.

Dr. Stone smiled. "There will be. Call me. I'm here to help."

Cat drove home slowly, thinking only of what must be done. Grocery shopping, opening and closing the garage door, climbing down the stairs to her house, carrying bags of food, putting away the food. She wasn't supposed to do any of it, yet she must eat.

When the details threatened to overwhelm her she thought of only one thing at a time. She would find a way. She always had.

She was a very good swimmer.

She turned into the driveway, looked at the closed garage door and shrugged. The Toyota's paint job would just have to suffer exposure to salt air until she could raise and lower the garage door again. She let herself out of the car and descended the stairs slowly, taking unusual care. As soon as she reached the middle level of the house, where she had left the phone plugged in, she called Jason's mother.

"Sharon? This is Cathy."

"Oh, God. Did Jason miss the school bus?"

"No." Cat hesitated. Asking for help came very hard for her, but she had no other choice. "I have a very big favor to ask of you."

"Name it," said Sharon cheerfully.

Cat spoke in a rush, trying to get it over with. "I have to take it easy for a while. Bed rest. No lifting anything, not even a camera."

"Cathy! What happened? Did you have a bad fall?" There was real concern in Sharon's voice. In his own charming fashion, Jason had stitched together the two women in his life.

Cat laughed oddly. "Not in the way you mean. I'm

pregnant, Sharon. And I want to stay that way. So it's bed for me until I stop spotting."

"Cathy . . . oh, Cathy, I don't know whether to congratulate you or cry," said Sharon. "Is Travis happy about it?"

"This is a solo flight." Her voice was flat, utterly colorless. "But congratulate me anyway. I want this baby. I'm going to move heaven and earth to have it."

Silence. Then, "I'll do whatever I can. I miscarried twice before I had the twins, and they were born five weeks too soon in spite of all I did."

Cat was silent, not knowing what to say. Then, softly, "Thank you. Knowing someone else has been through it makes me feel less . . . alone."

Sharon made a funny sound, half laugh, half cry; but when she spoke her voice was brisk and her words practical. "Hang up the phone and go to bed. I'll be over as soon as the babysitter arrives, unless there's something you need right now."

"No. I'm fine. Just fine. Thanks."

That evening Cat lay in her bed watching sunset transform the world. Colors flamed up from the horizon, spilling molten beauty over the sinuous waves. Then she saw the *Wind Warrior* skimming over the burning sea, ebony strength and beauty following the dying sun into darkness beyond the horizon. Going, gone, Travis riding into night on the back of a great black bird, leaving her with nothing but the shadow of the sun burning behind her eyes.

She slept finally, badly, twisting and turning silently. She awoke in the heart of night, a stifled scream on her lips. Falling. She was falling and there was nothing to hold on to except the hope of dawn.

Tangled in covers, she lay for a long time, afraid to move and risk vertigo again. Beyond the window, darkness stretched from horizon to horizon, unbroken.

Jason and the sun came at the same moment.

Cat sat up quickly, pulled on a robe and waited for the boy's brilliant smile. He appeared in her bedroom door, grinning and clutching several packets of instant cocoa.

"Mom taught me how to make this," he said proudly.

He vanished before Cat could answer. She heard sounds from the kitchen. A few minutes later Jason rushed into the bedroom carrying empty mugs and a tray of toast. He put mugs and tray on the bedside table and ran back to the kitchen. This time he returned slowly, carrying a pot full of hot cocoa. He poured with more determination than grace, but most of the chocolate ended up in the cups. With a flourish, he handed her a dripping piece of honey toast and a mug of cocoa.

"Thank you, Jason. You can cook my breakfast anytime." Cat smiled at the boy, thankful that her antinausea pills worked.

Jason smiled proudly. "I told Mom I could do it alone. Besides," he said, reaching for a gooey slice of peanut butter toast, "only a mother wants to eat with two screaming babies."

There was no tactful way to disagree with her benefactor, so Cat took a tentative bite of the toast. She half expected to have her stomach rebel. It came as a relief when her body accepted the toast without comment.

"You want something else before I go to school?" asked Jason, licking his fingers. A cocoa moustache gave his face a rakish air that complemented his tumbled black curls.

"No thanks. This is more than I've eaten for a week."

Jason frowned. "You're gonna get skinny."

"Slave driver," sighed Cat, taking another piece of toast and honey from the haphazard heap in the center of the tray.

She nibbled on the toast hesitantly, then with more confidence, pleased that food tasted good again. She reached for the pot of cocoa, only to have Jason grab it first.

"Mom said you're not supposed to lift *anything*." He poured more cocoa for Cat, frowning intently.

"Thank you," she murmured, discreetly licking up the rivulets of chocolate before they dripped off the cup onto the bed.

The phone rang.

Cat's heart turned over in the instant before she remembered that it couldn't be Travis. He had stepped into the wind, vanished as irrevocably as yesterday's sunlight. Automatically she started to get up to answer the phone. Then she realized that she wasn't supposed to get out of bed, much less climb a flight of stairs to the workroom where she had left the phone.

"I'll get it," said Jason, racing off.

He came back in a few minutes. "It was Mom. She's going to the store and wants to know if you need anything."

Cat reached for the tablet on her bedside table and tore off the sheet that held the grocery list. "Could you hand me my purse, please?"

Jason held the purse out to her with a smile as wide as the sun. The idea of being Cat's legs hadn't lost its attraction yet. She hoped it wouldn't. After seeing the *Wind Warrior* sail into the night, she needed Jason's blithe company.

She fished out her checkbook, wincing as her scorched hand scraped against the zipper. None of the burns were bad. Travis had yanked her hand out of the flames before blisters formed. She simply had painful streaks of red skin that would split and peel away in a few days.

She wished that the rest of her would heal as quickly.

"Give this to your mom," she said, handing him the check and the list, "and tell her thank you very much. When you get home from school you can teach me how to play Go Fish."

"Oh boy!" He turned and raced toward the back door.

"Wait!" said Cat, looking out the window at the advancing ranks of waves. "The tide's up. Use the front door."

"It's all right," said Jason cheerfully. "I just go between waves."

He was out the back door before she could object. Anxiously she watched him dart down the stairs to the beach. Because her bedroom jutted out beyond the deck and the slant of the bluff, she could see the bottom of her stairs and the bottom of Jason's stairs. She saw him wait on the last step until a wave retreated, then he scurried across the beach and up his own stairs before the next wave could wet his feet.

Relieved, Cat lay back on the bed. After a few moments sleep washed over her in a black tide, carrying her out to sea.

Chapter 11

THE PHONE RANG, WAKING CAT. SHE SAT UP AND started to get out of bed before she remembered.

"I'll get it," called Sharon from the kitchen.

She came into the bedroom a few moments later. In one hand she carried the telephone. The answering machine was tucked under her other arm.

"That was the framer. They've got some finished stuff for you to look at. I put the groceries away." Sharon looked around the room. "Where's the outlet?"

Cat pointed to the wall by her bed. "Thanks."

"No problem. What else needs to be moved?"

"Nothing urgent. When I'm less tired I'm going to sort and mail some slides." She grimaced. "Correction. I'll sort and you'll mail." She looked up suddenly. "Sharon, are you sure you have enough time to run my errands?"

"All the time you need. If it hadn't been for you these last four months, Jason and I would have driven each other crazy. Tonight I'll send Jack over to move whatever needs moving."

"Thanks." Cat laughed oddly. "Seems that's all I've been saying today. Thanks and thanks and thanks."

"So enjoy," said Sharon, smiling. "Heaven knows you've done enough for everyone else. It's about time you were on the receiving end."

The house seemed very empty when Sharon left. Normally Cat would have gone to the workroom and begun sorting slides, or she would have sat at her desk and handled the endless correspondence and bookkeeping chores. But nothing was normal anymore. She was confined to her bed with only her own thoughts for company, forbidden even to lift her beloved cameras.

Her thoughts were unpleasant company, caroming between Travis and checkbooks, the cramps that wouldn't leave her body and the spotting that frightened her now that she understood its cause. If thinking about those things was too painful, there was always money to worry about, or lack of it. In four days she had to write out checks for the twins and her mother, checks that would exceed her combined checking and savings accounts by $5,573.82. If she were able to work, the deficit wouldn't matter. She'd had jobs worth twice that lined up, but she'd had to cancel them. If the Big Check from Energystics didn't come . . .

Don't worry. It's bad for the baby.

Cat lay and stared at the ceiling, repeating Dr. Stone's advice and wondering if it was possible to think of nothing at all. She wished that memories of Travis wouldn't twist through her like black lightning, burning her until she wanted to cry. But tears wouldn't come. He had left her nothing, not even hope, and without hope there could be no tears.

The phone rang, startling in the silence. She groped for the receiver.

"Hello."

"Is that you, Cochran?"

"Hi, Angel," she said, clearing her throat. "It's me."

"Danvers around? I called his cousin's house, but no one answered."

Cat hung on to the phone until her hand ached, fighting to control her emotions. She would have to get used to hearing his name unexpectedly. She would have to get used to knowing that she would never again wake up next to his solid warmth, never again see his eyes brilliant with passion, never again see his lips smiling as he bent to kiss her, never again taste the salt-sweet flavor of him, never again—

"Cochran? You there?"

"Yes." She forced herself to swallow past the constriction in her throat. "I'm a little fuzzy. You finally caught me napping, Angel."

He hesitated. "Are you all right?"

"Fine," she said, sounding anything but. "Just fine." She took a deep breath. She had to tell Harrington something. At the very least she had to tell him that *The Danvers Touch* was a write-off unless the publisher would be satisfied with the photos she had already taken. "Angel?" she asked tentatively.

"I'm sitting down," he said dryly. "Go ahead."

"Travis is in the wind," she said, words tumbling out as though if she spoke quickly enough she could get it all said and over with before Harrington suspected how she felt. "I'll send you the slides I have for the book. If they aren't enough, you'll have to get another photographer."

"Hey," he said, his voice soft, "not to worry. Danvers gets restless, he leaves, he comes back."

"Not this time." Her voice was very clear, very certain.

There was a long silence followed by a sigh. "You sure you're all right?"

"I'm working on it, Angel."

"That's the ticket. Work. I'll line up a few foreign gigs for you. In fact, just this morning I was talking to Miller in Paris and—"

"No," she said, interrupting.

"What? Why not?"

She hung on to the phone and thought of the lies she could tell her green angel. But of all the people in the world, she owed him the truth. He had helped her when she had crawled out of the midnight sea, a naked stranger badly needing kindness, refuge. He had given both to her without hesitation or question.

"My doctor told me to stay off my feet for a while," she said. "No work. It's just temporary. I'll call you when I can take assignments again."

"Cochran, what the hell is going on?"

"I'm pregnant," she said bluntly. "And if I want to stay that way, I've got to spend some time in bed."

"Pregnant! Jesus—" Harrington swallowed the rest of his comment.

"Don't sound so shocked," said Cat, smiling despite her own pain. "Angel," softly, "not to worry. I thought I was sterile. This baby is a miracle."

"But—"

"Nobody said miracles were convenient," she added almost whimsically, feeling her emotions lift with the renewed realization of her own fertility, the unexpected gift growing inside her. With that she could survive anything. Even a rich bastard with a velvet drawl.

"Does Danvers know?" Harrington asked bluntly.

"Yes."

"Then why in God's flaming hell did he leave you!"

"Ask him when you find him. If you find him."

"I will. And he'll tell me, if I have to hire someone to hold him while I beat the truth out of him. No one treats you like that and gets away with it. No one. Not even my best friend." He made a disgusted sound. "Especially my best friend. To think I hoped he and you would— Ah, *hell.* I'm sorry, Cochran. I wish I'd never thought of a book about a sonofabitch called Danvers."

"I don't have any regrets, Angel—not like that. Everybody should ride a wild, breaking wave at least once."

There was a long silence. Then he asked, "Do you need anything?"

"Just the check from Energystics."

Harrington swore pungently. "That's why I called. Energystics is belly up in the bankruptcy court. They're paying their debts at six cents on the dollar. Our lawyer is filling out claim forms right now."

Cat heard little beyond the word bankruptcy.

"Cochran? You still there?"

". . . yes."

"What about the L.A. show?"

"There's a batch of prints at the framers," Cat said mechanically. "I didn't have time to select mats and frames."

"So let the gallery do it. They never like what the artist chooses anyway." He hesitated, swore. "I know you were counting on that Energystics check."

"I'll manage. I always have."

"You weren't pregnant. Surely Travis—"

"No." A single word, cold and precise.

"Then I'll give you—"

"No! Not Travis. Not you. Not anyone. *I earn my own keep.*" Cat heard the echo of her own voice, as savage as Travis's had been when he offered her the check for a million dollars. Kept woman. Whore. But Harrington didn't deserve her anger. She closed her eyes and worked very hard to keep her voice calm. "But thanks anyway, Angel. I appreciate the thought."

The silence stretched uncomfortably. Finally Harrington said, "We'll talk about this later, when you feel better."

Cat didn't answer.

"Cathy . . . ?" He sighed. "Take care. I'll call you soon."

"Sure," she said mechanically. "Bye, Angel."

The phone clicked back into its cradle. For a long time there was no sound in the room. Cat lay without moving, looking at the two prints hanging on the opposite side of the room. She hadn't shown them to Travis, wanting to wait until they were properly matted and framed. They had been ready when she got back from sailing with him. She hadn't had a chance to show them to Travis.

And now he was gone.

The first print was life-sized, a close-up of Travis taken the night he'd carved Jason's boat. Light from the gooseneck lamp slanted across Travis, striking gold out of his hair, making the color of his eyes the vivid blue-green of Brazilian tourmaline. Light bathed his hands, revealing the fine scars, the strength, the tension of his lean fingers holding the unyielding block, the steel flash of the knife coaxing dark curves out of wood. His intensity and intelligence resonated through the picture. The result was so real she had the feeling that if she called his name he would look up and smile.

The second print was as big as an open newspaper. It was one of the shots she had taken the first time she had seen the *Wind Warrior,* before she knew the ship's name or creator. In the print the sun burned across half the darkening sky. The ship was a shape out of ancient legend, ebony grace and power, daring to sail across the incandescent eye of God. It was an extraordinary image, one of the best photos she had ever taken . . . and there was no one to share it with.

Cat closed her eyes, yet still she saw the *Wind Warrior* flying through twilight into gathering night. Emotions twisted through her, shaking her. She knew then that she didn't hate Travis, couldn't hate him no matter how much easier that would make living without him. Anger, rage, fury—yes, all of that and more, feelings she had no easy labels for. But hate? No, not that. He had created too much beauty for her to hate him. He was a fire burning in the center of icy night. She had known his dangers, and she had stood too close to his flames anyway. Her fault, not his.

And when all was said, when the last word was lost in silence and ice, there was the fact that he had given her a beauty few women ever knew. For a few weeks she had been a part of his fierce and tender fire, as graceful and wild as a flame burning with him. Now the time of fire was gone, flames scattered in darkness and wind, nothing left but the memory of warmth . . . and a single ember hidden inside her, fighting to live. That ember deserved its chance to burn.

Slowly she turned to the telephone, picked up the receiver and pushed in seven numbers. There were three rings before a woman answered.

"Tidewater Auction House, may I help you?"

"This is Catherine Cochran. I have some cameras to sell."

Cat wrote out the last check, sealed the last envelope, licked the last stamp. She lay back on the massed pillows and stared at the neat stack of envelopes. She had paid everything but the rent, the processor and the framer. She would worry about them next month. She would worry about a lot of things next month, but not now. Not now. Today she would be grateful that she had enough money in the bank to live on for three weeks. Four, if she were very careful.

She eased herself onto her side, pressed an extra pillow against her abdomen and tried to ignore the cramps. The spotting had become somewhat lighter but had not stopped. The cramps came and went and returned, redoubled. Heat flushed her body, followed by clammy waves of nausea.

The sound of someone knocking at the front door floated down, followed by Dr. Stone's voice.

"Catherine?"

"The door is open," called Cat.

Dr. Stone came into the bedroom. Cat's bed had been moved so that it was right next to the full-length window overlooking the sea. Sunlight streamed in, picking out all the angular envelopes and scattered debris of Cat's bill-paying spree. On a bedside table was a drift of shells that Jason had found and brought to her. The shells made light and shadow curve into shapes that were both fascinating and serene.

"Working?" said Dr. Stone, looking at the envelopes.

"Just taking care of a few details," said Cat. "Sharon will mail them for me tomorrow."

"I'll take them on my way home." Dr. Stone gathered the envelopes and put them in her leather attaché case. Quickly, expertly, she examined Cat. When she finished she sat in the chair that had been drawn up to Cat's bed for visitors.

"It's not any worse, is it?" Cat asked anxiously.

Dr. Stone sighed. "It's been ten days, Catherine. Frankly, I'd hoped for some progress. You're staying in bed?"

"Yes. I only get up to go to the bathroom."

"Are you eating well?"

Cat handed over a list of her meals since Dr. Stone's last visit. The doctor read it in silence, nodding approvingly from time to time. "What about sleep?"

Cat looked down at her hands, willing them not to clench. She hadn't had a whole night's sleep since Travis had sailed the *Wind Warrior* over the curve of the world. She would sleep, yes, but only for a few hours. Then she would wake up cold and shuddering, her body reeling with the memory of having stumbled into the hole at the center of the universe. The disorientation was so great that she had started sleeping with a light on so she would know immediately where she was when she woke up.

Slowly she described the dream and the sensation to Dr. Stone. When Cat was finished she closed her eyes and waited. After a moment she felt Dr. Stone's warm, dry hand take her own.

"You've never talked about the baby's father," said Dr. Stone quietly. "Does he know you're pregnant?"

Cat's face became smooth, utterly expressionless. "Yes."

The doctor sighed. "You're not the type of woman to sleep with a man casually, Catherine. Do you still love him?"

"I don't hate him," said Cat, unwilling to assess her own churning feelings any more than that.

"Even though he abandoned you?" said the doctor bluntly.

Cat's breath came in sharply as she remembered Travis's rage and . . . agony. His sense of betrayal had been as deep as hers. Deeper. She could see that now, where before she had seen only her own terrible hurt.

"I don't hate him," she said in a soft, certain voice.

"That's why you want this baby. Other men, other babies just don't interest you, is that it?"

"Yes."

"No wonder you can't sleep. The man is gone, and you're losing the battle to keep the baby."

"No."

Dr. Stone's hand squeezed gently around Cat's wrist. "Listen to me. You must begin to accept what almost certainly will happen. Otherwise you won't wake up when you stumble into that hole. You'll just keep falling."

Cat closed her eyes, not wanting to see the doctor's compassionate face.

"Catherine."

Her eyes opened.

"Don't blame yourself," continued Dr. Stone gently. "It's a miracle that you're still pregnant at all. You have an amazing will. But even you can't keep willing miracles day after day, week after week." The doctor hesitated, then added, "I've seen thousands of pregnancies, delivered thousands of babies. I've learned not to question the wisdom of a woman's body, particularly in the first trimester of pregnancy. Learn to accept all the possibilities. Then, when your mind is calm, let your body decide."

Cat drew in a long, tight breath. "I'll try, doctor. But I want this baby so much . . . !"

Dr. Stone smiled. "Nothing would give me greater pleasure than to deliver a healthy baby into your arms twenty-six weeks from now."

Cat looked quickly at the doctor's dark, compassionate eyes. "I'll think about what you said."

Dr. Stone nodded and stood. "I'll see you in three days. Call me if anything changes."

The light flowing over Cat shifted from yellow to gold to deep orange as she lay watching the supple transformations of the sea, thinking of what Dr. Stone had said. Yet no matter how she tried, she could not accept the idea of losing the tiny ember inside her. So she thought of other things, mind floating in free association, adrift in twilight, seeking the black shadow of a vanished ship.

Ten days later the *Wind Warrior* sailed back out of the night. Cat watched the ship's return, then waited in an agony of hope that was greater than any pain that had come before. She waited for three days. She endured three more dream-haunted nights. Travis neither called nor came to see her. It was as though she did not exist, as though she was no more to him than spindrift torn from a breaking wave.

It was then she realized that even good swimmers could drown.

The fourth night after his return was no better. Silently, Cat endured both the nightmare and the black hours before dawn. With transparent gray eyes she watched color seep into the starless arch of sky. Slowly she rolled onto her side, ignoring the cramps that gripped her lower body. She felt the dampness and knew that the spotting hadn't lessened after three weeks of bed rest. If anything it was worse today than it had been yesterday. Like the pain of not hearing from Travis.

Beneath her bedroom window, surf leaped over black rocks. The ranks of waves were enormous, almost uniform, rhythmic. At erratic intervals a larger set of combers would come crashing and tumbling onto the shore, shaking the house with their shock waves.

Cat found herself holding her breath, waiting for the explosive beauty of the biggest waves, waiting for the clash of fluid force and rocky bluff. Eagerly her eyes searched for the telltale dark lines of the larger waves looming out of the brightening day. When the huge combers came in their fives or sevens, bringing their own wild thunder, she smiled triumphantly, glorying in the violent sea. It was like having someone scream for her when she was too proud to scream for herself.

She had just spotted another series of smooth-backed monsters humping up out of the sea when a slight motion at the corner of her eye distracted her attention. Cold horror broke over her as she saw Jason darting down his stairway to the beach, coming to visit her as he had on so many dawns.

She sat up screaming, "No!"

But Jason couldn't hear.

Cat was out of bed and racing for the back door before Jason took another step. She yanked open the door and ran across the deck to the stairway.

"Jason, go back! *Jason!*"

The boy couldn't hear her screams above the relentless battering of surf on the beach, cataracts of water foaming over the rocks and burying the lower quarter of her stairway in a deceptively creamy froth. Helplessly Cat ran downstairs, measuring her distance from the boy as he dashed over the foamy beach during a lull between the waves.

Somewhere in her mind a metronome counted the seconds since the wave had retreated, counted the steps he had made along the beach, counted the stairs he had to climb to be above the reach of the big combers humping up out of the sea in rhythmic explosions of blue-green violence.

Not enough time.

Too much distance.

She didn't scream again, even when she saw the wave come apart, burying the beach in a deadly frothing cataract. She simply ran faster than she ever had in her life, taking the cement steps with reckless speed.

She and the wave reached Jason at the same time. She wrapped her arms around him and the twisted iron railing and hung on. A wall of water slammed into her. She held her breath and Jason and the rail as the wave reversed, trying to suck her back down to the sea.

Coughing, strangling, blind, she staggered up three stairs with Jason under one arm. She neither heard nor saw the next wave. It exploded around her, burying her in a violent cataract of green and white. Before she could recover, the third wave hammered her to her knees.

Even then she didn't release her hold on Jason or the railing. The outflow of the third wave combined with the incoming power of the fourth, a cold ocean pouring over her and not retreating. Half-conscious, she forced herself to her feet, desperately trying to lift Jason's limp form above the reach of the devouring sea.

It was like trying to lift the world. The clock in her mind ticked off the seconds between waves, telling her that it was already too late. The fifth breaker consumed her, dragging her down, clawing at the boy who was too heavy for her to carry. Dimly she sensed a tiny second of calm while the wave was balanced between advance and retreat. She knew that when the balance shifted, when the wall of water rushed back to the sea, it would take her with it.

I'm sorry, Jason.

But she couldn't even say the words, nor could he hear her.

The wave hesitated, then began its powerful retreat. She felt the rough railing slip away beneath her unresponsive hands. Before she could renew her grip the world jumped crazily. At first she thought another wave had come, a wave so strong that it was washing her up the stairs on its crest. Then she realized that someone was carrying her, carrying Jason, taking them both beyond the reach of the exploding waves.

The instant she saw the deck beneath her she struggled free, reaching for Jason. She tried to tell her rescuer that Jason needed help breathing, but all she could do was choke and fall to her knees. Desperately she reached for the small, still form that had been laid down on the deck. She tried to give Jason artificial respiration but was coughing so violently she had neither strength nor coordination for anything else. A man's hands descended, hands crisscrossed by fine scars, hands strong enough to defeat the wild sea and gentle enough to coax life back into a small child.

Travis.

Cat watched his hands work over Jason and willed the little boy to breathe again. It seemed like a lifetime before he coughed, yet the clock in Cat's head had counted off less than a minute before Jason was breathing on his own. She coughed wrackingly again and again, clearing her lungs. Then she felt something break inside, warmth rushing out of her. With a small sound she sank to the deck.

Travis turned to her. His face was grim, his eyes haunted, his voice ragged. "You're bleeding, Cat. You must have cut your leg."

Cat saw the blood mixed with sea water on her legs, blood pooling on the deck, blood flowing out of her womb. She screamed terribly, but it was more than pain that clawed that scream from her throat. It was a denial that she could lose everything she had wanted out of life, that in the space of a few weeks she could be peeled like a bud until nothing was left but a fragile, transparent core.

The scream was still raw in her throat when another kind of wave surged up and broke over her. She gave herself to its blackness with an abandon she had once reserved for life.

When she woke up again she thought she was still caught in the wave, green and white surrounding her. Then she realized that the green was pale and calm, the white clean and smooth and dry. Sheets. Walls. A bed. Quiet. Her body ached everywhere. She moved to ease her muscles and realized that there was a man's hand holding her arm. She saw Travis asleep in a chair next to her bed, his hand around her wrist, fingertips resting on her pulse as though even asleep he needed to be reassured that her heart still beat.

With a small shudder she closed her eyes. At a great distance she heard the waves breaking, cataracts pouring over her, drowning her and the boy she couldn't have loved more if he had been her own. But Jason was safe now, thanks to Travis. Jason was safe, and she had drowned. Which meant, oddly, that she was safe, too. Nothing can hurt you when you're drowned.

The thought pleased her, surrounding her with numbness. She had lost far too much being close to this man, more than she thought she could lose, more than was hers to lose. Slowly she eased her wrist from his grip.

The motion woke him. His eyes opened, blue-green, vivid, seeing through her to her transparent core. Something inside her moved beneath his look, something very like pain. She could not bear that, his seeing her empty core, his pity. When he took her hand again she removed her fingers with unhesitating finality.

"Jason." A single word. All she could say, her throat raw from salt water and screams.

"He's fine. The doctor checked him over, read him the riot act about storm waves and turned him over to his mother."

Even as he spoke, the last part of Cat's emotions that had struggled against numbness quietly gave up. Jason was fine. That was all she needed to know, the best she could have hoped for since she saw blood pooling around her on the deck.

"Thank you for saving him," she said, closing her eyes, her voice toneless. "I wasn't strong enough."

Silence came to the room, haunted by the sounds of surf breaking against black rocks. But the sounds were only in her mind. Perhaps if she slept they would go away, leaving her in a silence to equal her numbness.

Warm fingers touched her wrist.

"Aren't you going to ask about yourself?" The fingers closed around her in hard demand.

She opened her eyes but saw nothing except the emptiness inside her where an ember of life had once burned.

"Dr. Stone told me you'd be depressed, even though you knew how bad the odds were against a successful pregnancy," said Travis quietly, his fingers loosening to stroke her wrist. "It will pass, Cat. Physically, you're fine. A little tired, a little bruised, but nothing that rest won't cure."

She said nothing. He turned her face so that she had to look at him. When he saw her eyes he took a sharp breath and gathered her against his chest to comfort her. She did nothing, neither response nor retreat, as still as a photograph in his arms.

"We'll be able to have another baby," he said urgently, smoothing her hair, then holding her far enough away that he could see her face. "Cat? Did you hear me?"

She looked through him to the hall beyond. She heard him, but his voice was far away, muffled by layers of blessed numbness, layer on layer of icy water enfolding her, an ocean to drown in.

"Cat," he said, holding her close again, rocking her slowly, his voice ragged. "I know that you hate me. I deserve it. I came back to you too late. . . . If not my baby, then another man's," he whispered. "Anything, Cat, anything, but don't look like that. Scream and call me names; I deserve all of them. At least cry. Tears will heal you faster than anything else."

He looked down at the woman in his arms. If he had not felt her weight, he wouldn't have known that he held anyone. She simply *was not there*. She had retreated beyond his reach, beyond the reach of anyone or anything. Nowhere did he see the woman whose photographs hummed with passion and intelligence, the woman whose mind and body had become a part of him, the woman whose incandescent fury had burned through all his hours since she had taught him how little money could buy.

"This isn't you, Cat," he said as he kissed the tumbled mass of auburn hair, plea and command at the same time. "In a few days you'll feel better. You'll be able to take your camera and catch the waves coming up over the edge of the world, waves that came thousands of miles just to touch your feet. Smart waves." His lips brushed her cheek. "Lucky waves. I learned from them, but I learned too late. . . ."

Tension moved through her body. Her pale eyes looked at him, through him, beyond him, seeing something that made his throat ache as it closed around futile protests. For an instant his arms tightened painfully around her, a reflex as useless as his aching throat. She was slipping away from him, carried out to sea on a wave that was too powerful for him to combat.

"I sold my cameras."

She rolled away from him, turning her back on him and the world, staring at the far wall without seeing it, seeing nothing at all.

"Cat . . . why?"

Even before his hoarse protest was out, he knew the answer. She had sold her cameras for the same reason that he had mistrusted her: money. She had sold her future to buy enough time to have his baby.

After his first, involuntary cry the only sound in the room was his ragged breathing as he measured the extent of his loss, her loss, their loss. His hand trembled as he reached out to stroke tangled coils of hair away from her still face. He sat for a long time, motionless but for his hand smoothing her hair with endless patience, his eyes as dark as hers were pale.

After the first time he didn't call her name again.

Chapter 12

WHEN CAT OPENED HER EYES THE NEXT DAY, TRAVIS was there. He had been there every time she awakened, night or day, since he had carried her and Jason beyond the reach of the storm waves. Travis said nothing when she woke up, demanded nothing of her, not even the simplest acknowledgment of his presence. She ignored him, instinctively knowing that he threatened the emotional numbness that was all that protected her from being overwhelmed. The rest of the world she could cope with after a fashion; but not Travis, not in any fashion.

"Sharon and Jason are here," said Travis quietly. "He thinks it's his fault that you were hurt. Sharon thought if he saw you he'd feel better."

Travis waited, unwilling to ask any more of Cat than he already had, knowing he had no right to ask anything of her.

She thought of Jason, young and laughing and so very vulnerable. "He doesn't know about—about—" She stopped, unable to say the word "miscarriage." But Travis understood, she realized distantly. He had always understood everything about her except the one thing that mattered. She had loved him.

"Don't worry," said Travis quickly. "All Jason remembers is seeing you reach for him just as the first wave hit."

"All right," she said.

Travis disappeared. A moment later Sharon and Jason came into the room. Cat looked at Jason's taut, too-old expression and troubled blue eyes. Emotion rippled beneath her numbness. She realized how glad she was that this small boy was alive.

"Jason," she said softly, holding out her hand.

A smile lit the boy's face as he ran across the room and buried his face against her neck in a fierce hug.

"I thought you'd be mad at me," he said, looking up at her with eyes made huge by tears.

She shook her head, unable to speak. Her hand trembled as she pushed thick black curls back from his eyes. She hugged him again. "I'm very glad to see you," she said simply.

Jason snuggled against her for an instant before he pulled back, energy overflowing in an electric smile. "This is for you. I found it this morning."

He held out his hand. In his small palm was a shell that had been rubbed smooth by countless waves and then flung casually up on the beach by the storm. The rough outer shell had been completely worn away, revealing the pearly layer beneath. It was an object stripped to its essential form, displaying the gleaming beauty that had been hidden until time and the waves had peeled the shell to its iridescent core.

At one time she would have itched to photograph the shell. Now, it was all she could do to accept it.

"It's beautiful, Jason. Thank you."

She saw Sharon look at Travis, who was standing in the doorway, then at Jason. Travis crossed the room in two steps and lifted the boy onto his shoulders.

"I saw a candy machine in the lobby," drawled Travis. "Bet they have your favorite kind. Watch your head."

Travis ducked, Jason squealed and the two of them successfully negotiated the doorway to the hall. The sound of Jason's giggles floated back.

"It isn't fair," whispered Sharon, crossing the room to take Cat's hand. "It just isn't fair that you should lose your baby to save my son."

Cat looked at the woman's clear blue eyes, eyes as troubled as Jason's had been. Cat tried to smile. "Jason is alive. That's all the 'fair' anyone can expect."

"But—"

"Sharon, I'd do it again. I love Jason."

Cat watched tears gather and slide down Sharon's cheeks. She felt a dim envy for the other woman's ability to cry.

"Thank you," said Sharon.

"Thank the man who carried Jason up the stairs."

Sharon smiled helplessly and shook her head. She squeezed Cat's hand, started to speak, then bent and kissed Cat's cheek.

Cat lay and looked at the ceiling after Sharon had left. She heard footsteps come and knew Travis was back. She neither moved nor spoke. After a time she heard Dr. Stone's voice talking to a nurse outside in the hall. When the doctor came into the room Cat turned toward her.

"I want to leave."

"You'd be better off with a few more days of rest," said Dr. Stone, looking at Cat's chart.

"I can rest at home better than I can rest here. Tell the cashier's office to make up my bill."

Surprised, Dr. Stone looked from Cat to Travis. Cat's emotions might have been frozen, but her intelligence wasn't hampered at all. She immediately realized that Travis was paying for her hospital room. Something close to anger flickered for an instant in her pale eyes. She looked at Travis.

"Rich man, I'll sell myself on street corners before I take one dime of your money." Her voice was smooth, empty. She turned back to the doctor and did not look at Travis again. "I'm leaving whether you agree or not."

There was no emotion in her voice, simply certainty. She would not stay here one moment longer than she had to. At home she would not have to put up with his presence by her bed, his tourmaline eyes following her every movement, counting each breath she took.

Travis made a sound of protest, telling her that he knew her true reason for wanting to get out of the hospital. Dr. Stone hesitated, then gave in to the inevitable. As Travis stalked out of the room, the doctor began giving instructions in a professional voice. Cat listened without comment until Dr. Stone mentioned a prescription for contraceptive pills.

"I won't need that."

"They're therapeutic. They'll help your body to recover its normal hormonal rhythms. Take the pills for three months, then flush them if you like. But don't get pregnant for at least six months. A year would be even better."

"There will be no pregnancy."

Cat said nothing more. She left the hospital in silence, driven by an equally silent Sharon. Once Cat was home she spoke to no one. For three days she allowed nothing to disturb her silence. The answering machine was left on. She returned none of the phone calls, listened to none of the messages.

Travis did not come over, though she saw him swimming each dawn. She wondered if his nights were like hers, if every time he fell asleep he stumbled into the hole at the center of the universe and woke up sweating, cold, disoriented. Then she realized what she was thinking and would have laughed if she could. Rich men didn't have nightmares. They didn't care enough about anything to let it disturb their sleep.

The phone rang. She looked at it for a long moment, knowing it was probably Harrington. Only a feeling of guilt forced her finally to put aside her lethargy long enough to answer the phone. She should have called him the day she got out of the hospital, or any of the days after.

"Hello."

"Cathy?"

Harrington's voice, his concern as clear as the rose light filling her room. "No," she said, her voice husky from lack of use. "This is Cochran."

Static crackled softly on the line, filling the silence.

"I talked to Dr. Stone," said Harrington bluntly.

Dimly, Cat wondered how he had gotten the doctor's name. Travis, probably.

"Are you still there?" asked Harrington.

She felt an absurd impulse to laugh. Of course she wasn't there. She had drowned days ago. Hadn't Travis told him?

"Cathy—damn it!—say something!"

"Hello, Angel. How are you? I'm fine, thank you. Just fine."

"Good," he said smoothly. "Then there's no reason why you can't finish the Danvers assignment."

Cat stared at the phone, speechless. Then, "You're crazy, Angel," she said flatly, feeling something finally stir beneath the numbness. "I sold my cameras."

"Not to worry. It's taken care of. You're a famous photographer now. Nikon is dying to lend you equipment."

"What are you talking about?"

"Didn't the gallery owner tell you? Your show sold out. You're back-ordered for more. You're a thirty-thousand-dollar hit, Cochran. And Ashcroft's publisher came through. If you don't like the gear that was sent out to the *Wind Warrior*, buy a different camera. Hell, buy twenty. Money doesn't matter anymore. You're over the hump."

Cat knew she should feel something, if only relief. She could pay off the hospital, the signature loans, her mother's expenses, everything. But she felt nothing, nothing at all.

"Cathy," softly, "I've never asked you to do something for me, have I?"

". . . no," she said, swallowing, afraid of what he would say next.

"I called in a lot of debts to get the Danvers book going. I didn't say anything before because there wasn't any way you could do the work. But Dr.

Stone said you were well enough to spend a month shooting the *Wind Warrior* under sail, as long as you took it easy the first few days."

"Angel." Her voice broke. She tried again, desperately wanting to refuse him but knowing she owed him so much more than a few photos. Her mind raced frantically, trying to find a way out of the trap. "On one condition," she said finally. "That Tra—" Her voice broke again. She couldn't say his name. "Only the crew," she said finally. "No one on board but me and the crew. *No one.*"

"Done," he said quickly. "Be at the harbor in an hour."

"That isn't enough time!"

"How long does it take you to drive to Dana Point?" he asked reasonably. "Everything you need is aboard, and I mean everything. Even clothes. Swear to God. I knew you wouldn't let me down. Bye, Cochran."

He hung up before she could protest.

In a daze, Cat dressed and stuffed a few things in an overnight bag. She drove to the harbor where the *Wind Warrior* rode quietly at anchor, its superb maroon wings furled. Diego met her, took her aboard and showed her to a cabin. She was relieved that it was not the one she had shared with Travis. She didn't think she could have stayed in his bed without remembering everything that she must forget.

As she opened cupboards looking for a place to put her few things, she found the camera equipment Harrington had said was on board. In silence she examined item after item—the latest model Novaflex, state-of-the-art Nikons and lenses, motor drives and film carriers—everything she might possibly need, more equipment than she had ever dreamed of owning. There were even four camera bodies and a lens system that duplicated the equipment she had sold, as though Harrington were afraid that she wouldn't be comfortable with different camera models and lenses.

She looked at all the equipment, adding it up in her mind. The wide angle lens she held in her hand was the latest model put out by Nikon. It cost well over two thousand dollars. She knew its price because she had promised herself one as soon as she had the money to buy it. She doubted Harrington's glib explanation that Nikon had loaned her the equipment she saw spread out in the tiny cabin. Either he had bought it himself, or Travis had.

She finished opening cupboards and stood silently, staring at what had been concealed by polished wood. The cabin had been fitted out as a seagoing photo lab tailored to her precise needs. There was a refrigerator packed with film. The Kodak slide processor had been cleverly suspended to counteract the inevitable surge of waves. The slide duplicator was new, far better than the one she had at home. The cabin was a photographer's dream, everything that money could buy.

Cat looked at it all and wanted to feel something, pleasure or anger or outrage or . . . anything. The camera equipment might have been bought recently, but the cabin itself couldn't have been designed and executed in a few days or even a few weeks. It had to have been done when Travis was trying to get her to run before the storm with him, before she told him that she was pregnant. Slowly she turned around, seeing him in every polished length of wood, in the cleverly designed lab, in the gleaming symmetry of cupboard and sink, mundane items recast by his mind into a beauty that sang beguilingly of their maker's skilled, sensual hands.

Emotion rippled through her, a feeling like a ghostly caress breathing heat over the ice surrounding her. She shuddered violently. Slowly, carefully, she packed away the camera equipment, closed the cupboards and went up on deck. She stood at the railing and watched Dana Point slide away behind her, felt the timeless rhythms of the open sea as the ship spread its wings and stepped into the wind.

When it was dark she went below, only to remember that she hadn't brought anything to sleep in. She went through the cedar drawers beneath her bunk and found clothes in all styles and only one size. Hers. Harrington had been right. Everything she needed was aboard. She found an emerald silk nightgown. She ignored it. In a different drawer, stuffed into a corner, she found a black T-shirt. It was soft from many washings and smelled of cedar. She pulled it on quickly. It was far too big. Only one person could have worn it. She put the thought from her mind. She would rather wear one of Travis's forgotten T-shirts than the silky, alluring gown.

She lay down and felt waves rocking her, heard only the wind and the hiss of water dividing over the bow. A vague sparkle of stars came through the lozenge-shaped porthole above her bunk. Finally, she slept.

Three hours later she woke up in a cold sweat, nausea turning in the pit of her stomach. She knew immediately that it wasn't seasickness. She had simply stumbled into the hole again, falling and turning endlessly. The feeling of disorientation faded as she saw the lighter shade of black that was the porthole.

She didn't go back to sleep. She didn't want to. It wasn't worth it, just to wake up sweating and shaking, holding onto herself so she wouldn't scream. She knew it would pass, eventually. It had before, darkness dragging slowly toward dawn. But in the icy center of night, time itself froze, sweating seconds as slowly as a glacier sweated water.

Quietly, desperately, she stared out the porthole and counted stars. Maybe tomorrow night it would be better. Maybe, at least, it wouldn't be worse.

She was up on deck before the last star faded into dawn. She spent that day and the following five days sitting at the bow of the *Wind Warrior,* staring into the horizon, seeing nothing, saying nothing, dreading the coming night when she would wake and stare out the porthole, looking for a dawn that never seemed to come.

At sunrise of the seventh day, Travis was waiting on deck for her. There was nothing but ocean in all directions, no ships, no shore, nothing to swim toward even if she had the strength.

After the initial overwhelming realization of his presence, her first thought was that Angel had lied to her. Though she said nothing, though she refused to speak to Travis at all, the accusation was written across the taut lines of her face. He saw it, as he had always seen so much of her. So much, and still not enough.

"Angel didn't lie to you, Cat. The captain is part of the crew."

She closed her eyes. Of course, and Travis was captain of the *Wind Warrior.* She should have phrased her demand more carefully.

"I tried to be patient," he said quietly. "I thought you would succumb to the lure of your cameras and the *Wind Warrior* sailing a long reach at dawn. But

in six days you haven't so much as unwrapped a roll
of film. You're not sleeping, and you're not eating.
Since you won't take care of yourself, I will."

She felt something shoved into her hands. She
opened her eyes and looked in disbelief at what he
had given her. It was a wet suit of the type surfers or
scuba divers wore in cold water.

"Put it on. If you refuse, I'll do it for you."

She saw nothing in his face but the hard planes
and angles of his determination. Once she would
have flung his suit and his pity in his face. Now it
simply didn't matter. Nothing did. She went below,
changed into the wet suit and came back on deck.

The ship was hove to, resting quietly on the rolling
back of the sea. She went to the diving platform at
the stern where Travis was waiting for her, a tall
black figure looming against the dawn. She climbed
down and dove into the water. He followed, swimming beside her. Diego watched from the railing,
ready to launch the Zodiac if it was needed.

Cat swam erratically at first, more flight than a
coordinated effort at staying afloat. Gradually the
ingrained rhythms of swimming claimed her. She
swam mindlessly, arms and legs churning, ignoring
the tiredness that had become as much a part of her
as her gray eyes. She didn't know how long she
swam. She only knew that when it came time to
climb back onto the *Wind Warrior* she hadn't the
strength.

Travis climbed aboard, lifted her easily out of the
water and carried her back down to her cabin. He
peeled off the wet suit, toweled her dry, dressed her
warmly and left. He returned in a few minutes,
carrying breakfast. The first thing she saw was the
little white pill Dr. Stone had prescribed.

"Take it," he said, holding out a glass of juice.

She didn't move.

"You aren't strong enough to fight me," he said bluntly. "If I have to, I'll shove it down your throat."

She took the pill.

When she made no move toward the food, Travis picked up the fork and loaded it with scrambled eggs. "Open up."

His words and action reminded her of the night at the restaurant. She looked at his blue-green eyes and knew that he was remembering too. Pain moved beneath her numbness. She took the fork away from him. She would eat, but not from his hand.

"I'm not leaving until the tray is clean," he said. "Take as long as you like."

She ignored him, but the plate was empty when he took it away. He returned for her almost immediately.

"Up," he said curtly. "Get your cameras."

She said nothing, simply looked at him, her pale eyes dazed with exhaustion and something more. He couldn't do this to her.

"No mercy, Cat," he said softly, leaning over her until she could see nothing but him, a tawny-haired giant filling her world. "I'm going to push you until you fight me. Somewhere under all that ice a fire still burns. I'm going to find it. *Get up.*"

She got out of bed, knowing that if she refused he would simply carry her on deck. She didn't want that. When he touched her she remembered things better left buried under layers of ice.

For the rest of that day and all the days that followed, Travis was her nurse and nemesis, driving her physically in the hope that she would be tired enough to sleep through the night. It didn't work. No matter how far she swam, no matter how many meals she ate, no matter how many exercises she did or how many pictures she took under his critical eye, the hole in the universe was still there beneath her feet . . . and when she slept she fell through, awakening to terror. She came to dread going back to her cabin to face the freezing core of night.

Halfway through the third week at sea she woke as she had every night, fighting not to scream. When she looked out the porthole she knew she could not take one more instant of fear, could not count one more star. With a choked sound she went up on deck. She found a place out of the wind and huddled there, staring blindly into the night.

Though she had made no noise, Travis appeared. He picked her up. She went rigid in his arms.

"No. I won't go back to that cabin. Do you hear me, Travis? I won't." Her voice was soft, shattered. It was the first time she had spoken to him in all the long days since he had appeared on *Wind Warrior*.

His arms tightened around her as he looked at her drawn face. In the moonlight she looked otherworldly, as brittle as hoarfrost. "It's all right, Cat," he said gently.

Slowly her body relaxed. He carried her to the cabin at the bow of the boat. His cabin. She didn't protest. She would do anything, endure anything rather than count the stars beyond her porthole again. He put her on the bed, covered her with a blanket and smoothed her hair back from her forehead. She flinched as though he had slapped her. His face settled into grim lines as he sat near the bed.

Eventually she slept, only to awaken shaking and cold and nauseated. Her low sounds of distress woke Travis. He lay down next to her, holding her. She didn't fight his touch. At that moment she could no more have turned from his warmth than the sea could turn from the pull of the moon. For a long time he held her, rubbing out the knots of tension in her neck and shoulders, murmuring comfort and encouragement to her.

"Cat . . . Cat," he said softly, his hands strong and warm on her. "Don't fight your feelings. Scream or cry or smash things, do whatever you have to. Let go, Cat. Let go."

Her only answer was a shudder that wracked her body.

He held her, warming her cold flesh until finally she slept again. This time she didn't wake up until long after sunrise. It was the most sleep she had had since she had told him she was pregnant.

Travis appeared in the cabin, carrying her wet suit. The daily routine began. Neither one of them said anything about how the night had been spent. At some point during the day Cat began to do more than go through the motions with her cameras. The beauty of *Wind Warrior*'s magnificent maroon sails swelling against the cobalt sky finally had seeped through her numbness.

She did not speak to him. When it was time to sleep again, she went to her own cabin. She woke up shaking and cold, trying not to scream. She dragged herself off the bunk and started for the deck.

Travis was waiting outside her door. Wordlessly he carried her back to his cabin. He laid her on the bunk, climbed in beside her and pulled her against his body. She accepted his embrace and his warmth. In time, the shuddering passed. He settled her more closely against him, looking down at her and trying not to cry out his own rage and anguish.

"Cat," he said softly, raggedly, "don't be too strong. Let me help you. Bend before you break."

She didn't answer. His lips brushed her forehead, her cheek, and he tried not to think about what might have been, love and time and the past, all the things that money can't buy. He watched moonlight and shadows move over her face, watched her as though if he looked closely enough he could see through darkness to the end of her pain.

It was the same on the nights that followed. They slept until she awakened, and then he held her until she slept again. But he did not sleep again, could not, for her nightmare had become his.

The eighth night she slept in his bunk she woke to nightmare soothed away by his presence, then slept again. She awakened again almost immediately, wondering what had disturbed her; there was no nightmare clawing her out of sleep. Then she realized she was alone in the cabin. Silently she went up onto the deck.

The night was like velvet. *Wind Warrior* had flown them south to warmth. She saw Travis leaning against the rail, naked but for the briefs that were all he wore to bed. He was half-turned toward her but he didn't see her. He was looking at the bow wave breaking endlessly around the ebony ship. Beyond him a school of dolphins leaped in silver calligraphy against the seamless midnight sea. A full moon was balanced on the horizon, pouring radiance over the night, over him.

Cat stood without moving, without breathing, the crystal beauty of the moment slicing through her until she almost cried out. She heard Travis make a harsh sound. He buried his face in his hands, but not before she saw the silver gleam above his beard.

Confused, shaken, she stumbled back to his cabin,

his bed. She lay awake, sorting through certainties shattered by moonlight and a man's tears. No matter how many times her thoughts scattered they reformed around one impossible truth—he had cried for her when she was unable to cry for herself. Guilt might make him replace her cameras, and pity might make him bully her into health; but neither guilt nor pity could squeeze tears out of his strength.

She lay very quietly, wondering how many nights he had comforted her and then gone out on deck alone with no one to comfort him. As silently as moonlight, tears came to her, burning her, melting through ice to the pain beneath. She heard him walk softly into the cabin and ease himself onto the bed. She turned toward him, fitting herself against him, holding him as he had held her so many times.

She tried to speak, but her breath came out in a ragged sob. She could only say his name again and again, crying as his arms closed around her, crying because he had cared enough to cry for her. He called her name once before he buried his face in her warmth, holding her as tightly as she held him, sharing the terrible wrench of emotions returning to her.

And when there were no more tears they still held one another, warmth in the cold center of night.

She awoke with the taste of him on her lips, bittersweet residue of tears. He was watching her. When she didn't turn away, his arms tightened to pull her close. She felt the pain twisting through his body, heard it in his voice.

"I should have been with you," he said. "I should have cooked your meals, bathed you, carried you into the sun, held you." His voice tightened into silence, then continued. "I didn't believe you loved me. I kept telling myself you'd call, you'd come to me, that all you wanted was to marry my money. Then you told me you sold your cameras."

He held her so close that she couldn't breathe, but she didn't care; she was aware of nothing but his face, his eyes, his words, his warmth.

"You sold your cameras to keep my baby and never called me, never spoke to me, never asked one thing of me." He closed his eyes. His face was bleak without their unique light. When he spoke again his voice was soft. "I thought that nothing could be worse than seeing that wave break over you and Jason, seeing your blood pooling on the deck, hearing you scream. I was wrong. The last few weeks have been like watching you die by inches, knowing I'd killed you but not cleanly, not quickly. Nothing I did could help. The nights, Cat. My God, the *nights*. And the nightmare will go on forever because I can't change the past. I can't take back the moment when you saw blood on the deck and you screamed."

"The nightmares began before that." She touched his cheek with her palm, gently turning his head toward her. "I knew from the beginning that I would almost certainly miscarry. I knew that it wasn't my last chance, that I could have other babies. But I didn't want another man's child. I wanted yours. I wanted you, but I'd lost you. That's when the nightmares started. When I lost you."

"Cat—"

"No," she said, covering his mouth with her hand. "Let me finish. Let me be like you, strong enough to bend."

His lips moved against her palm, but he said nothing.

"For seven years I prided myself on standing alone, and then I fell alone. I'm still falling. Don't leave me, Travis. Not yet. I know I'm not rich enough for you to trust, to love. I don't care about that anymore. All I care about is here, now, you. Let me run before this storm with you. And when it's over you won't have to say anything, do anything. I'll leave."

His lips moved from her palm to the pulse beating in her wrist. "You're richer than I ever was or ever will be. Fire and life and love. If I thought I could buy you, I'd sell even the *Wind Warrior*. But you can't be bought, can't be begged, and borrowing isn't good enough." His arms moved, fitting her body against his. "But you can be stolen, sweet Cat. And that's what I've done. The *Wind Warrior* owns three-fourths of the world. No one can find you and take you away from me."

He brushed her hair aside until he could whisper against her ear, holding her so tightly she couldn't move or speak. "But I promised Harrington I wouldn't keep you against your will." He heard her surprised exclamation and smiled. "You didn't really believe that your angel would force you back to work just to meet a deadline, did you? It was the only way we could think of to get you on board the *Wind Warrior*. The publisher told me your photos were so good that he'd cheerfully wait until hell froze over to get the rest of them."

"Some angel," said Cat, forgiving Harrington even as she realized how and why he had misled her.

"He's no angel at all," said Travis grimly. "He wouldn't help me until I promised to let you go when you were well, to let you find a man you could love. And he's right. You deserve that love, Cat. I'll let you go, I promise it."

"I've already found the only man I could love,"

she said, touching his face with fingers that trembled. "Nothing has changed that. Nothing ever could."

"Marry me," he said urgently, his beard caressing her cheek, her neck, his lips warm and firm on her skin. "Please marry me." Then he swore softly. "That isn't fair to you. You should have time to recover, but I'm afraid that once you're well you won't need anyone, and I need you . . . I *need* you. Marry me."

"Don't," she whispered, eyes closed, afraid that if she looked at him she would accept no matter what motivated his words. "The miscarriage wasn't anyone's fault, not yours, not mine, not Jason's. I'd lost before I ever went down those stairs. Don't marry me out of pity. I can take anything but that."

He laughed harshly. "I'd as soon pity a storm. You're so strong."

"Strong?" she asked in a husky voice. Her lashes opened around eyes luminous with tears. "Sure. That's why I wake up in a cold sweat every night."

"You spent a month going through the nights alone. I've spent only a few nights and it's tearing me apart."

"You've helped me just by being here, holding me," she said softly. "It's much better now. Don't feel guilty. Don't feel you have to marry me."

"I love you, Cat."

She looked at him helplessly, wanting to believe him. He felt the tremor that went through her, saw shadows of pain and doubt in her haunted gray eyes.

"To hell with words and fighting fair," he said thickly.

His lips brushed hers as his tongue licked at the corners of her mouth. "Let me in," he whispered between gentle assaults with his tongue. "Please, Cat."

With a small sound she opened her lips, let him fill her mouth with his breath, his taste, his tongue meeting hers until she forgot to breathe. She felt the sweet warmth of his skin beneath her hands, felt his body change, felt his heat wash over her in a shimmering sunrise of passion. His hands moved beneath the black T-shirt, his shirt, her only night-gown since she had boarded the ship.

He stroked her hungrily, his hands warm and strong, touching her with fire. She trembled and sighed, telling him how much she liked being touched by him. His hands moved from her hips to her shoulders and then over her head, taking the T-shirt. His hands returned, sweeping down her body, removing the scrap of lace that was all she wore.

She lay naked in the dawn pouring through the porthole, watching him, asking nothing of him but his presence here, now. He bent until his lips could touch her, his warmth touching her temples, her eyes, her mouth. His tongue lingered over hers for a time, moving slowly, deeply, sending desire quivering through her. When he ended the kiss she made a sound of protest. He called her name and buried his hands in the silky fire of her hair. She arched against him, asking him to touch her.

His fingers curled around her breasts, caressing her as his tongue rasped softly over her skin. With slow, unhurried movements he cherished all of her, moving over her like the sun, warming every shadowed hollow. She changed beneath his touch, his tongue setting fire to her until she moaned. Her hands clenched rhythmically in his hair as she cried out in the wordless language of ecstasy. With a deep male sound of pleasure he held her straining hips against him until the storm passed. Then slowly, reluctantly, his mouth moved back up her body, tasting the salt-sweetness that misted her skin.

"I didn't steal you out of pity or guilt," he said against her mouth, catching her lower lip in his teeth, moving his hips hungrily against her and drinking her ragged moan of pleasure. "I stole you because I had to. I want to sink into your soul the way you've sunk into mine. You taught me how to love, my Cat, my woman. And then I drove you away before I could discover how much I loved you. Now I know. I love you enough to heal you and let you go. If that's what you want. Is that what you want—to go? Tell me what you want, my love."

She looked at the tourmaline depths of his eyes, felt his arms hard and strong around her, the heat of his desire burning against her. He had given her everything, asked nothing, not her love, not even the easing of his own need.

"You," she whispered, pushing him gently over onto his back, her hands sliding down his body, peeling away the single piece of clothing he wore. "I want you."

"Do you still believe that this rich man can't love?" he asked, holding her against his naked warmth. "The money hasn't changed, Cat." His lips moved in a sad, ironic smile. "I'm rich and getting richer every minute."

"Screw your money," she said distinctly.

Travis looked startled, then he smiled. "Such an indelicate suggestion," he murmured. "And such a waste of time." He looked at her, silent laughter moving through his body until her hands found him and he groaned. He moved suddenly, rolling her onto her back until he lay between her legs. "I have a better idea. Marry me. Then the money will be yours and you can do what you like with it. Even"—he smiled crookedly—"that."

Before she could answer he moved against her lightly, stopping short of the union she wanted.

"Travis . . ." The word was both name and plea.

"Do you want me?" he asked, moving just a bit, touching her, teasing her.

"Not fair," she breathed, feeling lightning race through her again, burning currents that promised to consume and renew her in the same sweet flames. "Not fair."

His eyes were blue-green fire, fierce and loving. He laughed and moved again, touching her, but not enough, not nearly enough. "Whoever told you pirates fought fair?" he drawled.

She felt herself melting in liquid waves of pleasure. "I want you."

"How do you want me?" he asked, his voice husky, deep. "Husband or lover? Friend or partner? Companion or father of your children?"

"Yes," she said, closing her legs around him, trying to draw him into her liquid warmth.

"Yes what?" he asked, fighting the desire that shook his strength, showing what it cost him to wait for her answer.

"Yes. All you can be. All of you."

He whispered her name as he completed his gentle invasion of her. For a long moment he simply held her, murmuring his love over and over, hearing the words return redoubled from her lips. Then he began to move with the timeless, potent rhythms of the sea and love, melting her, melting into her, stealing her away.

Above them the *Wind Warrior* spread its wings and soared through the incandescent dawn, a radiant pirate ship skimming the edge of creation.

Silhouette

Intimate Moments

more romance, more excitement

— $2.25 each —

#1 ☐ DREAMS OF EVENING
Kristin James

#2 ☐ ONCE MORE WITH
FEELING Nora Roberts

#3 ☐ EMERALDS IN THE DARK
Beverly Bird

#4 ☐ SWEETHEART CONTRACT
Pat Wallace

#5 ☐ WIND SONG
Parris Afton Bonds

#6 ☐ ISLAND HERITAGE
Monica Barrie

#7 ☐ A DISTANT CASTLE
Sue Ellen Cole

#8 ☐ LOVE EVERLASTING
Moëth Allison

#9 ☐ SERPENT IN PARADISE
Stephanie James

#10 ☐ A SEASON OF
RAINBOWS Jennifer West

#11 ☐ UNTIL THE END OF TIME
June Trevor

#12 ☐ TONIGHT AND ALWAYS
Nora Roberts

#13 ☐ EDGE OF LOVE
Anna James

#14 ☐ RECKLESS SURRENDER
Jeanne Stephens

#15 ☐ SHADOW DANCE
Lorraine Sellers

#16 ☐ THE PROMISE OF
SUMMER   Barbara Faith

#17 ☐ THE AMBER SKY
Kristin James

#18 ☐ THE DANVERS TOUCH
Elizabeth Lowell

#19 ☐ ANOTHER KIND OF LOVE
Mary Lynn Baxter

#20 ☐ THE GENTLE WINDS
Monica Barrie

Silhouette Intimate Moments

Coming Next Month

Raven's Prey by Stephanie James

Honor Knight had to convince Judd Raven the two men who
had hired him to find her weren't her father and brother.
Only Honor hadn't realized Judd was holding her prisoner
for his own reason: he was in love.

Against The Rules by Linda Howard

At seventeen Cathryn Ashe had fought Rule Jackson and lost.
Now, more sure of herself and her new-found independence,
she was ready to challenge him again—only this time,
her heart was at stake.

The Fires Of Winter by Beverly Bird

As editor of a small paper, Heather Cavelle tried to write only
of the good in the world. Then David Sullivan took over and
plunged the paper into a search for crime and hidden truths,
and what they discovered was their love for each other.

Fantasies by Pamela Wallace

When Spencer Tait met the new studio president
Devon O'Neill they clashed immediately. Tensions were high
and the future at stake as the cameras rolled—because this
time, the real story was taking place behind the scenes.